Beneath

My

Skin

Lyn Duclos

Beneath My Skin, Lyn's fourth book, is yet another departure in genre from each of her previous books. Variety, so they say, is the spice of life and in this book there's quite some spice to delight her readers.
Now retired, Lyn's interests have widened to include ballroom and line dancing, cycling and walking, one of which you'll find in the book.
To learn more, readers can visit her at: www.lynduclos.com.au
& on Facebook at: www.facebook.com/lynduclos.author

Beneath My Skin

a novel

by

Lyn Duclos

PilandPress

First published by Piland Press
Melbourne, Australia 2021
2/11 Fowler Street, Chelsea, Victoria 3196, Australia
www.lynduclos.com.au

National Library of Australia
Cataloguing-in-Publication entry

Creator: Duclos, Lyn, author.

Title: Beneath My Skin / Lyn Duclos.

ISBN: 9780975780473 (paperback)

A catalogue record for this work is available from the National Library of Australia

The characters and events in this book are fictitious and any resemblance to real persons, living or dead, is purely coincidental.

Printed by Ingram (Worldwide)
February 2021

Cover design by Lyn Duclos & Aaron Wood
Author photo by Pilar Duclos Vargas
Typeset in 11 pt Garamond

SHATTERED REFLECTIONS

WHILE I CAN STILL REMEMBER

FUGUE

Acknowledgements

- Dr Janet Mason, MAPS (Consultant Psychologist), in the early stages to understand what makes June tick.
- Rob Williamson, train driver, for the long and fascinating interview that gave me such insight into what it's like to drive a train.
- David Andrew, Senior Advisor, Client Services, State Trustees Limited, for useful advice about the complications of wills.
- Zozie Brown, illustrator, who generously advised on the cover design.
- Ann Whiley, artist, who kindly offered to paint the cover before we changed our minds.
- My BETA readers who gave me such valuable feedback: Jane Russell *extraordinaire* (who read it twice and is up for another go!), Bob Newey, Merrilyn Hayes, Jan Hayes.
- Aaron Wood, who, despite his busy family/work life, made space for me and this book. He did a fabulous job on the cover with me and for that I'm forever grateful. (Andrés would have said: *noice*.)
- Norma Etchells [dec.], my courageous friend who couldn't wait to read the book but ran out of time.
- Mimi Sananikone, who's loyal friendship and belief in me has pushed me to continue when I least felt like it.
- Ulla-Britt Benner Larsen, my cousin in Copenhagen who's eagerly waiting to read yet another book of mine in English, even after struggling through the other three!
- Desirée Duclos, always encouraging and generous with advice all the way from Singapore, unless she's here nagging me, as cousins do.
- Janine Wood, my cousin whose enthusiasm and boundless energy is so contagious that you think you can climb Everest if she can.
- Allan Puroku, who gave me so much love, encouragement and support to finish the book (between dances).
- Pilar Duclos Vargas, my smart, witty daughter and best sounding board this side of the Black Stump, who helped to unravel the plot on countless occasions. I think I might have given up if not for her.

For my darling daughter,

Pilar Duclos Vargas,

who shares a scintillating intelligence with her brother,

Andrés Duclos Vargas,

whose presence still lingers.

Saturday, 7th January 2017

I bought this notebook because of the cover. It simply says: *For your memories —
the ones you already have and the ones you're going to make.* My memories make me
cry. I hope the new ones will make me smile.

I was born on the sixth of June, so Mum called me June. If I'd been born in
1966 instead of 1955, she said she'd have called me Six. Thinks that's funny,
even today. 'Six, six, sixty-six!'

How many times I've wondered why she had me. She certainly didn't/
doesn't want me. Ever. She's the most non-maternal mother you could find.
But, then again, that's just with me. What about precious Wayne and darling
Sandra? Moon and stars shine out of both their bums. My bum doesn't even
rate the ozone layer.

Yesterday, when I got home from work, there was a letter from Mum. Oh,
heavens! This had to be trouble. My stomach turned over, mixing what was left
of my lunch with a portion of dread. I turned the envelope over and there it
was: B. Cooper, Beechworth. No street address, but everyone knows the Coop-
ers. Been there for donkey's years. It strikes me - the omission - as somewhat
arrogant. A sense of entitlement. *I live here and you'd better know it! And you, you
worthless lump, you'd better know it.* That's me: the lump.

The last time Mum wrote to me (she never rings) was to say that Sandra
was marrying for the <u>fourth</u> time and what did I intend to give her and it'd
better be more generous than the last gift as that was pretty lousy.

I can't remember what I gave her for the last wedding. A sheet set, I think.
Or, was that for the 3rd wedding? It could have been a doona and cover. Who
cares anyway? I never received a thank you for any of her disasters.

I wondered if I'm expected to go to the 5th. There was no invitation en-
closed but that could come separately. Last time I pretended I had the flu and
the time before I said I'd broken my leg. Can't remember what I said for the
others. I'm sure they didn't lose any sleep over it. Didn't bother to find out if
I'd recovered, either time. Probably relieved I didn't go.

I opened the single sheet of paper with Mum's scrawl over a few lines.

Gran dead. Solicitor <u>demands</u> you go to his office. Cant see the point. Please yorself. Monday 16th 10 oclock ON THE DOT

No salutation or signature, of course.

I'm shocked. Gran's dead?!

I hadn't been all that close to her but, hey, I'm sorry she's gone but I guess it was her turn. I look up at a photo of her on my fridge. Not your Granny Davis type of old lady, though she had a good crop of snowy white hair with a natural wave you'd kill for, but that's where the resemblance ends. She hadn't had teeth in for as long as I can remember. The story goes that she left them on her bedside table every night until a new puppy got hold of them and crunched them up like chicken bones. She'd say every new year she'd replace them but never did. I reckon she'd look funny with them in anyway.

A faced lined like scrunched-up linen and little beady eyes that could slice right through you if she was angry. She was a tiny little thing, wiry, strong as an ox. Totally unafraid of anyone or anything. And she smoked. Gran sometimes laughed until she coughed and coughed, spat, coughed, took another drag, then coughed again amidst a cloud of smoke, ash falling down the front of her stained dress and cardigan. All the time.

Born Mae Queenie Rivers, Gran was nothing like her namesake, Mae West (Gran's dad saw all her films). Said what she thought; didn't matter who it hurt. She was not one to hand out compliments either, so I was flabbergasted at a backhanded compliment she gave me when I was a kid.

'She got what? Seventy one percent? That kid?' Gran said pointing at me. She peered at my report card, the one Mum had thrust at her. She inhaled again. I swear the smoke poured out of her ears as well as her nostrils. Hairs and all. 'Whose brain'd she get? Not yours, that's for sure!'

Mum scowled at her. 'Steady on, Mum,' she grated out as she dragged on her own cigarette. 'I've done all right.'

'Did I miss something?' Gran howled with laughter. 'You! Jesus, you can't even spell your own bloody name!' Coughing and spluttering. Lighting up again. Ashtray full already.

'Shit, I love you too, Mum,' Mum spat back.

I open Mum's letter again. Monday the 16th. I look at the calendar. There isn't a Monday 16th in February, so it has to be January. She has to mean Monday week! I'll have to ask Merv, my boss, to get a few days off.

I notice my hands are shaking as I make a cuppa. Stop it! I just wish I wouldn't get upset every time I have to go up there. And for a will reading of all things. Well, Mum didn't say it's a will reading. They don't have them anymore, do they? Why would I have to be there? The solicitor DEMANDS I be there. What on earth for? Has Gran left me something? A dirty ashtray perhaps. A chipped vase. The bloody gazunder! That'll be it. The one her parents had and that Gran always said was worth its weight in gold. Yuk! I suppose I could use it to stick a plant in.

Monday, 9th January

'I need the sales figures next Monday. You know that,' Merv complains. As a manager goes, he's usually quite amenable but he's a bit testy lately. He keeps belching and holding his gut and looking pretty lousy.

'I'll have them by Friday lunchtime,' I promise.

He looks up at me. 'Really?' I nod. 'Ah, good on you, June. You never let me down, do you?'

'I try not to,' I say as I turn to leave his office. I hesitate, then ask, 'Are you all right, Merv? You don't look a hundred percent.'

He holds on to his ample gut and grimaces. 'Bloody gastric reflux again.'

'Are you doing anything about it?'

'Gastros...gastrus...'

'Gastroscopy,' I finish for him. 'When?'

'Monday,' he gasps and then burps. Loudly.

'Well, you'll have the figures before that so you can relax,' I nod. 'You need anything else?'

'No, ta June. You go and have a lovely family get-together.'

Not likely, I mumble to myself as I close his door.

April looks up as I pass her desk. 'All OK for Monday?'

'Yeah.' I pull a face. 'Almost wish he'd said no.'

She laughs. 'What - miss out on the gazunder!'

'Shhh,' I hiss, looking over the partitions. Amy's on a call and Mel's nowhere in sight. Probably in the loo touching up her makeup before lunch. BBB's banging away at his keyboard like he's trying to break it. He's the one with a sewer for a gut. Bad Breath Bob I call him. I've never told anyone that.

April beckons me back. 'Can you take the same lunch break as me?' she asks. 'We have to do something about your wardrobe, remember. We could check out the Myer clearance sale.'

I look at her with grateful trepidation.

April

When April started work at Danks, I thought, here we go again. Another air-head. Wet behind the ears. Do I have to train yet another? God help me. But she proved me wrong. Smart as a whip, learns quickly and she actually seems to like me! Get that. Actually, despite her pushy, nosy attitude, she's got her heart in the right place. And I like her. First time I've liked anyone in all the years I've worked at Danks. She wears weird clothes, she's funny and hoots and snorts like a pig when she laughs. She makes me laugh. And that feels good.

Her first day was a bit traumatic, actually. She arrived very late - I'd rung the agency who had no idea why - and turns out she'd witnessed an accident where a tram hit a woman on Swanston Street. April had hung onto the woman's hand until the ambulance arrived and pronounced her dead. They had a hard job getting April to let go of her because she couldn't believe the woman had gone. It was on the news that night. April was dubbed a hero. She said it was bullshit.

I didn't know how to deal with her when she arrived at the office. I tried to send her home but she said it was okay and that she wanted to get 'stuck into her new job' before lunch. She gave a bit of a snort and said, with her two front teeth protruding, 'That was so cool! I've never seen anyone die before. It was the loveliest thing - be with someone who goes to the other side. I wonder if she's having a party over there now?' I didn't know what to say so I showed her to her desk and got her to fill out some new employee forms.

That was a few years ago and, since then, she's bullied her way into my life but in a nice sort of way. I really can't imagine my life without her now. For a while she nagged me about having a drink after work on a Friday night. I NEVER go to bars. Past tense. Never did. Do now. I just got sick of the nagging. 'Oh, come on, June. How about this week? You've got nothing better to do, do you? I'll bet you don't. Or have you got a boyfriend tucked out of sight? Have you? Have you? Come on! Just one drink. Well, maybe two. Oh, who gives a fuck.'

Yes - the 'F' word. She throws it around like an 'April shower' - get that. Couldn't care less. I was offended at first. Really got under my skin. Then one night she actually got me to say it.

'Come on June. Say fuck.'

'No.' I could feel my lips tightening. Like a schoolmarm.

'It's just a word!'

'No.'

'Open your mouth and say after me,' she goaded, 'FUCK!'

'No.'

'Well, for fuck's sake, spell it, then,' she hooted, downing a good mouthful of beer. 'Say after me: F...'

'No.'

'June ... if you don't at least spell fuck, I'm never going to speak with you again.'

'April...'

'Ah, ha,' she snorted. 'I sense capitulation!'

'I'm not...'

'F, for fuck's sake! What's wrong with that? Say F!'

'Have it your way. F!'

'Excellent,' she gloated with a hoot, finishing her beer. 'Now - say U!'

'You,' I said with the word 'you' in my mind.

'Well, how bloody hard was that?!'

'Well ...'

'Now, June, try a C.'

'See,' I spat out, thinking of sight, sea.

'There you are,' she laughed. 'How hard can that be? Now try K.'

'Kaye,' I thought, of my Aunty Kaye on Dad's side of the family who lived a bohemian life.

'Now,' she said. 'Say: F ... U... C ... K!'

'F ... U ... C ... K,' I spelled out.

'Well, you've as good as said it,' she snorted. 'You may as well say the whole bloody four-lettered word: FUCK!'

'Fuck,' I said, in an explosion of air and spit. I can't believe it. It was so liberating!

'I'm proud of you,' she said with unaccustomed sobriety.

Wednesday, 11ᵗʰ January

April skips out of the lift just like a school girl on an excursion. She pushes her shiny dark hair behind her ears and runs her tongue over her top teeth. She does this when she's excited or worried. Today she's excited because, as she put it the other night, she's on a mission for a 'June makeover'. Ever since I told her about my having to go to Beechworth for the solicitor's appointment, she's determined that I make an impression on my family. She insisted she go home with me to have a look in my wardrobe. I didn't want her to. I made all sorts of excuses. Have to get dinner. Feed the fish. Get ready for work. Fill in the crossword.

'We can get Chinese takeaway,' she said.

I don't get Chinese on a Wednesday!

'Let's get a bottle of Riesling,' which wasn't a question.

I don't drink Riesling. I drink moscato!

'You need some new clothes,' she said after we'd polished off sweet and sour pork, Szechuan chicken (which nearly blew my head off, much less strip the lining of my oesophagus) with fried rice, and nearly a bottle of that Riesling stuff. I was so out of sorts that I didn't know what to do and, stupidly, let her bully me into a tour of my wardrobe, such as it is.

'You've got the same dress five times,' she commented slowly as she turned from the hangers.

'Well...'

'You mean you don't wear the same dress every day?'

'What do you mean, the same dress,' I replied defensively. 'I wear a clean one every day of the week.'

'But, why is each one exactly the same as the others?'

'I don't have to think about what I'm going to wear,' I said. 'It's like having a uniform.'

'And two cardigans exactly the same,' she said, holding them up.

'Yes, and they've lasted all these years because I look after them.'

'How many years?'

I had to add it up. 'Let's see. I left school at the end of 1974 and started at Danks in the new year, when it was in Malvern. I went up to the city and bought the dresses and the cardigans in Myers Bargain Basement.'

April's mouth dropped open. 'You don't mean to tell me,' she said slowly, 'that you've had them since 1975?' Her voice rose an octave. 'That's forty-two years!'

'Well, I suppose it is,' I said.

'Forty-two years! Fucking hell!!'

'April, please. The neighbours'll hear you.'

And then she started hooting and snorting until she collapsed on my bed in a fit.

'Are you all right?' I began to tap her between the shoulder blades.

'June. June,' she snorted. 'I can't believe what I'm hearing.'

'What is this,' I enquired testily, 'the Inquisition?'

'No, but, let me get this straight. These dresses and cardigans are forty-two years old.'

'Well, they're the third lot.'

'What do you mean?'

'I've had to replace them twice over the years.'

'Not the same style ... colour ...'

'As close as I could get.'

'Aren't you sick of them? Make you throw up every time you see them? Make you want to commit sewerage pipes?'

'What's sewerage pipes?'

'Top yourself. Knock yourself.'

I must have had a blank look on my face.

'Commit suicide, June,' she said, suddenly serious.

'Why would I do that?'

'Never mind,' she said. 'What about your shoes?'

Thursday, 12th January

So, here we are in Myers flicking hangers frantically looking for I don't know what. April seems to have some idea. She rips a hanger off a rack, holds it up and then beckons me over to slap the garment over my chest. 'The right colour,' she says. 'Wrong look.' She discards the item as if it's a bit of rubbish. Puts it anywhere. I've given up trying to rehang her discards and attempt to adopt her don't care attitude though it goes against my nature.

'What about this one?' she asks her, not me, despite me providing the body. I look at the dress in a mirror as she holds it up against me. Actually, I'm looking at the price tag. $159.99! I've never, ever, spent even a fraction of that on clothing.

I look at her aghast. 'You can't be serious!'

'Yeah,' she says considering my reflection. 'Too sombre. You need to zap 'em with something bright.'

Here I am, parading in front of my wardrobe mirror after we've had two medium pizzas and a bottle of shiraz. I never drink red wine. The first few sips were so strong and sour I nearly spat it out but, after April poured more wine into my glass, I didn't care anymore and, actually, it got a bit better. I never have pizza on a Thursday. I get it on Saturday nights at 6:30 from Tony's Pizzeria. I have ham and cheese pizza, even though Tony has tried for the last umpteen million years to get me to try something else.

'Why would I get that if I like ham and cheese?' I tell him every Saturday when I pick it up. 'If it's not broken, don't try to fix it,' I say with panache.

'Try the Pepperoni,' he begs, 'or the Chicken and Feta, or the Gran Supremo (whatever that is),' he keeps begging.

I tough him out and he's just about given up, though he does sometimes fling a few more exotic pizza names at me like 'Capricciosa'.

Then I go home, open the pizza box, have one slice standing up as I check on Merv (my goldfish - not my boss - though they do have some things in common: they're both easy to get along with, both have red hair/scales, and they both burp), check the TV guide, switch on the tellie, watch the news, and then settle down with the pizza on my lap and watch a good romance or some reality TV. If the films are too violent, I get *Notting Hill* or *Message in a Bottle* or *An Affair to Remember* off my shelf and enjoy it all over again.

Tonight's pizzas aren't ham and cheese, by the way.

April barks instructions at me. 'Pull it down. Pull it up. Ruche it up.' (Ruche? What's ruche?) 'Gather it so it hides all the bad bits, June. Like this,' she demonstrates. 'Hold your stomach in. Shoulders back. Turn around. Stick your boobs out.'

I'm exhausted. There's a pile of Myers bags all over my bed and she's making me try on everything, I mean everything! I'm so embarrassed I have another sip of that red wine. She even made me have a bra fitting! I've never done that in my life. The woman was pushing my ... breasts ... into all these bras, tightening, loosening straps, having me bend over, checking my armpits for overflow. April convinced me to buy a BLACK bra with matching underpants!!! And a skin coloured set, a red set and then a bright blue set. Where on earth am I going to wear them? I look at my old comfy beige bra crumpled up in the rubbish bin (of course I'll get it out when April's gone) and look at my raised breasts sticking out under a bright red jumper. Actually, I think they look like they belong on a Hollywood movie set. Without me.

'Now the shoes,' she instructs.

I look at her in confusion. There are FOUR new pairs of shoes.

'The black leather ones.'

'Oh,' I say weakly as I sit to get them on. 'How am I supposed to walk in these heels?'

'Hold yourself erect and ... I can't believe you've never worn heels!' she hoots. 'Not even when you were young and went to dances?'

'I never went to dances,' I say quietly, looking at the floor.

She bends over and looks up at me from the floor, her hair scraping the carpet. 'Never?'

I shake my head and have a sudden impulse to cry. I can't believe it and blink furiously.

'June?'

I stand up and take a look at my reflection. Well, it doesn't appear to be me, except from the neck up. There's this rather lumpy person, suddenly taller, wearing a black straight skirt topped with a long, bright-red, cowl-necked woollen jumper which hides the lumps and bumps. I think it's rather flattering, surprisingly enough. I remember to hold my shoulders back and, whoops, out comes the bust line again.

She's looking at me critically. 'Yes,' she says, 'that'll do nicely for the solicitor thingy and that family of yours. Sober but classy. You need some jewellery, though. Shit! We could have got it at Myer as well.'

'I've got...'

'Don't even bother, June. You said you've just got the silver chain and pendant? No bloody earrings, no rings, no brooches except the VERY DATED cameo. Right?'

'Well, yes, but..'

'You need modern, stylish jewellery, June. Big, not piddling tiny.' She undid her huge costume necklace.

'I don't think it would...'

'Just to get an idea,' she insists, placing it around my neck and standing back to appraise the result. 'Not bad,' she says. Actually, I agree with her. Even though it's a cheap-looking bit of nothing, it sets off the jumper. 'You can borrow this until we go shopping again tomorrow.'

'Tomorrow!' I'm aghast. 'I have to get those sales figures to Merv ...'

'How long'll that take you? Can I help with that?'

I look at her doubtfully.

'An hour or two tops,' she says confidentially. 'He'll have it by lunchtime and we'll go off to get your accessories.'

Friday, 13th January

Merv's very happy with me as I place those figures on his desk at 11:30 am. 'Good on you, June,' he grins, obviously feeling a bit better today. 'After you and April disappeared for the afternoon yesterday, I thought you'd both been abducted, tortured by terrorists, and thought my gut would explode with worry.'

'Not about us,' I laugh. 'Your sales figures, more like it.'

He picks up the figures and nods satisfactorily as he reads. 'Why don't you take the rest of the day off? You never have any holidays,' he says thoughtfully, 'and yesterday must have been good for you.'

'Okay, thanks boss,' I say. 'I'll be taking April with me too.'

Sunday, 15th January

It's Sunday morning at Southern Cross Station. It's 7:05 am and I'm starving. No time for breakfast this morning, so I made a couple of sandwiches to eat on the way. I have to get off the train at Wangaratta and get a bus to Beechworth. It's going to take about 3½ hours. I'll be there in time for lunch at Mum's.

I rang her the other day. When she picked up the phone it was like, well, who the heck is this? I had to remind her it was her daughter calling. The one in Melbourne.

'I'm arriving around 10:40 on Sunday,' I told her.

'What're you coming on Sunday for?' she complained. 'Your appointment with Little Malcolm (he's big Malcolm's son who was the town solicitor since the ice age) is on Monday.'

'Yes, Mum,' I said patiently, 'but there's no connection to get me there at that time.'

'Humph,' she said.

'So ... I thought I'd stay the night at home (<u>was</u> my home = place of abode) and get there in time on Monday.'

'Well, if you have to,' she grumbled under her breath.

Well, thanks, Mum.

'What time are you leaving Monday?'

'I hadn't planned on leaving that early,' I protested. 'I thought I'd catch up with Sandra and Wayne.'

Silence.

'Mum?'

'They lead busy lives, you know.'

'They're not the only ones,' I ground out. 'I'm coming up from Melbourne after all. Got the time off.'

'Should of asked 'em.'

'Really?' I splutter. 'Really?'

So, here I am, gnawing my way through the second of my sandwiches which has gone dry because I ran out of Glad Wrap. The corned beef is okay with the chutney, though, so I'm peeling off the crusts. The bus is only half-full, so I've got plenty of room to stretch out. I don't want to sit next to anyone and have to talk. I've got my head buried in a book, just in case, to ward them off.

We've just gone through Milawa. I look down at the farms and imagine the people who live there now. Have their children left for the city? How do they keep going? I feel nervous. Excited. What has Gran left me? I have to remind myself it'll be nothing because of who she was and how little she probably thought of me. I can't remember the last time we were in contact. Certainly not between visits to Beechworth.

I've just woken up on the outskirts of Beechworth. I think I've been dribbling. Looks pretty-much the same. Some road works going on. There's Mr & Mrs Williams' place. The Taylor's. The old milk bar. We go along Camp Street. There's the bakery. No sign of Mum. Or anyone.

I get down and retrieve my small suitcase. I pull down my skirt and straighten my top. I catch my reflection in the bakery's window. It's nothing like me. I scan the street. What am I supposed to do now? I told her the time! Geez. Let's sit for a while. I cross and uncross my stockinged legs. They feel slippery. April made me shave my legs so I could wear them. The crutch of the pantyhose feels tight and gravity's pulling it down a couple of inches. Tom Adams walks past me without a glance. He hasn't got a clue it's me! We fought in the playground at primary school and yet I don't strike a chord. Good. I wonder if it's that brown eye shadow and mascara April taught me to use. And the lipstick. My lips feel greasy and, yet, when I look in the mirror, I see someone who has colour in their face. Not that it's a pretty face, but at least it's got colour. I feel a bit embarrassed wearing it but April insisted.

'Give 'em shit,' she said, 'even if it's just showing them how different you can look.'

It's 11:30. I suppose I'll have to get a taxi to Mum's.

'So, you got here,' Mum observes. She looks over at me in the doorway with a raised eyebrow as she continues to baste the Sunday roast.

'Well, yes,' I reply, trying not to act insulted.

'You're almost late for lunch.'

'I had to get a taxi.'

'Sandra's in the middle of wedding preparations,' she says. *My gut feeling was right.* 'So she's got no time to see you before you go back.'

'Ah...'

'And Wayne has some business deal he has to tie up tomorrow...'
'What about today?' I ask.
'Oh...something about the kids and their footy training.'
'Just as well you're here,' I say weakly, trying to make light of the situation.
'Well, come and stir the gravy,' she says. 'Make yourself useful.'

Monday, 16th January

I'm sitting in Little Malcolm's reception area. His secretary is making an attempt at typing something on her keyboard. I can tell she hasn't a clue. The phone rings. 'Hello?' she answers. *Very professional.* 'Yes, Mr Malcolm Power's office.' She listens for a while. 'He's tied up at the moment with a client,' she says looking at a closed door. 'Can I take a message?' And this goes to a series of questions and answers which rival a federal investigation. She hangs up with a sigh. It's obviously way and above her capabilities. The door suddenly opens and Little Malcolm shows out an elderly lady.

'June?' he asks. 'June Cooper?'

'Yes, Mr Power,' I say, standing up.

'Really?' There's no recognition on his face. I don't know whether to take this as an insult or compliment.

'Malcolm,' I admonish him, less formal now. 'June from high school.'

'Well!' He looks me up and down. 'I wouldn't have guessed...'

And I bless April for her magic.

'So, that about wraps it up,' Little Malcolm says.

I stare at him in shock. 'So, you mean to tell me...'

'I'm not telling you anything,' he says. 'It's your grandmother telling you.'

'I don't believe...'

He turns the document around in front of me. 'Read it for yourself.'

I scan the lines until I read what he's just told me.

'*...so, sorry to tell you Darl but your mum isn't your mum. Your mum is your aunt. That is to say your Aunty Helen is your mum...*'

'But...'

'What a kick in the guts,' Little Malcolm observes.

I'm sitting in the window at the Beechworth Bakery with a pot of tea, reading Gran's letter again. She's telling me from the grave that I'm a bastard. That Aunty Helen got up the duff at the age of 16, went and stayed with Aunty Kaye (Dad's bohemian sister) in Mildura once she started showing, had the baby up there and then bloody-well disappeared.

I look up as a motor bike roars past the window, breaking my absorption with Gran's revelations. A waitress asks if I want a top-up. I nod yes. I wait for her to bring me a fresh pot and watch the people passing by wondering if any of them are grownup versions of kids who bullied me at school.

'...and you once asked me why your mum didn't love you. Now you know. Helen's baby (you) ended up on her doorstep and she had to explain, married or not, how come she had a baby (when she didn't have a baby) to all of Beechworth. Thank Christ she's always been like a tub of lard and pregnant or not no one would know the difference. Actually Brenda couldn't stand you. Still can't. So the secret's out. Not that Brenda is going to tell Beechworth about it. Family. You have to stay loyal to the family. I didn't tell her that I was going to tell you. You do with it what you want. I'm not going to be around to be part of the fireworks. Maybe I will see it playing hop scotch over coals or sitting on a cloud, which I doubt very much. To this day I don't know if your real mum is alive. I always hoped Helen would come back. Kaye was zipped up like a clam about Helen. She died early so Helen's whereabouts remain a mystery. She might be dead too.

And so she might. Or not.

April bounces up and down on my kitchen chairs. 'Come on,' she implores. 'How long are you going to make me wait?' She has a sip of that shiraz she brought. So do I.

'I hardly know where to begin,' I say.

'Geez. Just start at ... oh, I don't know ... what was your mum's reaction to your new look?'

'Speechless.'

'What do you mean speechless? How could she be speechless?' April runs her tongue over her top teeth. I know she's excited.

'She never said a word,' I say, 'but I saw her raise an eyebrow.'

'An eyebrow,' she hoots. 'A fuckin' eyebrow?'

'April. Language,' I admonish.

'Oh, come on! A bloody eyebrow for a total makeover.' She thumps the table and I jump.

'April,' I say quietly, smoothing my new skirt over my knees. 'She's not my mother.'

April's mouth hangs open. I can see her uvula which is totally gross. Now who's speechless?

Tuesday, 17th January

I leave Merv's office after he's actually given me a compliment on my new look. It's raised a few eyebrows with the rest of the staff. It must be a trend. April wants me to have a haircut, but not with my normal hairdresser. I've been going to her for, oh, I don't know, twenty years? How can I turn my back on her now? April says I need to cover the greys and look more trendy. At 62??????? Well I suppose it's not too late to start, though I'm nervous.

After an extended lunch hour (Merv will have a fit) I can't get over the new me. More than the new clothes. This is me with a neck and a short cut that frames my face and glasses. I have to admit I look younger. My moist dark mauve lipstick says something - I don't know what, but it does. I'm scared to look at myself in case people think me vain but, really, I don't look like I used to. Will I wake up and find the old one on my pillow? I'm scared to look back because I really like this. April seems to know what's good for me. I'm discovering things about myself that I had no idea about. Not just my appearance, but food, drink, attitude. Well, fuck me dead! Did I say that???!!

Now she wants me to get new glasses. Says the frames are *shithouse* (her word). I shudder to think what new ones may look like, though I'm coming to trust her judgement. This is fun :)

She also wants me to go searching for Aunty Helen - Mum.

'How do you know she's dead?'

Good point.

'I don't know,' I reply.

'Then let's see if we can find her,' she says, taking a large gulp of that nice shiraz.

Wednesday, 18th January

Tonight I'm at April's place. It's a flat on Barkly Street, Fitzroy North. I'm surprised how nice it is. It's modern, has lots of natural light, and is close to everything, including work and shops. I didn't realise how old my flat's looking. Well, I suppose having been there for the past 30-odd years, it would look dated. I don't complain much and the owners are pretty good at fixing anything. I have to walk 20 mins to get to the station though, whether the sun's cracking my skin open or the rain's diving straight into my underwear.

After work, we went to April's on her bus, then stopped at the shops nearby. We bought some wine, some chicken breasts and a sachet of Madras curry sauce. This is a bit of an adventure for me. I feel wound up. Apprehensive. I haven't been out at night, other than picking up my takeaway, since forever (that's an April saying). She shows me around her place and I'm trying to come to terms with the April I know and the April who lives here. This is really lovely. I know she's got a neat desk at work, but this is spotless. I wonder for a moment what she thinks of my sloppy place. Well, she goes there, so it can't bother her too much.

She soaks some rice and dices the chicken. 'Can I help?' I ask, but she shakes her head as she swallows a mouthful of shiraz (becoming a favourite with me now).

'No, June. You just make yourself at home and I'll have this on in a jiff.'

I lean against the kitchen doorway, glass in hand, as she whips out some green things (vegetables I never buy - I'm too embarrassed to ask what they are) and some carrots. Onions and garlic too. I'm curious as I cook very plain food for myself in between my takeaways. This is a very competent April, this young woman in her kitchen.

'So, what do you reckon, then?' she says, looking over her shoulder at me as she stirs the dinner.

'I don't know that I'm ready for this,' I say, looking anywhere else but at her penetrating gaze.

'Why not? Shit, you find yourself with a mother who's <u>not</u> your mother and an aunt who <u>is</u> your mother!' She stirs vigorously with emphasis. 'Geez, I'd be wanting to know *everything*.!'

'Yes, I know, but ...'

'And there are websites where you can do a search...'

'April - I just don't know,' I say weakly. 'I need to digest it first.'

She looks at me quizzically. 'It's bothering you?'

'Well, yes. Wouldn't it you?

'I suppose...'

'I feel my whole world has turned upside down. It's been a lie.' Tears threaten to betray me. 'I don't know who I am anymore.'

'Shit, June,' she says looking at me closely. 'You look miserable. You didn't like the old cow anyway! Isn't that a bonus?'

'You have such a skill for saying it as it is, don't you,' I smile. 'No, I didn't - don't - like her, as you say, and never felt a connection.' I inspect my glass minutely. 'I understand why now - and why she hated me so.'

'Did she really hate you?'

'Well, that's what my child-self felt.'

'What about your dad?'

I shake my head. 'He was always good to me. I liked him a lot.'

Liked? Is he dead?'

Influential Men

Kevin (my dad) was in and out of my life consistently (he was a sheepshearer) until I was around seven, and then he died. Something about a ram chasing him all over the place, pushed him into a waterhole and sat on him until he drowned. Karma for something Dad did? Who knows.

My grandfather was a tall, thick-set man who always wore a hat. He used to stand in his Beechworth estate agency doorway, jiggling the coins in his pockets, a reminder of the power of the money he no doubt had. He never liked me. I remember one Xmas when we were waiting for lunch to be cooked. We were in the kitchen when he gave Wayne and Sandra *real* watches. I was flabbergasted, as kids in those days didn't have the real thing. I stood there with my mouth hanging open. Our grandfather turned and looked at me. Got an attack of the guilts. For a fleeting second. He dug into his pocket and threw a note and some coins at me. Then turned back. June forgotten.

So, those were two of the most influential men in my life. Impressive, eh?

But then there was old Mr Wilson. He was my shorthand and typing teacher at high school. He also taught bookkeeping. He thought I was the ant's pants and wanted to train me up to be a judge's secretary.

'What, you?' Mum had chortled. 'And how are you going to manage that? Go down to the big smoke, find a judge to give you a job, and then get fired because you're a dunce. Now,' she'd said, putting her hand on my little sister's head, 'Sandra could do it standing on her head, couldn't you, Darl?'

The fact that Sandra was only interested in fiddling with boys behind the shelter sheds and playing sport, not to mention she had nothing between her ears, escaped Mum totally.

I saw the regret in Mr Wilson's eyes as he listened to the message I relayed from Mum. A big fat NO.

'June, please ask your mother to come in and have a chat with me,' he'd said, imploring with his liquid, basset hound dog eyes.

'She won't come, Mr Wilson,' I'd said, fighting tears of frustration and hurt.

In fact, she never visited the school, except for my first day when she dropped me at the gate and turned without a word of encouragement. I didn't mind. I looked up at the building and thought it would give me something I never got at home: belonging. The teachers actually smiled at me, talked to me, and made me feel that I was as important as any kid in the class. I used to offer to help clean and tidy the classroom, when everyone else had left each day, because I felt useful. No one waited for me at the gate so it didn't matter how late I was. I loved the conversations with my teachers. I accepted that their lives and families were different from mine - poles apart, in fact. They fascinated me with stories of holidays all over Australia, sometimes even in other countries. It was incredibly foreign to me as our family never went anywhere.

There was a sign over our back door which said 'Home is where the heart is' and for years I wondered where that heart was kept. I asked Gran once if she knew where it was. She looked at me with her open gummy mouth and cracked up laughing, coughing, spitting, then dragged on her fag. 'Jesus, June. You ask the craziest questions!'

I never found that heart, except a half used-up one in Gran's chest. She never showed any affection for me in front of the rest of the family but, now and again, she'd ask me how school was and if I was going to escape from the nut house. I assumed that was the Beechworth Lunatic Asylum (originally known as the haunted Mayday Hills Lunatic Asylum) on top of the hill, and was scared to death Mum was going to put me there and throw away the key.

Actually, I asked Gran if she'd go to my school on grandparents' day one year but, even though she'd said yes, she ended up in hospital with a bleeding ulcer and I was afraid to ask her again in case it was my fault she'd got so sick and she'd die.

Mum never went to parent/teacher meetings. Not for me, at least, but she was there when Sandra and Wayne's teachers summoned her. 'They're so clever,' she would say to the walls, making sure I was captured in the wallpaper. A smug smile would curl up her lips. I wondered why she was never that proud of me.

Wednesday, 18ᵗʰ January [continued]

April hands me a plate of chicken curry and rice that she's conjured up in her tiny kitchen. It's spicy hot but it's tasty. This is so different from my normal diet. I wonder if I'll be sitting on the toilet for an extended period tomorrow morning.

'Who taught you to cook this?' I ask.

'No-one,' she grins. 'I get some recipes on the net, sometimes on YouTube, and then copy what they do. It's easy.' She takes a large spoonful and manages to get it into her mouth. 'Mum died before I was old enough to have the mother/daughter thingy,' she grimaces. 'Cancer,' she states matter-of-factly, when she sees my shock.

'I'm so ...'

'Doesn't matter,' she shrugs. 'I didn't know her, so I don't miss her. 'Dad was the stand-in most of my life, but he's moved on. Has his new family - I've got step-brothers, two of 'em - and a step-mother who'd rather I wasn't around.' She shovels another fork-full into her mouth and chews thoughtfully. 'So, I came to Melbourne ...'

'Where from?'

'The Gold Coast. Mermaid Beach.'

'Do you miss it?'

'Not really,' she says thoughtfully. 'It can get bloody cold here but I think I'm acclimatised already. I should after two years.'

'Have you got any family in Melbourne?'

April shakes her head.

'So, why Melbourne?'

'It seemed like a good idea at the time,' she laughs. 'Shoved a pin in the map of Oz with my head turned, and it was stuck in Melbourne.'

I get a taxi home as I'm too scared to go on public transport after ten o'clock. Costs me a fortune, but I'll make it up next payday. Not that I regret it. I really enjoyed my evening with April. She's, what, nearly 30 years younger than me, and yet she seems so more worldly and mature than I'll ever be.

Before she started at Danks, my days were all the same. Walk to the station. Catch the train. Walk to work. Spend eight hours at work, catch the train home. Have dinner with Merv watching me while I watch the telly. Go to bed around

10:00, read a Mills & Boon for about half an hour, turn off the light, and then it starts again the next morning. Except for weekends. Saturday morning I wash my 5 work dresses and 2 cardigans. Put the telly on. Watch the breakfast programmes, news, gossip. Read the rest of my book. Clean out Merv's tank, walk up to the library, borrow another 5 Mills & Boon books, buy what I need at the supermarket, go home. The rest of the day and Sunday stretch interminably in front of me.

April turns up and turns my life upside down.

I like it.

Thursday, 19ᵗʰ January

Today is a Thursday, like any other Thursday. I walk to the station. It takes me 17.5 minutes if I walk briskly. The same people are on the platform, as they are every other day. We shuffle to our customary spots. If an interloper turns up and dares to encroach upon our imagined spots, we (my fellow passengers and I) glare at them. *This spot belongs to me*, our eyes and faces yell at them.

There's this young upstart in 6" red heels, jiggling away to whatever junk she's listening to in her earphones. I nudge up as close as I dare to the yellow line. The train driver honks his horn at the crossing. I see his face momentarily as he flashes past me, the train slowing to a stop. I don't have to even think about which door I'm going to open. I'm in my usual spot where I know the door will line up. My right foot extends towards the door. The 6" heel, preceded by a pointed toe, rams past me and bright red nails grip the door handle.

I stumble backwards in shock. *The nerve of the creature*, I mumble to myself.

The carriage is almost full but I can normally find a seat, mostly in the same area, but the creature barges in and plants her bum on MY seat! I'm furious. *Hey, I've been travelling in this carriage for more years than you've been alive, you little upstart, and you've taken my bloody seat!* This is, of course, what I'd like to say, but don't have the courage. My mouth opens and shuts like Merv's.

I find a seat opposite her. I open my book but the lines swim across my vision. My hands are shaking with fury and I have to grip the book hard so that no one can see.

She takes a small bag out of her giant handbag, opens a mirror, and begins to apply makeup. She appears to be totally oblivious of the other passengers. She's so wrapped up in her image and the layers of gunk that she covers it with, that she seems to be in another dimension. Blink and she'll be somewhere else. Her world is her face and the portrait she paints.

How she applies so much mascara is a wonder to me. The constant rocking of the carriage doesn't seem to be a problem. She times each stroke between jerks, thick black layers building giraffe lashes which she batts at her mirror. Now she's applying foundation, after putting a head band in place. She spreads it like peanut butter all over her face from her forehead to her neck. Her fingers stroke her skin, unhurried in their worship of her image. She removes moist wipes from a packet and slowly cleans her fingers.

A lip liner traces her full mouth, and now she applies a lipstick that matches her nails and shoes. She pouts at the mirror, turning this way and that, until she's satisfied with the mask she's created. It all goes back into the cosmetic bag and is tucked away into the maws of her handbag. Now she straightens, shoulders back, bust extended, lips pouting, eyes flicking from male to male. *See me*, her mask demands. *See how gorgeous I am.*

Her gaze settles on my book, her top lip curling as she reads the title, and she meets my eyes, mocking me, before deliberately, slowly, sweeping across my clothes and down to my shoes. She snorts, actually snorts, as she puts her head up to the ceiling and laughs throatily. Honestly, if I had a hammer, I'd smash it down between her eyes until her surprise would melt into oblivion. That would have to satisfy my silent rage.

She gets out at South Yarra and the rest of my journey returns to normal. I still can't concentrate on my book but it doesn't matter as there's not far to go before I get off at Flinders Street. A shaft of sunlight blinds me as the train crosses the river and turns left towards Richmond. When I can see again, a nice man in a charcoal grey suit is smiling at me. I've seen him before but he's never smiled at me. He looks back down at his newspaper before I can smile back in return. When the carriage pulls into Flinders Street, he disappears in the crowd as I go up the escalator.

Merv's all smiles. He waves me into his office and grins as he reads out his medical report. 'No ulcers. No cancer. Nothing sinister. Still just a bit of gastric reflux,' he says. 'The doc is prescribing some different pills and reckons I'll be as right as rain in no time.'

'Fantastic,' I enthuse. His relief is palpable. I'm happy for him. Really.

'So, Trish and I are going to celebrate with a holiday to Bali.'

I look at him, my mouth open. I shut it before a hovering fly pops in.

'I know,' he laughs, looking at my reaction. 'I've not had a holiday since...'

'You got married,' I say. 'You went to Merimbula for your honeymoon.'

'Jesus, June. Of course you know when it was!' He burps his approval of my ability to recall the momentous incidents in his life.

It's not that hard, really, as he and Trish never go anywhere. Her mother keeps them chained to Melbourne with her many and varied triggers of emotional blackmail. They returned early from their honeymoon (probably mid-coitus) as Trish's mother broke her leg and needed to be cared for in her home. Actually, it turned out to be a sprained ankle, but that became obvious only after they returned.

Then there was the other time when they'd booked to go to Alice Springs, see Ayers Rock, do Kakadu, the lot. A fabulous trip. Wish I'd done it. Well, they didn't. Marj (the mother) rang in a panic the day before departure saying that she was being stalked and needed a safe haven. Their place would do, but she couldn't possibly be there on her own. No! Couldn't possibly. So the holiday was cancelled. They lost their dough, or a greater part of it, due to the 'situation' not being covered on their travel insurance.

The most recent attempt to get away (5 years ago), Merv reluctantly paid for a cruise from Budapest to Amsterdam. This was going to be it! Far enough away to ignore any calls for help. They were about to board their plane, mobile phones off, when over the loudspeakers came a call for Mrs Patricia Potter to take an urgent call. Merv took one look at her (so he told me later) and sagged back into a seat facing the runway. People were boarding their plane. He could see the pilot and co-pilot checking their instruments. Marj had struck again. This time she was about to be picked up by the ambulance to take her to a palliative care hospital for her last moments on this earth. Merv asked Trish how that could be when Marj was in the restaurant with them last night eating voraciously and drinking every drop of goodbye champers that filled her glass. Trish had looked confused. Merv asked why couldn't her brother take care of it but, just in case, Trish wanted to be there when dear Marj was due to depart this earth. Amazing: Marj's recovery after the travel insurance paid for <u>some</u> of the holiday. Merv swore he'd never go overseas again. Never mind the fact he'd not actually <u>been</u> overseas before. Poor Merv.

'So, you're going to Bali,' I say slowly. 'Have you paid for it yet?'

'Yes, I have. But guess what?' He has a gleam in his eye.

I try to guess, but can't.

'Marj doesn't know,' he announces triumphantly. 'And Trish doesn't know.'

'You mean...'

'Yep,' he says. 'Trish thinks she's going out for dinner and a film on Friday night. She won't be back for a couple of weeks. Neither will I.' The look on his face is priceless. The burp is victorious.

'You think you'll get away with it?'

'I can but try, dear June. I can but try.' He swivels his chair towards me. I know what he's going to say. We've had this conversation before. 'Will you hold the fort while I'm gone?'

'Of course,' I say with no conviction whatsoever. 'Good luck.'

Friday, 20th January

These past two days have been hectic as I go through the motions of cancelling Merv's appointments for the next couple of weeks, rearranging meetings, getting him to sign off documents, copying his itinerary and contact points. I'm half-hearted about it all as it seems a pointless lot of upheaval for something that's not going to happen. Still, Merv is burping along happily looking forward to kidnapping his beloved Trish. Good on him, I say. Let's hope this one works.

We haven't told the others yet. BBB's in his own world of managing the inventory, shifting new stock around the warehouse and such.

Mel's his sidekick, recording the stock in a mostly efficient manner (when she's not in front of a mirror or talking to her latest boyfriend on her mobile).

Amy's our ambassador on the phone and at the reception desk. Not being blessed with much between her ears, Amy nevertheless somehow transfers callers to the right person and charms anyone who enters the office with a lovely Doris Day smile.

April's good at accounts, so that's what she does.

I'm Merv's right-hand general dogsbody. My job evolved with me when I started work at Danks as a junior and I've been generally happy here, except when we moved to the city. I didn't like the extra travel - and still don't - but I can't imagine doing anything different. Merv's all right as a boss. Doesn't interfere with what I do and is generous with a bonus every Xmas. He keeps telling me to have a holiday but in the same breath says he doesn't know how he'd cope if I did take leave. I've got a bucket load of leave owing me but where would I go? What would I do?

Monday, 23rd January

Merv's actually pulled it off! They snuck out of the country and landed safely in Bali. Called me on Skype at lunch time today and I paraded the staff in front of the laptop screen in Merv's office. You should have seen their faces. They were so surprised to see him and Trish in singlet tops and holding colourful cocktails up like trophies.

'Where the bloody hell are you?' BBB spluttered.

'Guess,' chortled Merv, punctuating his glee with a massive burp, his double chin wobbling in agreement.

'I give in,' BBB sighed. 'It looks better than here, though.'

'Hawaii?' squealed Amy.

'Nope.' Trish gave Merv a quick cuddle.

'Tahiti?' was Mel's offering.

'Nah,' Merv laughed. 'Bali! Bali! Bali!'

April looked at me suspiciously. 'You knew?'

'Well, of course I did,' I said.

'But you didn't...' I could see the hurt on April's face.

'April, sweetie,' Trish interrupted, 'June was under strict instructions not to say anything to anyone.'

'She didn't tell me,' Mel pouted.

'Me neither,' Amy sulked.

'I'd have given her the sack if she had,' Merv grinned.

I glared at him.

'Well, maybe not that drastic,' he admitted.

BBB didn't see the joke. 'So, what am I supposed to do about the end of month stocktake? If I'm not kept in the loop my situation will become untenable.'

Merv and Trish lowered their cocktails to a nearby table. 'Look, Bob,' Merv said. 'This is a once-in-a-lifetime holiday for the two of us. We had to do it in secret. You know why.' He kissed Trish resoundingly on the lips. 'And I don't want you, any of you, to say anything to anyone until we return.' There was silence in the office. 'I mean that.'

BBB's lips were in a thin line. 'Humph,' he retorted.

'Do I have your word, Bob?'

BBB nodded.

'And the rest of you?'

'Yes, Merv,' they said in unison, shuffling their feet as if they were doing a routine on stage.

'June's got it all in order, so there's no problem,' Merv finished. 'See you in a couple of weeks!'

They shambled out of the office and I closed the door behind them. I sat on Merv's chair, swinging it around. 'Hey, boss, I could get used to this,' I said.

'Don't count on it,' he grinned at me. 'Sayonara!'

'I think that's Japanese, Merv...' I said, but he'd already cut the connection.

Wednesday, 25th January

Merv and Trish are having a good time. There's a frantic call from Marj, which I deflect with a rehearsed lie that workmen cut the electricity and phone line outside Merv and Trish's house, that Trish is spending hours in the city trying to sort it out – hence her absence – and that Merv's taking her to a hotel at night.

'Well, what hotel is it?' she demands.

'He forgot to tell me.'

'Why isn't Trish calling me from whatever bloody hotel it is?'

'She didn't want to worry you.'

'Worry me?' Her voice rises to a screech. 'I'm out of my mind here.'

'Can I help?'

And Marj blurts out a litany of disasters that plague her existence but I don't buy them. Emotional blackmail's wasted on me.

'How about I get Trish to call you when their mobiles are found?'

'Found? What do you mean found?'

'Oh, well,' I continue, 'they were in their overnight bags which they left in a taxi and ...'

Already I'm sick of going in to the office early and leaving later at night. The extra money doesn't really compensate for the inconvenience. I don't really need it. I mean, what do I spend my salary on? Food, public transport, the occasional taxi, fish flakes, utilities, and now all this expense on clothes that April has bullied me into buying. Look, I don't regret it and, really, it's hardly put a dent in my savings.

It's threatening showers this morning as I stand on the platform waiting for the train. I'm at my usual position but having to fight for it with a young man who's wearing jeans and a sloppy jumper with holes in it and he stinks. God knows what it'll be like in the carriage if I can smell him out here. I don't think he's quite all there as his eyes are darting all over the place and he keeps sniffing. His hands are jerking as if he's been electrocuted. No wonder, listening to some awful noise plugged into his ears that even I can hear out here on the platform. I'm avoiding actually coming into contact with him as I ease my left foot forward to gain my rightful spot. His right shoe jumps in front of me. I almost lose my balance. I glare at him and he sniggers.

The train arrives and I get into a carriage full of strangers. I hate this earlier train! I feel out of place and bad tempered. The only good thing is that there's more seating available. I sit between a girl with her head stuck in a book, earphones plugged in, and a man with his legs wide apart, *The Age* spread out over his lap. Bloody cheek taking up my personal space. I paid for my fare just as he did. I don't know how he's reading the paper because his left leg is jigging up and down. It's so annoying!

Directly opposite me, with his knees mere millimetres from mine, is a very handsome man of about my age. He's got salt and pepper hair, which looks quite distinguished, especially around the temples. His grey suit looks to be good quality and he's wearing a a light blue shirt underneath it . I peek down at his shoes. They're polished black and are spotless. A briefcase is on the floor between them. I look at him under my eyelashes, pretending to be turning the page of my book. He's got a tablet that he's reading from. I don't think it's emails, messages or Facebook, because he's not using his fingers much except for scrolling.

The girl gets out at Caulfield, so I move over to the window seat. An Asian girl sits where I was and is engrossed in messages, her thumbs going like crazy over her phone's keypad. I'm able to look in the window's reflection to study Mr Handsome. He's clean-shaven. His fingernails are impeccable. I wonder what job he has. A banker, insurance executive, CEO of some multi-million dollar business, surgeon, psychologist, TV announcer? There's a ring on his finger.

April's fidgety tonight as we sit in my kitchen with Chinese takeaway and a bottle of chardonnay. I regard it suspiciously as she pours it. It looks a bit like urine. I smell it and it's not far off.

'Why'd you change to this stuff?' I ask her.

'What, the chardonnay?'

'Yes. I've only just got used to the shiraz.'

'Well, it's about time you tried something else,' she says matter-of-factly.

'What if I don't like it?'

'You will,' she shrugs. 'You got used to the shiraz, didn't you?'

I notice a slight tension between us. Actually, it's been in the air since yesterday. I can't quite put my finger on it. 'April,' I say. 'Have I done something to offend you?'

She looks up at me quickly, runs her tongue over her top teeth, shovels a forkful of pork and rice into her mouth. 'What gives you that idea?' she asks, grains of rice escaping from her lips. I wince.

'Well, April,' I say, sounding like a bloody Sunday school teacher, 'it's just that you're not your usual bubbly self and I wonder if it's me or if something else has upset you.'

She regards me for a long moment, swallows her food, takes a sip of that chardonnay. 'Well, yes, actually. I thought we were friends.'

'Friends?' I'm surprised. 'Friends? Of course we're friends!'

'Then why didn't you tell me Merv and Trish had pissed off?'

I look at her in dismay. 'But he swore me to secrecy. Even Trish knew nothing about it.'

'I thought you trusted me.'

'I do! I do with *my* secrets but I can't share those that belong to others.'

She looks at me with those large, hooded, tawny-brown eyes of hers, sucking air between the gap between her two front teeth.

'In the business world, there are certain things that need to be kept confidential...'

'Oh, puleeez,' she says rolling her eyes.

'No, really, April. It doesn't matter whether it's something to do with the business or something personal like Merv whisking Trish away from his mother-in-law. He confided in me. It was important to him and I had to respect that.' I look at her imploringly. 'It has nothing to do with you, me, or anyone else. I didn't think for a minute that I would tell you, Mel, Amy or BBB...'

'Who?'

'Oh,' I curse my slip of the tongue. I take a sip of my urine wine, buying time to see if I can worm out of this one.

'Who?' she demands.

'Well...BBB is...Bob.'

'Okay then, June. What does BBB stand for?'

'Promise not to tell?'

'Well, that's a bit rich, isn't it, coming from Ms Secrecy Herself.' She glares at me.

'Bad Breath Bob.'

April suddenly chokes on her wine, so badly that I have to go behind her and whack her on the back. She's going purple in the face. 'April! Are you all right?'

She coughs and coughs but finally gets herself under control. 'It's perfect!' She coughs again. 'I wondered if it was only me who noticed.' She looks at me sharply. 'Does anyone else know you call him that?'

'No, I swear,' I say.

'Not even Merv?'

'No, I wouldn't. It's a bit cruel, don't you think?'

'Jesus, June. I could think of worse things to call him than that but BBB'll do nicely. Sometimes I think I'm going to throw up when he stands over my desk. I hold my breath until I'm ready to pass out.'

'Same here!'

We laugh together. The tension is gone.

Thursday, 26th January

I'm wearing my nice black skirt and bright red jumper with my new shoes that I haven't worn much as my bunions stick out when I wear heels and hurt like hell. I didn't know I had bunions. I stand on the platform in my usual spot waiting for the train. There's only today and tomorrow that I have to get the early train before Merv and Trish get back. My hands are a bit clammy. I can feel butterflies in my stomach as I wonder if Mr Handsome will be in the carriage again. The train pulls into the station and I stand back as a nice man opens the door for me. I thank him. Not many do that these days.

I get a window seat. I settle down, take out my book and glance around. I can't see him and am disappointed. Maybe he's in another carriage. I feel tears pricking my eyes. I can't believe not seeing him again makes me feel like this. What's wrong with me?

There are two young fellows chatting as they stand, hanging onto overhead handles. They get off at Malvern and suddenly I see Him! He's sitting over the other side of the carriage at the far end with his back to me. My heart's in my chest doing cartwheels. I wait until we stop at Armadale and pretend I'm leaving the train. I walk up to where he's sitting but there are no empty seats. A student gets up for me and suddenly I'm sitting next to him. I don't know what to do. I look sideways to see what he's doing on his tablet. Just what I thought yesterday. He's reading *The Age* online. His left shoulder is touching my right. I'm acutely conscious of my red bra and underpants as his aftershave wafts over to my willing nostrils. His briefcase is tucked between his legs but I can see some gold initials carved into the leather. I turn sideways to read them. I think they are MD. MD as in medical doctor? Or M for Michael, Matthew, Mason, Max? D as in Dawson, Dwyer, Duncan, Dixon? I'd love to ask him but am too afraid.

I sit paralysed until the train zips into Flinders Street Station. As I get up, I drop my book. I bend to get it but MD picks it up for me. 'You dropped this,' he says in a voice like a newsreader's. He looks at the title: *Summer Sizzle*, blazoned across a couple in a passionate embrace. MD raises an eyebrow and smiles down into my eyes. His fingers brush mine as he hands me the book. I open my mouth to thank him but he's been taken up by the crowd and is gone.

I'm finding it hard to concentrate at work today. Amy has a cold but came in anyway. I tell her to go home rather than spread her germs around. Mel's not happy that she has to do reception. I relieve her when she goes to lunch. I sit lost in thought about MD who has the most delicious smile. I imagine he's the hero in the book I'm reading. He's got his shirt off and is running his fingers through my hair as he bends over me, his lips apart. I close my eyes to block out the flickering fluoro light over the front door that I keep meaning to get fixed. Amy whinges about it constantly.

'Have you got a headache?' April's voice cuts into my daydream.

'What?' I say, startled. 'No, I'm fine.' I sit up straight.

'Well, you don't look it. What're you pulling at your hair for with your eyes closed, then?

I look up at her not knowing what to say. 'Just thinking.'

She stares at me thoughtfully before saying: 'You want to go look for that jacket when Mel gets back?'

I nod. 'Where's the best place to go?'

'Myer again. They've got another clearance sale.'

'Oh, good. I'd like to get some perfume, too. And a nice nightie,' I add.

Her eyebrow goes up but she says nothing.

'I'll give you a yell when Mel's here,' I say.

We find a smart business jacket. Black. And I buy the most decadent nightie I've ever seen, let alone owned. 'Who's this for, then?' April quizzes.

'Just me,' I say, trying to hide a half-smile on my face.

That eyebrow again. She's sucking air between her teeth. A sure sign there's trouble brewing.

Next we go to the Guerlain counter near the entrance on the ground floor. The sales lady hovers like a dragonfly. She sprays a sample of at least six perfumes on my inside wrists until my nose is utterly confused. I finally choose *Champs-Elyses* as it's on special. It smells all right to me.

As we walk back to work, April asks: 'So, who's the boyfriend?'

'Boyfriend!' I act suitably shocked. 'Boyfriend!'

'Yeah, June, boyfriend. You're holding out on me. Another bloody secret.'

'Well...'

'So, what's the deal?'

Friday, 27th January

Merv's looking at me with a mournful expression. 'Don't look at me like that,' I croon, scattering some fish flakes into his tank. 'You're number one with me. Always will be.' He sucks some flakes into his mouth and does a few excited twirls around reminding me of that sexy fish in the *Nutcracker Suite* part of *Fantasia*. I always fancied goldfish after I saw it the first time. 'But that doesn't mean to say I can't have another man in my life.' I do a twirl of my own around the kitchen in my sexy black nightie.

Today changed my life.

And Mr Handsome - MD - Matt - changed it for me.

My new black jacket is long enough to disguise my lumpy stomach and hips. I look almost slim. I saw my reflection in the carriage window as the train edged along the platform. I patted my hair back where it jumped out over my forehead. I licked my lips nervously as I entered the carriage.

People everywhere on their mobiles or tablets. One man stood shouting into his mobile: 'Of course I finished it. Didn't you...?' Everyone trying not to look at him whilst at the same time listening to his conversation whether they wanted to or not. 'Jesus Christ, Pete. Do I have to wipe your arse for you too?' Lovely man. Imagine working with him. Two young girls giggled at the arse reference. He glared at them as he continued his rant at poor Pete. '...and how many times...?' His face was turning a nice shade of purple. 'Well, fucken'...'

I bumped into his phone hand so hard he dropped it. 'Oh, sorry,' I said, pretending to lurch again with the train. 'Bumpy ride this morning.'

He went after his mobile which had been kicked under a seat. I turned to look straight into those delicious sky blue eyes smiling at me. He laughed and said, 'Good acting,' inclining his head towards the no-longer-shouting man still trying to get his mobile that passengers were kicking all over the place. He shuffled over to make room for me beside him.

'I felt like slapping him,' I said. 'What a crass individual.'

'I'd rather have you on my side than not,' he smiled.

And then we struck up a conversation that lasted until Flinders Street. I don't remember everything we said because I was in such a state of wonder and happiness. Here I was, June Cooper, Ms Nobody, talking with the most handsome man this side of the Black Stump and he seemed to like me. We stood up as the train pulled in and we gravitated to the escalator, still chatting, easy as pie.

'How about a coffee before work?' he asked. 'That's if you have the time.'

'Of course,' I said, looking at my watch without reading it. 'I'd like that.'

We took a seat inside a laneway café where it was quieter.

A waiter hovered.

We sat with our coffees, biting into scrumptious muffins, covering just about every subject you could possibly think of. His name's Matt (Matthew) and, despite the wedding ring (apparently his wife doesn't understand him), he's very friendly. He's in banking and is looking for an assistant he can rely on. He was impressed how I handled shouting man. He's also impressed with my employment record: one job = reliable.

'I'm going to have to go, June,' he said reluctantly as he finished his second coffee. 'Meetings.'

'Of course,' I said, holding my breath.

'You won't be on the same train next week, will you?'

'No,' I shook my head. 'My boss returns on the weekend so I don't need to go in so early.'

He smiled at me. 'Would you be prepared to meet for a job interview after work one day next week?'

A job? Me? Leave Danks - and Merv - to do something else? Suddenly I'm scared but exhilarated at the same time.

'Yes, I think I would.'

'Good,' he said, dipping his head down to my level to zap me with those sky blues. I'd do anything for them - for him! 'I've got your mobile number now, so I'll be in touch.'

We stood. I felt awkward. Should we shake hands? Kiss on the cheek? God - on the mouth??? He touched me on the shoulder as we parted. 'Talk soon.' And then the laneway swallowed him up.

Saturday, 28th January

So, here I am today, Saturday, wondering when/if he'll ring me. I'm flabbergasted. I've NEVER been offered a job before. I stand in front of the mirror trying not to see my body under the transparent nightie. What did he see in me? The new me? Well, he didn't know the old one, thank goodness, but is it ME or the assistant he needs? Most probably the latter but ... maybe he needs some comfort as that awful wife of his treats him so badly. I could give him the comfort, says the new me, but the old one is scared shitless (no doubt this expression has come from April). What would I know about comforting anyone, much less Mr Sky Blue Eyes - Matt? What would he like? How would he like it? My heart races. What do I know about anything? I mean - ANYTHING???

My love life, if you could call it that, adds up to a huge zero. Not unless you count ... no - don't go there. My love life, if you could call it that, adds up to ...

Stop it!

Stop thinking!

Go feed Merv.

No. I've already fed him.

Ring April.

What for?

Change of pace?

Thinking?

'Hi there, April,' I say. 'I hate talking into these answering machines. It shouldn't make any difference from talking naturally but it does.' I clear my throat. 'Anyway, if you get home before ten, give me a call.'

I wait.

'Bye.'

I shake a few flakes into Merv's tank - just in case.

The phone rings.

'June!' I slump back into my chair with relief. 'What's up?'

'Oh, I just thought I'd see if you're busy?'

'On a Saturday night? Geez, June. I'm beating the boys off at the door as we speak.' She chortles. 'What've you got in mind?'

'Oh, I don't know,' I say, fighting back tears. 'Have you eaten yet?'

'Nope.' I can hear her sucking air between her front teeth. 'You want me to go over to yours?'

'Well, April,' I sigh, 'that'd be just lovely.'

'Okey dokey, I'll pick up some takeaway on my way through. You got some wine?'

'Actually, I do.'

'That'll be a first,' she snorts. 'I'll get some more, just in case. I want to hear all about this bloody boyfriend of yours that you've been hiding under a rock.'

'So that's it in a nutshell,' I say, collapsing back into my armchair. I reach over to my glass and take a good sip. I'm dry in the mouth after telling April all about Matt.

She's sitting regarding me with those hooded eyes that appear to be hiding lots of thoughts, both good and bad. I can actually see the tip of her tongue darting between her front teeth.

'Are you going to take it?' she says eventually.

'What, the job?'

She nods.

'I haven't got it yet,' I say cautiously. 'Besides that, I don't know if I want to leave Danks anyway.'

'What!' she screeches. 'Miss the chance of a lifetime? Maybe even an affair with him?'

I look at her, my heart racing. I feel breathless because she's put what I want more than anything out in the open. 'An affair?' It comes out as a squeak.

April's head goes to one side as she looks me up and down, sucking at her teeth. 'An affair shouldn't be a problem for a woman your age. You've still got time...'

'Oh, thanks a lot!'

'What I mean is,' she grimaces, 'you haven't gone totally to fat...'

My mouth drops open in shock.

'...and with a bit of exercise we could get you fit enough.'

My mouth is still open.

'How long since you last had a man?'

My mouth closes with a snap of my teeth. I'm speechless.

'No bullshitting me, now,' she admonishes. 'When?'

'I...'

'Yes?'

'I really don't...'

'Yes?'

'April, I can't...'

'Oh, Junee, I didn't mean to make you cry!' She comes around and pats me on the shoulder. 'Really.' A couple more pats. 'Why are you crying, anyway?'

She leans over and looks me straight in the eyes. Then I really start to cry. 'I can't talk about it,' I blubber.

'You've had a broken heart?'

'No ... no ... '

And I'm suddenly back fifty years.

Bloody Disgrace

I'm 13, I think. I'm bailed up behind the shelter sheds at school. There are four boys. They're goading me on. 'June the goon, June the goon, show us your prune!' They're pressing me up against the back fence, pushing my dress up, pulling at my underpants. I'm fighting for all I'm worth - silently - as I bite, scratch, hit, punch. But two boys grab my wrists. They pin them against the fence. The other two pull my pants down.

'Get a load of her bush!' one boy laughs.

'Get a load of her flab,' another giggles. He grabs my spare tyre and wobbles it. 'Pork belly!'

'Oink! Oink!' they jeer.

The ringleader is unzipping his pants.

'No!' I yell, but one of them clamps his hand over my mouth. I try to bite him but he wacks me across the face. 'Shut up, porky.'

I feel his penis try to gain entry between my legs. He pushes against me, grunting. 'Jesus,' he mumbles. 'Tight as a fish's arse.'

I feel something tearing. A red-hot pain sears me. I gasp. He keeps pushing until his thing gets inside me. I will myself not to cry. Then he's thrusting, again and again, until he collapses against me and is pushed out of the way. Another of the four grabs hold of my bum and pulls me towards his erect penis. 'Come on, June, give us what you've got.' And he pounds his way into what makes me different from him. I have a cavity that he can fill with his essence, despite the fact that I don't want him to. I have no say in it. This is what makes me female. The weaker sex. Dominated by the urges of the vile male.

I spit in his face, looking directly into his red eyes.

'Bitch!' he yells, punching me in the stomach as he unwillingly exits me.

I double over as his fist strikes under my chin.

And then I don't remember anything. Except finding myself in a heap against the fence.

Alone.

I somehow get home.

Mum takes one look at me. She says, 'Jesus Christ. What a bloody mess. What the hell have you been up to?' She makes as if to hit me. 'Go and clean yourself up. You stink!' She turns back to the stove.

I feel blood running down my legs. 'Mum!' I cry.

'Coming home like that,' she says out of the corner of her mouth. 'Bloody disgrace. Thank Christ you're not my...'

And I miss that comment.

As always.

A broken heart?

I can't answer April.

I've never told anyone what happened that day.

I just shake my head.

She looks at me and knows. Somehow she knows.

'It's your secret, June,' she whispers. 'You don't have to tell me.'

And she hugs me.

I cry like a baby.

Monday, 30ᵗʰ January

'Now for the next folder,' Merv says, reliving his excitement over his holiday. This is the fourth folder in his gallery that I've had to sit through. Neither he nor Trish are good photographers. They cut off heads and have some interesting views of asphalt and sand. It doesn't matter to him. He thinks every one of the hundreds of photos is fantastic.

'What did Marj say?' I ask.

He grins. 'We didn't tell her.' He holds up his hands against my expression. 'You did such a good job lying your head off that we decided to keep it that way.'

'What about your tans?' His forehead's peeling and the rest of his face and neck are bright red.

'We told her we went to a solarium and they cooked us. Wants us to sue them. We said we're thinking about it.'

'I declare your nose is getting longer by the minute,' I scold him.

My mobile buzzes in my pocket. I take it out to see who's calling. It's HIM!!

'Ah, Merv, I have to answer this one,' I say as I back out of his door. 'Sorry.'

He looks deflated but soon turns back to his screen and smiles at whatever photo he's looking at.

'Hello?' My hand shakes as I take him into the ladies bathroom.

'June,' he says in his mellifluous voice. 'I'm glad I caught you.'

Me too, I think. *You don't have any idea how much.*

'Is this a bad time to talk?'

'No. No, it's fine,' I say trying to keep the emotion out of my voice.

'About our conversation the other day. A job interview.'

'Yes,' I croak. 'I remember.'

'Would you like to come in for an interview Friday after work, say at 5:30?'

'Yes, that'd be fine,' I say slowly, going cross-eyed in the mirror.

'That's if you're interested,' he breathes into his phone. 'We didn't really talk about the conditions, pay, etc., but we can fill you in on Friday.'

'That's okay,' I smile at my reflection, trying a pout on for size. 'We can sort that out then.'

The door opens with a bang and Amy rushes to an empty cubicle.

'Sorry, Matt,' I grimace. 'I have to go now.'

'Of course, June,' he says with a smile in his voice. 'Until then.'

I spend a good five minutes sitting on the loo imagining telling Merv that I'm leaving. After all these years. Maybe I won't get the job. Maybe I'll just be Matt's ... what ... friend???

'Lunch,' I hiss out of the corner of my mouth as I pass April's desk.

She looks up confused. 'Today?'

I nod, looking back at her. 'Shopping.'

A huge grin grows all over her face. 'Ahhh,' she says softly with a knowing expression.

'What's that?' BBB mutters as he glares at his screen.

'Nothing,' April and I say at the same time.

The lift is full as we descend. April can hardly contain herself. 'So, what's up?' she squeals, as soon as we burst out of the building.

'Matt rang.'

Her mouth opens wide. 'He did?'

'Job interview. Friday.'

'Awesome!'

'Well, yes,' I say, cautiously. 'But I can't imagine ...'

'... leaving Danks?' She's almost shouting. 'Really? Junee, this is a step up the corporate ladder. Advancement. Pay rise ...'

'I don't need a pay rise.'

'Everyone needs a pay rise!'

'I don't.'

'What the ...'

'Not that I get a huge salary, mind you,' I say, dragging her over to a Myers window. We look in but our minds don't register the mannequins. 'But I just don't need it.'

'You've been spending a heap on clothes, shoes and perfume lately. Aren't you running a bit short?'

I shake my head. 'No. I've hardly made a dent in my balance.'

She turns from the window. 'What do you spend your money on, besides rent and takeaway?'

'Fish food.'

She pulls a face.

'Gas, electricity, water, phone.'

'What else?' she demands.

I think hard. 'Public transport. Underwear ...'

'Oh, yeah. I saw your hundred-year-old bras and knickers, don't forget. You haven't spent much on them lately.'

'I went to Beechworth for Gran's letter.'

She runs her tongue over her top teeth as she stares at me. 'Not that it's my business, but what *do* you do with your money?'

'Save it.'

'Invest it, you mean?'

'Yes. I have a couple of term deposits.'

'Property?'

I shake my head. 'I'd be terrified.'

'What - you'd rather pay rent than own your own?'

'It's the risk, April. I wouldn't know what to do.'

'You haven't been to a financial advisor?'

'Oh, no.' We make our way towards Myers entrance. 'They charge too much.'

She grabs me by the arm as we pass the perfumes. 'Since you began work, how many holidays have you taken?'

'None, really.'

'Why not?'

'Nowhere to go. No one to go with.'

'Geez. All those years and no holiday. What does Merv think?'

I step on the escalator. 'I've no idea,' I say as I look down at her. 'We've never discussed it.'

We step off the escalator and make our way over to the clothing racks. April flits from one to the other. 'Classy but understated,' she mumbles to herself. I fumble ineffectually around the clothes having not the faintest idea what to look for much less imagine how it would look on me. I thank my lucky stars that April's in my life. For the thousandth time.

April tops up my glass again. 'Careful,' I say, 'I don't want to get drunk.'

'Well, why the hell not? About time you let your hair down, Junee,' she snorts, 'but I think you're doing it in other ways.'

'What do you mean?' Though I know what she's thinking.

'The boyfriend.'

I look at her through the wine in my glass. 'He's not my boyfriend.' I try to hide my fear. 'Yet.'

We go through the pile of clothes, shoes, handbag, scarf. More underwear. Enough to make me look different from when I last saw Matt and hopefully halfway attractive. April's been showing me how to apply eye makeup and use a lip liner too. I've never had anyone be that generous with me.

Mum - not my mum - would never spend that much time with me. I don't remember her ever reading to me, helping me with my homework, showing me how to cook, how to weed the garden, even. She just barked orders and expected me to know what to do.

My first period was a total surprise to me. I thought I was bleeding to death until Sandra started laughing her sides out. She knew but she didn't enlighten me. I thought it might have had something to do with what those boys did to me. I went around to Gran's place with a wad of rags between my legs crying my eyes out. 'Oh, you silly sausage,' Gran said in mock seriousness, 'that's you turning into a woman.'

'I'm not ready to be a woman,' I wailed. 'I just want to be a normal girl.'

'Well, you are, Darl, but this is the next step in you growing up.' She patted me on the back. 'Didn't your mum tell you about it?'

Mum never told me anything. Period.

April leaves after she's satisfied I know how to dress and put my makeup on. 'Don't forget the nail polish Thursday night,' she reminds me. 'Last time you put it on, you had more on your fingers than your nails. At least there'll be time for you to chisel it off.' She's laughing, but *with* me. There's a difference.

I decide to go through my mail before I go to bed. There's another letter from the bank asking me to talk to one of their financial advisors. Again. Funny that April mentioned getting advice. It's more new territory which I don't know I'm ready for. My statement has arrived today as well. I check my balance. It stands at $788,942.43 which I realise is a sizeable amount. Well, it should be after all these years of saving.

I'm lying in bed wondering what will happen at the interview. I admit to myself that I don't want a new job and that if Matt says I can have it, then I'll decline nicely and see you later alligator! But what if ... what if ... it's ME he's interested in?????

Don't be stupid, June. Of course he's not. Who are you kidding? Not me, that's for sure. I know what I look like in a mirror. Double chin. Pasty skin. Big fat stomach, spare tyre, wobbly thighs, mousy hair (well, it was until April dragged me to a different hairdresser). The list could go on - all negative - until the cows come home. Makeover or not, you can't hide the real me. And that's not much.

But I'm a nice person, aren't I? I mean, I don't think I'm a bitchy person. Merv wouldn't have kept me on for so many years if I was stupid, would he? I must be all right if I can manage the office when he's out. Is that what Matt sees in me? Really? An efficient office worker? They're a dime a dozen. One who can handle crass train passengers? Oh, come on! Anyone could do that, couldn't they? Well, they didn't. It was just me. That must stand for something.

Don't count your chickens before they hatch, June. Wait until Friday and see what happens.

I turn my lamp off. There's the dim glow from the driveway lights that shines into my bedroom. I like it that way. I can make out the ceiling fan as my eyes become accustomed to the gloom. I scan the walls for alien shadows and realise I have nothing at all on them. Not one picture. Not one photo. I'm pondering the question as I fall asleep.

Friday, 3rd February

I step off the train and take the escalator to get me up to Flinders Street. I look down at my fingernails on the handrail. They're (almost) perfectly painted - or is it 'polished'? Either way, the cyclamen enamel covers a multitude of sins, including ridges. The left middle fingernail is smudged a bit, but I'll keep it out of sight. I'm conscious of the matching lipstick that is moisturising my lips and lifting the colour in my otherwise pale face. I got up really early to apply the eye makeup. That was a marathon. I jabbed my left and right eyeballs multiple times with the mascara wand until they watered eyeliner all over my foundation. Stupid! I should have listened when April told me to do the eye makeup first in case of 'waterfall', as she called it. Now I know what she means.

The lip liner had a mind of its own when I sneezed, streaking across my cheek and landing in my ear. I have no idea how I did that. Ask me to do it again and I probably couldn't. It took lots of soap and scrubbing to get the line off my face. That was after I'd reapplied the foundation after the mascara debacle, so I had to do it all again.

Luckily April insisted I buy half a dozen pairs of panty hose. I put my fingernail through the ankle of the third pair I've ruined this week. Why wasn't I born male?

BBB studies me as I walk past his desk at morning tea time. 'Going somewhere special?' he asks, as I dodge the airspace between his mouth and my rapid passage by him.

I answer with a mysterious smile. Well, that's what I think I plastered on my foundation-stiff face.

Mel leans back in her chair to see what BBB is talking about. She makes no comment.

Just before lunch, Merv calls me into his office. 'Is it your birthday? I thought it was the sixth of June.'

'Of course my birthday's sixth of June,' I laugh. 'Gee, Merv. You ought to know that by now.'

'Well, I do,' he concedes. 'Why are you dressed up like that, then? A special occasion?'

Quick as a flash I say: 'Lunch with a cousin from Beechworth.'

'Hmmm,' he remarks, his attention already on his laptop. He traces something on the screen.

'Merv!' I admonish.

'Huh?'

'How many times have I told you not to put your dirty fingers on the screen. It isn't a touch screen.'

His fingers leap back as if scalded. He's got a silly grin on his face.

I find an empty bench outside the State Library in Swanston Street, not far from the office. I open my sandwich and sit eating it as I watch the passengers going in and out of Melbourne Central. I feel pretty confident no one from work would visit the library. None of them are big on books.

April's at the dentist, expecting at least one filling, poor thing. She was fairly nervous, which is the first time I've actually seen her not her usual self. Not for the first time, I wonder about her private life. She talks about her dad back on the Gold Coast, her schooling, her childhood without a mother, but she never talks about what she does here in Melbourne. She's always available to come to my place, or happy for me to go to hers, but there's no hint of a boyfriend, friends, relations. Nothing. She's not an oil painting but she's not ugly by any means. She'd attract a certain type. She's very worldly (can teach me a thing or two), sharp as a whip, and has an opinion on just about everything. A young woman her age should be thinking about settling down and having kids before it's too late. I hope she doesn't end up like me.

I'm surprised when I look at my watch. I've been daydreaming for ages. My stomach is tied up in knots when I realise it's just over four hours until I see Matt again. My heart races as I go over all the pros and cons of actually turning up. I try to walk confidently along the footpath but my bunions are killing me and I've got a blister on one heel. I'd give anything for my comfy flats.

'See you tomorrow,' Amy calls out as she turns the switchboard over to night mode.

Merv left early and BBB snuck out after him. Mel followed suit.

There's just April and me left to turn out the lights and lock the front door. She checks me over. 'You'll do,' she nods.

'Thanks,' I whisper.

We take the lift down without speaking. When the door opens, we head for the exit.

'You promise to call the minute you're free?'

I nod, devoid of all saliva. She pushes a chewing gum into my hand. 'Just spit it out before you get there.'

There are three of them: Matt, a beautiful blonde woman of about forty years, and an older man who looks to be on his last legs. He's grey and his eyes are red-rimmed.

'June, I'd like you to meet Rebecca, our HR manager, and this is our office manager, Alan Fortescue,' he says, indicating the sick man. 'We're a close-knit group here so we rely upon each other a lot.'

I shake hands with them over what looks to me to be a red gum table, highly polished. Beautiful. Classy. I sink into the pewter-coloured carpet. I could sleep on it, it's so deep and soft. The furniture matches the table. The view from the eighth floor is to die for. None of this reminds me of Danks. I feel totally out of place. I'm scared stiff I'll burp like Merv or wet my pants.

The interview goes very well, I think. I can hardly remember what we talked about, other than my rescuing an entire trainload of passengers on their way to the city from a foul-mouthed terrorist. This seems to make me overly qualified for whatever job it is Matt is offering me. I just don't know what to say. The salary they suggest is obscene. So are the perks.

'I'll need some time to think about it,' I squeeze out from my deflated lungs. 'If that's all right.'

'Of course,' they chorus. 'Take your time.'

In no time at all, Rebecca and Alan disappear leaving Matt and me alone with the polished table. 'Can I get you a drink?' he asks. 'Whisky? Brandy? Wine? A liqueur?'

I'm dazzled by the choice. 'Wine's lovely, thanks. A shiraz, if you have it.' I know he will.

He pours a generous helping into a bulbous glass that looks like it cost at least $200. Just the glass. Never mind the wine, which I'm sure comes from the best vintage and vineyard in Australia. I know, because when it hits my taste-buds I'm a goner. He joins me on my side of the table. Swirls the same wine in his glass and clinks it against mine. 'To the future,' he toasts. 'To you.' He hits me with a smile that would melt an Eskimo's heart. 'To us.' This with a question mark pulling up one eyebrow.

He's looking at my mouth. I lick my lips nervously.

'You know, June,' he breathes close enough that I can smell his aftershave, 'I sense your reticence over leaving your current position but, whether you come to work with us or not, I hope that makes no difference to what could be - that I hope will be - something that you and I can make of a beautiful and rewarding friendship.'

I've forgotten how to breathe. His face, his eyes, are just inches from mine. My glasses are fogging up and I'm not sure if he's looking at me or something behind my head. The fumes from the wine are gushing out of my nostrils and burning the lining of my mouth. I feel a little dizzy.

He gently removes my glasses and moves even closer to me, looking into my eyes, though his are blurry without my glasses, and suddenly I feel his lips brushing mine. This happens so unexpectedly that I jump and my glass jumps with me. The wine in my glass shoots out and hits Matt on his white shirt collar, down his jacket front and onto his lap and - oh, my goodness, his fly!

Sitting in the taxi, my lips still tingle with the feel of Matt's on a part of me that's never been touched. My lips that speak, that smile, that close upon a mouthful of food, that deny germs access to my digestive tract. I can hardly believe that such light contact can invoke these powerful sensations. I marvel at how close it is to the descriptions in the countless Mills & Boon romance novels I've read. It's true, after all. A kiss is a gateway to the promise of more delicious, more enticing, more frightening emotions. I've read it a thousand times - the impact of a first kiss. None of the books have a 62 year-old heroine, though, who's never been kissed.

Where do I go from here after such an abrupt ending to our little tête-à-tête? Will he ever speak to me again? He must think me so clumsy! So useless. So ... I don't know ... nothing like that Rebecca who's so sophisticated (but nice). He assured me that he'll give me a call soon. That he hopes I'll take the job. Was he just being kind?

I hold it together until I see Merv's happy greeting - does he love me just because I drop fish flakes into his tank? 'Sorry Merv,' I blubber as my tears drip into his fortified/sanitised/homogenised tank. 'I'm such a klutz. I'll change your water tomorrow.'

I'm staring at the ceiling as I go over the interview in my head. I try reading my latest Mills & Boon but it depresses me. Most of the covers show gorgeous females and males pawing each other, no-one like plain old me. I dig my old cotton nightie out from the back of my wardrobe where April wouldn't find it. I don't feel even half-way glamorous enough to put on my new sexy night attire. I think I'll laugh at myself and I don't need that right now.

Maybe I should go back to Beechworth where I belong.

No I don't.

Forget Matt.

Forget trying to tart myself up.

What's the use?

You can't get a flower to bloom from a dried-up old stalk.

Who are you kidding?

I'm trying to climb a ladder that disappears into clouds. The higher I go, the more afraid I become. I'm scared to look down, scared to look up. I'm shaking as each rung crumbles in my hands and I cling to the sides of the ladder to stop falling. I'm in the middle of nowhere. Terrified. A noise shakes the ladder as I reach for the next rung. It crumbles and I scream.

The phone wakes me.

Thank goodness.

'June?

'Oh, I...'

'Are you all right? I've been worried sick.' April's almost shouting.

'It's ...' I turn to look at the clock, '... twelve thirty!'

'You promised, you promised me you'd call,' April splutters. 'I was going to call the police.'

'Oh, April,' I start crying. 'I'm so sorry. I completely forgot.'

'You forgot! How the fuck could you ...'

'It's just that it ended up such a disaster,' I blubber, 'that I drowned Merv.'

'What? You drowned Merv! What's the fuck's going on?'

Considering she's so worried about me, I let the language go without comment.

'Merv the fish, April.' I start hiccupping and laughing at the same time.

'It's about time you changed that bloody fish's name, for Christ's sake,' she says crossly. Then she starts laughing too. 'So, why the fuck are we laughing?

Saturday, 4th February

It's Saturday night and we're both sitting back watching *An Affair to Remember*. I can't believe April's never seen it before.

'I don't think I've ever seen a movie *that* old,' she says, pulling a face when I suggest we watch it.

'It was made in 1957,' I tell her, and point out how handsome Cary Grant is.

'I suppose ...' she concedes, '... in an old fashioned sort of way.'

Just to please me, she sits through it and actually cries at the end. I always do.

'Wouldn't have happened if they had mobile phones.'

'No, of course not,' I reply, 'and modern medical science would have fixed her up in no time and she'd be running in the Olympics.'

April snorts and tops up our wine. I'm feeling quite heady as we've gone through a bottle by now.

'And there'd be no romance in the world,' I finish.

She flicks through a book from the latest pile of Mills & Boon that I picked up from the library last week.

'What do you read this shit for?'

'It's not shit!'

'It's not real, either.'

'Who says?' I retort, disappointed she's having a go at what I enjoy so much. 'If there was no romance, there'd be no dreams, no weddings, no babies, no population.'

'Well, it hasn't happened to you, has it?'

'You either,' I say quietly.

Monday, 6ᵗʰ February

Of course I'm not going to take the job, even if Matt offers it to me again. I'd be so embarrassed and so out of place. No use kidding myself. So, should I call him or wait for him to call? Hang on! It was a job interview. I don't think it was all up to Matt. Why would Rebecca and Alan have been there if not to check me out? Matt would have had to confer with them and, of course, they'd have confirmed what a klutz I am. Story over. He seemed so sure I had the job if I wanted it, though. Oh, I don't know. I'm out of touch with how they run things these days. I haven't had to look for another job since Adam was a pup.

Merv's rabbiting on about Bali again. 'It's so cheap, June. You should go. Take a holiday for a change. See how the other half live.'

I open my mouth to tell him I wouldn't go there in a fit, but he's already onto the food, the genuine imitation watches - he holds his fake Rolex up for me to see - and the monkeys, the massages, the views, the pools, the surfing - '... not that Trish and I had time for that ...' and so on. He'd look like a beached whale if he tried surfing. As a matter of fact, so would I.

He's turning his screen around to show me more photos when my mobile rings. I've been keeping it in my pocket, just in case. It's Matt.

'Sorry, Merv.' I hold up the mobile and make a quick exit.

Back to the toilets. Thank goodness no one else's in there.

Matt asks if I'm okay. If *I'm* okay. What about his wine-stained fly???? How considerate can a man get? I ask him if he's calling about the job interview. He tells me Rebecca and Alan were impressed with me. Really?! I'll bet his nose is growing rapidly.

I say: 'Are you telling me that I have the job?'

'Of course!' he smiles through the phone. I can feel it.

'But ...'

'When would you like to start?'

OMG - I've learned that from April. 'Matt, I'm sorry. Really. But I can't take the position.'

'Oh, June ...'

'No, and please don't think I'm not grateful, but I couldn't possibly leave Danks.' There, I've said it. 'I'd be letting my boss down and, actually, I'm happy here, attractive though your proposition is.'

There's a bit of a silence at his end.

'Matt?'

'Yes. Yes,' he says. 'Of course I'm disappointed - so will Rebecca and Alan be - but I respect your decision.'

I blink away tears. I'm rejecting the best offer I've had in my life. I can't believe it.

'However,' he adds, 'I meant what I said on Friday night.' His warm breath leaks from the receiver. 'I hope that we can still be friends.'

I take a deep breath of my own. 'I'd like that, Matt.'

'Excellent! Would you be free for dinner on Wednesday evening?'

I make myself a coffee and one for Merv as well. I put his down in front of him and see that he's still mooning over his Bali photos. 'Did I tell you about ...?'

By the time we've drunk our coffee, we're up to their flight back to Melbourne. I think my eyes must have glassed over.

'June?'

'Ummm?'

'Are you looking for a new job?'

'What!' Just as well I'd finished my coffee or it'd be a replay of last Friday night - coffee vs. red wine. 'What makes you ask that, of all things?'

'Secret phone calls ...'

'Oh, that,' I laugh. 'Solicitor. Gran's will. Legal stuff.' I see a worried look on his face. 'Merv, I'd never leave Danks. You'd cark it without me and I'm not about to be charged with your murder.'

'Oh, June, you had me worried for a minute,' he grins and belches for good measure.

Wednesday, 8th February

During the next few days, April and I work out what I'm going to wear on my first dinner date ever. Of course we did that in Myers. I bought an elegant midnight blue Basque dress, a silver grey coat, shoes, bag, jewellery. April looked concerned at the price tags but I reassured her there's no problem. Well, there isn't, is there? My bank balance, for once, is doing something for me. She salivated over her favourite unreachable (money-wise) perfume as we were walking out. I made a mental note to buy her a bottle as a surprise. It's the least I can do.

I have my hair tinted, trimmed and blow dried on Tuesday. April said to do it the day before so I don't look like a try-hard having it done the day of the dinner date. 'Look casual about it, Junee, like you go out for dinner all the time. A hairdo is the least of your concerns.' She sucks air between her teeth and grins.

I look at her in amazement. 'I think you're an old soul.'

'I told you I'm not religious,' she retorts.

'No,' I tell her. 'I think you've been here before.'

'In Myer?'

'Silly.' She makes me laugh sometimes. Well, actually, quite a lot. 'An old soul has been around the block a few times when it comes to lifetimes on Earth. They gain knowledge from their past lives and apply it to their present life.'

'That's weird. Do you really believe that stuff?'

'I just think you've been here before,' I tell her. 'You know so much more about life than I ever will.'

We're in a bar after work. She holds up her glass to me. 'And you're one of the most innocent, unspoiled persons I know. Even an old sort like you.'

'Gee, thanks.' I pull a face.

'No offence.'

'None taken.'

We sit in companionable silence for a while - well, if you could call piped modern music (noise), silence. We're comfortable with each other most times.

'You know, I was reading a book ...'

'M & B?'

I have to think about that for a minute. 'You mean Mills & Boon?'

'God, June, you're sharp tonight.'

'Oh, shut up!'

'No offence.'

'None taken.'

'So ...?'

'Oh, the book. Yes, it was about that sort of thing. The heroine is a lot younger than her would-be lover but she can see through him, understands him ... in fact it reminds me of a film I was watching ...'

'Junee, have you ever read or watched anything that is not a romance? The classics, for example? Something to get your teeth into?'

'Like what?'

'Oh, I don't know - *Moby Dick, Wuthering Heights, Lord of the Flies, Treasure Island, Robinson Crusoe, Oliver Twist* ...'

'Well, I've heard of them. Do they have nice endings?'

'It depends upon what you class as *nice*.'

And so begins my classical education, according to April.

Matt arrives at my flat at the appointed time in a shiny dark green car. He looks at me admiringly, tells me I look beautiful (oh, come on, I can see in the mirror!), takes me by the hand and guides me onto the car's luxurious seat. I feel like a million dollars but know I'm only worth two and six. I tell myself I can pretend.

He orders for me (thank goodness because I don't understand the menu and I can't even see it as the print is so small and pale) and sits back for the waiter to pour our wine. Thank goodness April has schooled me, to some degree, in appreciating wine. At least I don't cough and splutter and say it's too bitter. In fact, it's delicious. It coats my mouth with warm berry flavours (don't I sound the professional?) that explode my senses (I've read that somewhere). I've never tasted anything like it. I could get used to this. The food is beyond my expectations and Matt guides the conversation to include my opinions and comments that I didn't even know I had. By the time we leave the restaurant, I'm on Cloud 9.

I'm nervous when he pours me back into the car. What's going to happen now? Somehow, we end up in a beautiful hotel suite. The bathroom is bigger than the whole block of flats I live in. I pamper myself in my alcohol-infused state and I don't care a bugger.

Que Sera, Sera,

Whatever will be, will be
The future's not ours, to see
Que Sera, Sera.

What that man does to me I'll never forget. He shows me what it is to compliment a man with my woman's body. It doesn't matter that mine doesn't look like Julia Roberts' body. Mine is mine and that's the best I can do. And he pulls delights from my insides that I didn't know I possessed. This is the stuff of M & B. All those romantic books didn't exaggerate. This is the real deal. My body, my mind, are singing.

I sleep with his body around mine - spooning - and his warmth, his smell, his everything, keeps me from thinking about tomorrow. I wallow in the now and grab it with both hands. Well - more than that, I'm embarrassed to say. If I never see him again, at least I have tonight.

Thursday, 9th February

Amy calls me on the intercom in such an excited voice. 'June! You've got a delivery.'

'Thanks, Amy. I'll get it when I finish my emails.'

She squeals. 'No! You *have* to come and get it *now*!'

What's wrong with the girl? She sounds like she's about to have a fit.

I go out to reception to find her cradling an enormous - and I mean *enormous* - bunch of yellow roses. She hands them to me.

'What?' I'm stunned. 'There must be some mistake.'

'No,' she squeals, 'look at the envelope. It says it's for you!'

Sure enough, my name's on it. Who would send me flowers? No - it can't be ...'

I open the envelope and the card says: *My thanks for a beautiful, romantic evening. M*

I try desperately to control the blush that is surging up from my throat. BBB and Mel swivel their heads at precisely the same moment. Their mouths are hanging open.

BBB smirks. 'Got an admirer, June?'

'Mind your own bloody business,' I snap.

That wipes the smirk off his face. 'Jesus, I only ...'

I ignore him as I go to the kitchen to put the flowers in a vase. Mel and April follow me. Mel's trying to get at the card but April snatches it first, holding it close to her chest. She glances at it then grins at me knowingly.

'Well? Well?' Mel's miffed.

'A congratulatory gift,' I say, 'for some studying I've taken up.'

'What sort of study?' Mel frowns.

'Human resources' April snorts. 'Good marks?'

I turn to the sink trying not to laugh.

They are the first bunch of flowers I've ever received. I'm pathetically grateful, excited, gobsmacked. I just don't understand. What does he see in me? Was I good in bed, despite the fact I had no idea what I was doing? Instinct, I've discovered, is a good attribute to nourish. And, of course, he was a good teacher.

I arrange the flowers lovingly and take them to my desk. They are a constant reminder of last night. I can't concentrate on my work.

'Who are these for?' Merv asks as he passes my desk on the way to the toilet.

'Who the bloody hell do you think they're for?' I ask.

'Well,' he says, 'who's the tetchy one today?'

'Sorry,' I mumble. 'It'd just be nice if more than one person on this Earth thinks I'm worth sending flowers to.'

'Oh, June.' Merv is contrite. 'Of course - you deserve flowers all the time; you're such a good person.'

I smile up at him. 'Don't take any notice of me.'

'No, really,' he says. 'I think we've all been taking you for granted. Here,' he continues, digging into his pocket. 'Go and buy yourself some red roses from me.'

'Gee, ta, Merv.' He has no bloody idea.

I go to April's for dinner. She's already got Chinese takeaway and I bring a bottle of something that I like because of the label. It's got something to do with a swaggie and the land the vineyard is on. I go home first to drop off the flowers. Merv gives a definite swish of the tail as I place them near him.

'Get an eyeful of these, Merv.'

Another swish.

That deserves a good shake of fish flakes.

'We'll enjoy them together,' I coo at him. 'I hope you like yellow.'

April wants to know *everything*, of course. She punctuates my account of the night with musical snorts between mouthfuls of food and wine. She pronounces the wine *passable*. She's impressed about the hotel.

'Week night - hotel - easy to disguise for a meeting interstate. The wife won't be any the wiser.'

That sounds so mercenary. Is that how it is? Should I feel guilty? Somehow I justify it thinking that if it wasn't me it would probably be someone else. Let's not beat around the bush here. Reality slips in guided by April. I voice my disbelief about his choosing me and his motives.

'Well, let's face it, Junee. If it was for a quick fuck ...'

'Must you!!!??'

'I'm saying it how it is.'

I try not to shudder at the thought as I take a sip of the passable wine.

'Look - dinner, great night in bed. All okay for a casual night. But the yellow roses? I don't know,' she says, shaking her head. 'Sounds more serious to me.'

'Really?'

'Well, yeah. The rest of the night is bodily functions ...'

I grimace.

'Eating, drinking, screwing. But flowers spell romance. Commitment. Though how he can do that with a wife onboard is beyond me.'

'Maybe they're about to split up?'

'Oh, puleeeeez!' She tops up our glasses. 'Don't ever fall for that line.'

'Well ...'

'Has he got kids?'

'Three ...'

'Then forget it. He won't leave the kids - never mind the wife - for you. Ever.'

So I wait.

My old nightie has returned to the back of my wardrobe and I'm looking at myself in the mirror. If I squint, I see the sexy night attire. I try not to see what's stuffed into it. If I take my glasses off, I can't see more than a coloured outline. That'll do.

Monday, 13th February

I've noticed lately that a set of male twins gets on the 8:05 train that I take, usually through the same door. But today it's through different doors. I find it strange, as if they don't know each other. They clearly look the same so I don't know who they're fooling.

I like to think that they live together but they don't work together. Do they take it in turns to drive to the station? Is it because they spend so much time together, they sit/stand in different spots? I suppose the more the train fills up, the more people wouldn't notice that there are two identical people in separate parts of the carriage.

They have identical haircuts. Short, mid-brown hair. Restless hazel eyes. Medium height. Stocky bodies. Probably mid-late thirties. Mirror images, except for their clothes.

Could they be Heckle & Jeckle? Laurel & Hardy? Daniel & David? Jacob & Joshua, Isaac & Isaiah, Jayden & Jordan, Ethan & Evan? Oh, stop it! Don't be ridiculous. They could be Malcolm and Evan.

Today Twin #1 sits next to me. I smell his aftershave. Nice. He holds his mobile tightly, like he's afraid of dropping it, as he texts rapidly with his two thumbs. Maybe he's texting Twin #2, who's at the end of the carriage, not looking at his mobile. I try to read what he's texting out of the corner of my eye. I see: *same fucking ... last nights ... drinks on the ... see you @ ...* I haven't a clue. They both exit the train at Richmond. I notice they don't speak to each other on the platform and touch off with their Myki cards at least 10 passengers apart.

Intriguing.

Merv has his feet up on his desk, looking very self-satisfied. 'Come in! Come in,' he invites expansively.

I look at him suspiciously. 'What?'

'June. June. Don't look at me like that.'

'Well, how am I supposed to look at you.' I take my glasses off. 'There, the rose coloured glasses are off. What's up?'

He sighs. 'Shakespeare said: *Familiarity breeds contempt ...*'

'You're sure it was Shakespeare?'

'Well, never mind,' he says, taking his feet off the desk. 'I just thought I'd let you know that Trish and I are off again for another holiday.'

'You're kidding.'

'Nope.'

'Does Trish know?'

'Nope.'

'Ahhh, I see it all. You're about to whisk her away again.'

'Yep. Marj won't have an inkling until it's too late.'

'Don't bet on it.'

'I know. I know. I'm being very careful.'

'Where to this time?'

'A campervan trip around Kiwiland.'

'How nice for you.' I try to show some enthusiasm. 'How long and when?'

'First of March for three weeks.'

'Hmmm ...'

'You'll hold the fort again, June?'

Later that day I send Merv an email:

Actually, according to Google, Aesop said: Familiarity breeds contempt. Mark Twain changed it to say: Familiarity breeds contempt and children. I wonder if that includes mothers-in-law as well?

'Spot on,' he replies.

Tuesday, 14th February

Laurel and Hardy are in my carriage again - at opposite ends looking detached. Without standing over the one seated opposite me with a magnifying glass, I have no idea which one he is. Do they take it in turns to sit/stand? He's wearing black pants and a black windcheater-type jacket over a blue collar. I'm calling him Hardy as that comes first in the alphabet.

He looks over at me and smiles. He smiles. He smiles at me.

'Hi,' he says.

'Hi,' I say.

'You always take this train?'

'Yes, I do.'

And then he leans forward, elbows on knees, and conducts the most amazing conversation with me until he and his brother get off at Richmond. We talk about his parents and his job - he's in IT. He says I remind him of his maths teacher in Year 12. I don't know whether to take that as a compliment or not but he tells me that she had the most influence on his future career than anyone else. I take it as a compliment. He looks up at me and whispers, 'You're better looking, though.'

Silly boy.

Nice boy.

His name is Rob.

I don't tell him that I know he has a twin. I'm leaving that up to him - if we ever meet on the train again.

Wednesday, 15th February

Next morning, sure enough, there he is.

'Gidday June,' he grins. He offers me a muesli bar. I see he brought two. Was one really for me or was it for his twin? I take it anyway.

He asks me if I'm good at maths. 'Reasonable,' I tell him. 'Nothing like you, though.'

Then he asks me how old I am. I'm a bit shocked as I still think it rude to ask a woman her age. Does it matter these days, though? I tell him.

'You're a few years older than my mum,' he says, cocking his head to one side as he studies my face. And everything else. I blush.

'Who do you barrack for?'

'You mean the football?'

'Yeah.' His leg starts jiggling up and down. 'Tell me it's not Collingwood.'

'It's not Collingwood.'

'Who then?'

'I don't follow the football.'

'Whaaaaat? You have to have a footy team.'

'Well, I don't.'

'Why not?'

'I don't like it.'

'Bet you would if I took you to a match. The Hawks, of course,'

I stand over April's desk. 'We have to go to Myers.'

'How many of them?'

'What do you mean? Myers in Bourke Street.'

'There's only one Myer in Bourke Street.'

'April, what *are* you talking about?'

'Why do you always call it Myers? It's Myer. No 's'. Singular.'

I have a think about that. 'Oh. People my age do. I've always called it Myers.'

'About time you didn't.' She swivels back to face her monitor. 'What project do we have to dress for this time?'

'The football.'

For once she's speechless.

I now own a pair of blue jeans. They stretch, thank goodness, though I had to lie on my bed to pull them up. April says they have to be that way or else they're too loose. I now know how women in colonial days felt in their stays. No wonder they fainted.

A dull red woollen jumper underneath a navy parka, and a collared shirt under the jumper. Brown leather ankle-length boots. A Hawthorn scarf to make Rob feel happy.

I can't believe I'm going to the footy.

Saturday, 18th February

We arrange to meet at Richmond Station. I spill out of the train with the crowd that jostles in its excitement to get off the platform and walk across to The Melbourne Cricket Ground (MCG). People in the know call it The G, so now I'm in the know. Rob's at the top of the platform ramp. I'm a bit nervous because I know nothing about footy but I can see Rob is determined to enlighten me.

We squash into the gate entry; Rob points out the toilets as he guides me to our seats. Wow! It's a big arena when you sit there facing the ground. And so many people! Everyone seems so excited, and when the players run through a barrier of paper ribbons, a roar erupts from the stands. I imagine I'm at the Colosseum in Rome and at any moment lions will emerge from the depths of the stadium and face gladiators. These footballers could be gladiators, they're so tall and muscled. You don't get a sense of it on the TV (not that I've spent more than a fleeting moment watching them on TV) but when you see them in person they look gigantic.

I have a vague idea of the rules of the game - I can't have missed all of it as Wayne played when he was a kid. Mum (who's not my mum) and Gran carted Sandra and me to the game to support him. I don't think he was very good at it. He got lots of blood noses and grazed knees and grass stains all over him. Sandra didn't mind going as she had her eye on the footballers.

I thought I'd be bored to snorts by the first quarter but I somehow get caught up in the game. Probably Rob's enthusiasm rubs off on me and I end up cheering for the Hawks along with him. I don't know any of the players but I pretend. At half time we have a traditional pie and sauce and a drink of beer. I burn the roof of my mouth on the pie filling and can't stop burping, like Merv, from the beer, though I burp into my scarf as a lady should.

By the time the game ends - the Hawks beat the Magpies, much to Rob's delight - I have no voice left and am exhausted. Rob is anxious to know if I enjoyed myself. I nod, without lying, that I did, indeed, have a good time. After the return journey back to my flat, I give Merv a quick hello in fish language then pass out cold on the couch. When I wake up, I turn the TV on and see the highlights from the match. Wow - I was there! Would I do it again? I have no idea.

Monday, 20th February

Matt calls me this morning. He invites me for dinner on Wednesday night. He mentions an overnight bag.

'Does Myers ... Myer ... have overnight bags?' I ask April.

She rolls her eyes. 'For?'

'Overnight.'

'Well, yeah, I guessed that. Is this Rob or Matt?'

'Matt.'

'Don't you have one?'

'What?'

'An overnight bag.'

'No, unless a shopping bag will suffice.'

The eyes roll again.

Tuesday, 21st February

This morning, Rob flops down beside me on the train. He tells me that he got pissed on Sunday and couldn't make it to work yesterday. I almost ask him whether his brother was in the same condition but stop myself in time. I can see him standing at the end of the carriage looking out of the window.

'So ... if you liked the footy on Saturday, how about trying something else?'

I look at him in surprise. 'Something else?' Why would a young fellow like him want to spend time with a woman my age? I'm slightly suspicious.

'Yeah, how about sky diving?'

I feel my mouth drop open and catch it before it ends up in my lap.

'Nah, just kidding,' he laughs. 'You like dancing?'

'Ahh, I don't...'

'I don't mean at a trance club or to the latest hip hop track on the charts. I mean ballroom.'

This is the stuff dreams are made of. Dancing in a swirling, gorgeous, long gown that responds to my movements, to the messages passed from my partner to my body so that I know instinctively where to place my feet. I can hear the *Blue Danube* waltzing between my ears, a slow fox trot, a *Pride of Erin*, the *Barn Dance*. My brain scans all the M & B books that I've read where the heroine dances through the pages until she's taken, ravaged, swept off her feet by the hero of the story. Those pages flutter the heartstrings, tickle the senses, provide fodder for the hopeful.

I'm taken back to gatherings when, as a child, I would watch Beechworth couples swirling around the local hall, faces radiant with the joy of the dance. I don't know why my parents never joined in. Gran would sometimes have a hand extended to her in invitation from her chair on the rim of the hall. She'd get up and suddenly transform into a graceful swan gliding across the floor, no longer the coughing, spitting version of her other self.

Never having had the opportunity or an invitation to dance, the dream receded into the grey zone where all my dreams and aspirations ended up. However, the times I was glued to the TV when the DanceSport championships were shown, the dream dragged itself back to be relived for a whisper of a moment. It would retreat again with the flick of the power switch, TV and grey zone joined in the same conspiracy: dream exposed, dream erased.

And, yet, here is this young fellow offering me something I never knew would - could - possibly be mine.

'I don't know how,' I say. I feel a momentary rise of hope fall flat with a thud in my chest.

'That doesn't matter,' he says. 'I can teach you.'

'You can?'

'Of course,' he says. 'I've been dancing for years; I teach as well.'

'Oh,' I manage to breathe, 'and what would that cost?'

'Hey, June,' he laughs, 'this is on the house.'

'Why would you teach me for free?'

He tilts his head to one side, studying me closely. 'I like you,' he says simply. 'I think it would be good for you.'

I don't miss his gaze that glances over my spare tyre and belly.

'Aren't I too old and unfit?'

'You're never too old to dance,' he says with conviction.

I hold my breath for a few hours and then exhale slowly. 'I would love to.'

Wednesday, 22nd February

Matt arrives tonight at the appointed time in his dark green car. He takes my overnight bag (new, thanks to Myers - sorry - Myer) from me and puts it into the boot. He opens the passenger side door and hands me a single dark red, fragrant rose as I settle into my seat. He slides into his side and leans across to kiss me lingeringly.

'I've been waiting for tonight,' he says, his eyes melting into mine.

'Really?'

And so we sit over a candlelit dinner at god-knows-where in the city. It's a swanky restaurant, I can tell, by the fawning waiters, the menu with no price tags, the dim, secretive cubicle where we're out of sight of the rest of the diners. This is Cinderella gone crazy. A 62 year-old frump being wined and dined by a gorgeous, handsome, wonderful man. What the hell is going on??????

I stop asking internal questions when we arrive at the hotel suite. I'm already half out of my mind with delicious food, equally delicious alcohol and then, of course, the company. I'll bet any woman in that restaurant would have cheerfully gouged my eyes out for a night with Matt. Yet, he seems mesmerized by me - yes, little me (if you don't take into account my measurements) - and he's not about to be deviated.

He plants the most scrumptious kiss on my lips that I melt into as the door closes upon our hideaway. M & B covers flash past my mind as I find myself inside those covers living the romance that I've always craved. Here am I, June Cooper from Beechworth, living an M & B story. Nothing's impossible or too outrageous. I'm the most attractive, seductive, wanted woman in the Southern Hemisphere.

Matt tastes every part of me (I'm blushing), he kisses every part of me (I continue to blush), and he sighs along with me as we're transported to another realm. Yes, I know, I sound like an M & B book but, honestly, that's how it is.

I wake up Thursday morning to more of the same. The last thing I want to do is go to work but Matt's getting ready. He's had his shower, we've eaten breakfast, he's onto his second coffee whilst knotting his tie. He looks fabulous. How does he do it? I'm not game to look in the mirror in case I break it. I wallow in the thick cotton sheets as I watch him.

'June,' he breathes into my neck. 'I don't know where you've been all my life, but I'm glad I have you now.'

I look at him through half-closed lids. 'You've no idea how glad I am.'

'Can we do this again?'

'What - now?'

He laughs. 'No, my seductress. I'm not *that* fit.' He kisses my forehead. 'Dinner - another overnight?'

Thursday, 23rd February

'Don't you look like the cat that swallowed the canary,' grins April as I drift past her on a cloud that lets me down with a thump in front of my desk. I look up at her in an exhausted haze.

'A bit tired, are we?'

I nod, smothering a yawn. 'Are you busy at lunchtime?'

She looks at me through narrowed eyelids. 'Shopping?'

'Yes.'

'Myer?'

'How did you know?'

'What theme this time?'

'Ballroom dancing.'

Her eyes almost pop out of her head.

Friday, 24ᵗʰ February

Tonight I meet Rob at 7:00 at a studio not far from my place. Lucky. After extensive calls to dancing studios about what to wear, I'm sporting a slightly flared knee-length black skirt and a simple red top. I was told to wear something comfortable. Rob meets me inside and introduces me to the studio owner. I'm to have a private class with Rob tonight.

Two hours later, I'm more foot-sore and exhausted than I've ever been. Rob, poor dear, is more than patient. He's diplomatic too. I wonder if he's ever taught anyone more stupid, less coordinated, less rhythmic, or less able to follow instructions. I try to remember the steps. I think I'm following him but I keep stepping on his toes, starting off on the wrong foot, turning left instead of right, putting weight on the wrong leg and wishing I was never born with bunions. We stop regularly for a drink when I swig a cup of iced water in a split second. How do people do this? It never looks *this* hard. Dancers always fling their heads back with a huge smile plastered on their faces, whereas I could just throw myself in a heap on the floor and sob my heart out in frustration.

'Maybe I'm just not made for this,' I mew at him piteously. I want to go home.

'Nah,' he beams at me. 'This is your first lesson. What did you expect? Did you think you'd dance like Ginger Rogers tonight?'

'Well, I thought I'd at least get some steps right ...'

'Don't worry, June,' he says, taking my hand. 'It'll come.' He should join the foreign service as a diplomat. 'It just needs practice.'

How many decades does he think I have?

'One more try and then we'll go get a drink.'

I do a passable one-two-three steps in a simple waltz but, by the time I begin to repeat those three steps, I've turned the opposite way to Rob and ended up crashing into a wall, which is actually a mirror, where I leave my lipstick smudged in a line that traces my decline to the floor.

We're in a bar not far from the studio. Actually, I'd prefer that we were in another state - no, another country - than where we are. I'm mortified. However, I've had two brandies which burn down my throat into a warm, reassuring internal hug. Brandy could be my favourite drink from now on. I order another. The night no longer seems a total loss.

Rob leans over to tell me something and then suddenly latches onto my mouth. My eyes spring wide open in alarm. What's he doing?! He puts his arms around me and pulls me close to his chest. I don't know what to do. Here I am, old enough to be his mother, and he's kissing me. I push my hand against him and come up for breath.

'Rob,' I gasp. 'I don't understand ...'

'Oh, June, you turn me on,' he says breathing heavily.

'You realise, of course, our age difference?' I croak. 'This doesn't make sense.'

'It doesn't have to,' he smiles. 'Besides, I like older women.'

Saturday, 25th February

'So, what happened then?' April's beside herself. The tip of her tongue darts between her front teeth and she's snorting slightly. 'This is sooooo cool!'

'Cool, you call it!' I'm indignant. 'How can it be cool that a fellow young enough to be *your* boyfriend tries to make love to me.'

'*Did* he?'

'Well, not quite.' I sip my brandy and dry. April's very impressed I'm drinking spirits now.

'I told him I wanted to get a taxi and that's exactly what I did.' I look at her out of the corner of my eye. 'End of story.'

'Juneeee, it is not,' she snorts. 'You're lying. What else happened?'

'Well, if you must know,' I admit, 'he had me bailed up against a wall while we waited for the taxi, kissing me until I thought I'd have no lips left.'

'And?'

'His hands were all over me. I was so nervous someone would see us but he didn't care. In the end, I didn't either.' I giggle. 'The taxi came too soon.'

'You shameless woman!'

'I am, aren't I?'

'So, when are you seeing him again?'

'Monday night for more torture.'

'Dancing lessons?'

'And the rest.'

Sunday 26th February

I'm sitting at my table in front of Merv. He's swishing around seductively. If I was a fish I'd go for him in a big way. I think about that. I wonder if he'd like a companion? Maybe he doesn't know he would like a companion because, like most fish, so we're told, he can't remember past 20 seconds. If he thought about it half a minute ago, then he'd be in a different mind space 10 seconds later. But what would the next 30 seconds contain? More of the same? Oh, poor Merv. Maybe he's miserable and seeing me is the best part of his day. Now that would be just awful. I promise I'm going to shop for a girlfriend for him. He glides in front of me, mouth opening and closing in grateful kisses.

That gets me thinking about my situation. A 62 year-old virgin - past tense - well, you can't count that schoolyard rape - finding myself with two men who really fancy me.

Me.

June Cooper.

Let's face it - look in the mirror and what do I see? Nothing special. As a matter of fact, nothing.

And yet, these two vastly different men think I'm the ants pants.

Why?

Love is blind?

Don't kid yourself. It's not love - it's pure and simple SEX.

What's changed that has these men seeking me out? I look down at my jeans and pull up the sleeves of my red jumper. That's it! April's makeover. I look different. I walk different. I feel different. Something's woken up inside me that maybe sends out a message, an SOS, to any available male who wants a bit of romance, an M & B romance. Is it pheromones? In a primitive sense, am I sending them out, chucking them out - okay - flinging them out to all and sundry? Now, that's a thrilling thought. Imagine the whole train carriage - male of course - seeking, connecting, throbbing with my own special pheromones that've just been pumped up and gift wrapped for them. Sixty-two years worth of them.

A scary thought: does that mean I can have more affairs? OMG (that means 'oh my god')! If more men hook onto my amazing pheromones, would that make me unfaithful to Matt and Rob? Probably not Matt - he's got a wife he's being unfaithful to anyway. Rob's probably having affairs with anyone he teaches. Why wouldn't he - they?

That leads me to think about Rob's twin. He hasn't mentioned him; neither have I. That's a bit of a mystery. I wonder why he doesn't talk about him. His twin is more than a brother. I don't talk about my brother. Why would I? I don't see him, I don't like him, but he's not a twin. Maybe I would talk about him if he was my twin. That would have to be fraternal. If Sandra was my twin - therefore, identical - would I talk about her? They say twins feel the same things and are inextricably connected (in a good way) and, if they live close, they spend a lot of time together. Rob and his brother obviously live close or together, because they catch the same train and get off at the same place. Do they work together doing the same thing? I'm itching to ask Rob but something tells me to hold off. If I feign ignorance, I may have an advantage up my sleeve. Goodness knows what for.

I think back to the change in my life which has happened since April took an interest in me and my appearance. She's educated me in a way I could never have imagined. I wonder at her knowledge - her savoir faire - if that's what I mean. And then I wonder about her own life which is a closed shop to me. Because she knows so much about how to dress, accessories, makeup, hair, etc., why doesn't she apply all of that to herself? She dresses down, if anything, hardly wearing any makeup, and her shoulder-length hair is invariably drawn back into a half ponytail. She almost reminds me of the old me.

What does she get out of making me over? For the first time, I speculate about her motives. Is she an ASIO spy? An industrial spy? I hardly think so. What could I tell her, or anyone else, that would make the slightest difference to how Danks muddles its way through the years with Merv at the helm? And, on a scale of 1:10, would that affect anything or anyone on this Earth? Is she a good Samaritan? I hardly think so, as she gives a pretty good demonstration of being anti-religious. Political leanings? That wouldn't even remotely connect with our friendship. I don't lean either way and, from what I can tell, she doesn't either. We've not even discussed politics.

And then I stop. Oh, no! Dare I ask? Sexuality? OMG (yes, again), could she be - could she - could she be - a lesbian? I go cold. Could she be grooming me? No. This is April. My friend. Not a lover. She's not shown anything that would lead me to suspect that, especially since I've become very much a heterosexual creature of late.

I look at the clock. It's just turned nine. I punch the speed dial.

'Hi April,' I say to her answering machine. 'If you're home, I just thought we might catch up.' I wait. She doesn't pick up. Maybe she's out having fun with some people her age. I hope so.

'Well,' I mutter, 'never mind. I'll catch you at work tomorrow.'

I look at the phone after I hang up. She's normally so available - so, where is she now?

I reheat the pizza I picked up on my way home. I put it on the plate and look at it. It's full of fat. I should stop eating this sort of thing. I open my pantry. There's hardly anything in there that you'd call healthy. I need to change my diet if I'm to do anything about this horrible, disgusting, spare tyre, big fat belly, big bum, saggy thighs. I think ballroom dancing could help the cure. Stuff the bunions.

Monday, 27th February

April hovers over my desk. 'Sorry.' She pulls a face. 'I heard your message too late to call you back. What's up?'

'Oh, nothing much. I just wanted your opinion about dieting.'

'I don't diet.'

'Then why are you so slim?'

'Genes?'

'I wish I had the same.'

'What brought this on? After work activities? Men? Sex?' She's laughing, not in a bad way. *With* me - not *at* me. Unlike Sandra and Mum (not my mum). They always laugh/laughed at me.

I laugh back. 'Something like that.'

'Ditch the junk and takeaway food, June, except for the Asian.' She sits beside me. 'All that cheese and pasta's no good for you.' She eyes me up and down. 'And you could do with a gym membership.'

'Gym?' I croak in alarm.

'Yeah, gym, not Jim.'

'Do you go to one?'

'Not all the time, but I could join you up in the one I'm at. We could go together.'

'Do I have to go to Myers ... Myer ... for the gym?'

'Probably.

I meet Rob at the studio again. He's very professional, repeating and repeating and repeating the steps. I will my brain to concentrate. It's not very willing. My confidence hits rock bottom when I step on his foot yet again. He's so patient. I wonder how he does it. It must be a bit like driving lessons in my twenties when I failed miserably. That's why I don't have a car. I don't seem to have inherited much in the way of coordination. I think back to Mum (who's not my mum) and her sister Helen (who is my mum) and Gran. I know Mum and Gran never drove. Did Helen? April keeps on pestering me to try to find out more about my real mother. Perhaps I should.

'June,' a voice cuts in on my thoughts, 'come back to me.'

'Oh, sorry, Rob, I was thinking about ...'

'Concentrate or you'll have a fall.' Rob looks at me unsmilingly. 'You're here to dance, not to think about your shopping list.'

'I wasn't ...'

'Never mind,' he snaps. 'Now, let's try again. Back with your right, back with your left ...'

I survive the two gruelling hours somehow despite my bunions screaming at me. I'm surprised that I finally get through the *Evening 3 Step* without any major mishap. I don't know what's going on with the waltz. I thought that was just 1-2-3 and Bob's your uncle, but I find myself galloping round Rob trying to keep up. It's nothing like you see on TV when the dancers glide around the floor effortlessly. Maybe that's in the next lesson. Rob introduces the slow fox-trot but I beg him to just concentrate on one thing at a time until I get it right. When I begin learning another dance, I've already forgotten the one before. I'm happy doing the *Evening 3 Step* for the next month if Rob agrees.

I hobble out of the studio in my flats surprised there's no trail of blood behind me. We go back to that bar again and, after a few brandies, I feel less like the world ending will begin in my feet. Life's a bit more rosy now. Rob's youth doesn't bother me so much when he starts kissing me again. Nor does the bartender looking on. I suppose he sees this sort of thing all the time.

'You wanna come back to my place?' he murmurs as we come up for breath.

'Hmmmm ... where do you live?'

'Around the corner.'

'Have you got any brandy?'

'A cupboard full.'

And so my night of debauchery, with a man young enough to be my son, begins. I fall into his car - it's red - and we arrive at his flat a few minutes later. Honestly, I don't think either of us could have waited longer. There is such an urgency between us. Rob kicks the door closed as he rips off my clothes. *Hey, careful there! I paid good money for this outfit. Oh, to hell with it - I can afford another.* I make short work of his clothes too. His body is muscled, taught, YOUNG. I try not to think about what he sees and feels as he devours my body. If it's so repulsive, he'd stop, wouldn't he? Maybe he likes skin that resembles crêpe. Maybe he likes rolls of fat filling his arms, his hands, his mouth. I know he likes the rest of it. He makes damned good use of it. And so do I. OMG I'm blushing as I write this.

Having sex with Rob is totally different from that with Matt. Matt is slow and gentle. Rob is fast, urgent, rough. I like it. I like both. Does that make me a hussy? Do I care?

Waves of ecstasy radiate from my nether regions. My forehead tingles, as do my fingertips, and then the wave extends as far as my toes that flutter with pleasure. 'Can I have more?' I beg, a slave to this wonderful world of bliss that I'm now a part of. I'm insatiable. Wanting. Needing. And I get more.

I don't remember how I get home. I have a vague recollection that Rob drives me here. We both have work not many hours from now, so I think we part at my door. My legs are shaking and I look like something a desperate bandicoot would bury. Merv doesn't mind. He blows kisses at me so I reward him with some flakes. I wake up hugging my pillow, wanting more of what I had last night.

Tuesday, 28th February

April looks at me sideways as I prop my head up by the chin at my desk. She grins as I try to smother a huge yawn.

'A big night, no doubt.'

'You could say that,' I grin back.

'You look like you got no sleep.'

'Not much,' I agree.

'Worth it?'

'Oh, yes,' I sigh.

Merv calls me on the intercom. I spend the next few hours going over everything before he takes off with Trish tomorrow. He takes a good look at me. 'Are you feeling all right?'

'Hmmm.'

'June? Forgive me saying this, but you look like shit.'

'Oh, really?' I giggle.

'Yeah,' he's saying, looking worried. 'Are you going to drop dead, by any chance, so that I have to cancel New Zealand?'

'I wouldn't do that to you, would I?' My hand slips from under my chin and my head almost hits the desk. 'Never have. Never will.'

He looks at me doubtfully but hope takes over. 'Take it easy, will you? Don't do anything I wouldn't do.'

I imitate April with a full-blown snort.

Merv follows with a detonation from the lower reaches of his gut and beams with relief. 'Sorry.'

April arrives with a Thai red curry and some rice. It's very hot but fragrant. We drink a sauvignon blanc with it. See - I'm branching out. It seems whatever new experiences I'm trying these days, I'm enjoying, whether they're food, alcohol or activities - well, we won't go into that.

I bring her up to date and then we settle back to watch *Notting Hill*. We laugh at Spike's antics and agonise over the road blocks thrown in the path of the would-be lovers. Of course, I've seen it countless times before but I never tire of it.

April sighs at the end contentedly. 'It's such a perfect ending.'

I turn to face her. 'And what about your perfect ending?'

'What do you mean?'

'Your love life. How's that going?'

'Oh, I ... er ...'

'Come on, April,' I say, 'I tell you everything about mine, but you tell me nothing about yours.'

She stops to think. 'There's nothing to tell.'

'Don't you trust me?'

We go back and forth about this, not getting anywhere. A wall of tension springs up between us and ruins the night. I'm sorry I brought it up. She makes an excuse about having to get to bed early and leaves soon after.

'There's something not right about that girl,' I tell Merv, 'and I mean to find out what it is.'

Thursday, 2nd March

I'm at April's for dinner. She's cooking a lamb casserole in the oven. The aromas coming from her little kitchen are mouth-watering. I contributed the vegies and wine, the least I can do. She won't let me help, not that I'd be much good anyway. She's been asking me about my Aunty Helen, my real mother.

'Are you any closer to wanting to see where she ended up?'

'I haven't given it a great deal of thought,' I lie.

April looks at me with an eyebrow up under her fringe. 'Yeah, right.'

'Well, not a lot,' I concede. 'I don't know where to start and don't know if I want to know. You know what I mean?'

'Maybe,' she says without conviction.

April's all bull-at-a-gate fearless. But it's *my* family history she's wanting to delve into, not hers.

We sit down to eat. The flavours are delicious.

'Did you cook this from scratch?'

She shrugs.

'You're a good cook,' I enthuse. 'Really good for someone who's self-taught.'

Her head goes down towards her plate. She's not good at accepting compliments.

'Do you have many visitors?'

She shakes her head.

'Does your dad come down to see you sometimes?'

Another shake of the head.

'Anyone?' No reply, so I let it go.

We eat in silence for some time.

'Look,' I say, 'I'm sorry. I didn't mean to pry. It's not my business.'

She looks up at me wretchedly. For once she's the one fighting tears. I put down my cutlery and take a sip of wine. 'I know how hard the past can be. Actually, you want to put it behind you, forget, only think of the present. The future, even, can sometimes be scary.'

And then I tell her about when those kids raped me at school. It summons up moments I would rather not have to face. I've buried it. Stomped on its grave. Shaken my fist at it. And here I am exhuming the bones of a rape. My rape. It's the first time I've told a soul. Tears scuttle down my face to drip onto the serviette draped across my lap. Very soon it's a sodden mess. April's mirroring my distress. We stand at the same time to hug each other. We sob our individual sorrows, shared, even though not articulated.

Snot runs down April's mouth and chin until I dab at it with a serviette. 'Here,' I say. 'I'm sorry I upset you.'

She hiccups and sort-of smiles through her tears. 'You didn't, Junee. You just brought my shit to the surface. '

'Is that a good thing or bad?'

'I don't really know.'

And then my dear April unleashes a torrent of words, spilling out over each other, as she relives her childhood. Desperate, unspeakable, horrifying words of an abuse so appalling that I am sickened to my marrow.

'... and ... and the day after Mum's funeral, I was curled up on my bed crying my eyes out. Dad came into my room and said: "Open your hands and close your eyes and see what God will give you." I put my hands out and closed my eyes waiting for him to give me Mum back, but I felt something soft and heavy in my hands and opened my eyes to see that I held his penis. His eyes were lit up with excitement. I'd never seen him look like that before. He told me that Mum couldn't hold his penis anymore, so it was my job in future to look after it. He said it was lonely and needed somewhere warm to comfort it. Then he put it between my legs - rammed it between my legs - until I screamed with pain and fear. This was not my darling daddy who'd never raised a hand to me. This was another man who just looked like him and who held his hand over my mouth while he ripped my six year-old body apart. When my mother died, I thought she must have taken him with her and left this imposter. I was all alone.

'We moved somewhere else so that no one would know us and he kept me out of school. He locked me in my room with a tin bucket every time he went to work or had to go out. "You be a good girl, he would say, because Mummy is looking down hoping you're looking after Daddy." I believed him. I had to learn how to cook and clean and give him my body. I was a replacement for my mother.

'After some years, he met a woman with two sons. She became my step-mother and they were my step-brothers. At first I thought it was a good thing. Joan took over the cooking and most of the cleaning and, I assumed, looking after his fucking penis. I was wrong. When Joan was at work and the boys at school, he would come after me. Joan wanted to know why I wasn't in school. He said I was backward and couldn't learn but, one thing I'll say for her, she made him enrol me in the local school. Of course I was backward. I was traumatised, had no social skills and no education. I think the school shrink suspected something but I never blabbed.

'One day the boys came home from school early and found Dad sticking it to me. They were delighted and insisted they join in or they'd tell Joan. In the end I stopped biting and scratching because they just held me down. I couldn't fight three at once.

'It took me quite a few years to catch up but I was determined I would learn. Somewhere I'd heard that an education gave you freedom - and that's what I wanted. I kept promising myself I would learn enough to escape. Most days I stayed back at school and did my homework in the library. I drove the teachers nuts asking for more and more work to do. They accelerated me and eventually I won a scholarship to Bond Uni. I couldn't take it, though, because it was too close to home. I cried for days over that. When I graduated from high school, I pulled out my savings from between some bricks at the side of the house, took a backpack and got on a bus to Melbourne. Those fucking bastards have no idea where I am.'

No wonder she'd escaped interstate. No wonder she'd cut off any contact with them. No wonder she kept to herself. Until she let me into her life.

We cry until our quota runs out. We snivel and sigh, our bodies and minds exhausted. And then we look at each other with understanding. We've shared our deepest secrets and, in the telling, our bond is cemented tightly, our previous friendship nothing in comparison to this. If I had ever had a child, a daughter, then this girl would be her. And I would protect her with everything I've got.

April tops up our glasses. 'To us,' we say together.

'See,' April points at her laptop screen, 'there's no Helen Rivers in the Mildura cemeteries.'

'That doesn't mean to say she's not dead. Just not dead in Mildura. And there's no Helen Rivers in the Mildura white pages. She could be dead anywhere but Mildura, or alive anywhere but Mildura.'

'Don't be so negative, June. We've only started on the hunt.'

We both stare at the screen willing my real mother to make an appearance.

'Do you know where your Aunty Kaye lived in Mildura - where Helen went to have the baby?'

I shake my head.

'And her surname was the same as yours?'

'Yes, but I don't know if she married and then changed her name. I remember going there when I was quite young but I don't remember a man being in the house.'

Dad was at the wheel of our Holden station wagon. Mum - not my mum - was beside him. Gran was in the back with me. It was stinking hot so we had the windows down. We arrived at Aunty Kaye's around lunchtime and were so glad to get out of the car and sit under the shade of an enormous gum tree which just about covered the whole of the higgledy piggledy brick house.

I remember it was dark inside. At first I was scared to enter but pretty bead curtains waving in the breeze enticed me in as well as a strange but nice smell from, what I now realise, must have been burning incense. There was a room, however, that was full of light. It was practically all windows and there were paintings everywhere - on the floor and walls, and an unfinished one on an easel. The strong smell of turpentine and, what I now know was oil paint, saturated the air. I spent some time studying the paintings. I liked their bright colours, their movement, their subjects - mostly people and animals. Two friendly dogs played with me and licked my face and made me laugh and chased me through the house and out the back.

Dad downed a couple of beers with his sister. Mum and Gran had some too. Aunty Kaye gave me some homemade lemonade. I still remember it because it was so cold it took my breath away. I held the frosted glass up to my burning cheeks and she smiled at me. Her eyes were so green I asked her if she'd painted them. She wore bright red lipstick and drop earrings with bells on the ends that tinkled when she moved her head. Her long dress swished around her when she walked and the neckline was so low I thought her boobs would drop out and surprise us all. I tried not to look at them but I'd never seen so much of a boob as those wobbling two. I'd not seen Mum or Gran's - perish the thought - but they didn't wear drop earrings or bright lipstick, so my child self decided they weren't qualified to show their boobs.

Our lunch wasn't the usual Sunday roast which would have made us hotter than ever. Aunty Kaye got me to help her carry out lots of bowls and dishes from her enormous fridge. We put them on a table outside that was built around the tree. Despite it being such a hot day, under the tree was cool. I felt so important helping my aunt and couldn't wait to try all the strange foods that she'd prepared. Mum and Gran looked at the lunch suspiciously. Dad tucked in without waiting for all the plates to appear. He must have known what the dishes were because he ate everything and went back for seconds. I think thirds as well.

When I saw Dad and Aunty Kaye together, I could see they were brother and sister, though Dad's eyes were more a faded green than her startling ones. Their hair was the same muddy brown colour, thick and wavy; hers was up on top of her head with a tortoise shell comb holding it in place. And they both had pointy chins and long faces. I'm glad my memory of them that day is so vivid because I never saw a photo of either of them.

Dad and Aunty Kaye chatted about everything and nothing, including about me and how I was going at school. She conversed with me as if I was a person of worth, not just some unloved kid who constantly got in the way. And she looked at me with those incredible eyes when she talked with me. I fell in love with her. She was probably the most beautiful woman I'd ever known, inside and out.

After we'd finished eating, Dad drank some more beer with his sister, while Mum and Gran sat over a big pot of tea. Things got a bit tense. Gran was quizzing Aunty Kaye about someone and Mum's lips almost turned blue while she held them in a thin tight line. My aunt kept shaking her head and saying something about business - not her business, I think. It's hard to remember now, but I felt sad that Gran was shouting and it wasn't such a nice time as before. I got up to go and wash the dishes but, as I reached over the table to pick up some bowls, one went flying through the air and hit Aunty Kaye on the shoulder. Beetroot juice dripped down her dress and into her lap and the pieces disappeared into her cleavage. She stood up digging into her boobs and flinging the beetroot back at Gran. Mum shouted too as she picked up some sliced meat and threw it at Aunty Kaye's face. The dogs were onto it in a flash as it fell to the ground but I could tell they didn't like what was going on, flying meat or not. They were circling the table and barking but at a sign from Aunty Kaye they settled beside her.

Dad got up saying something like:

'You silly bloody women, can't take you anywhere or you have a bloody fight and don't have a civil tongue in your bloody heads and what's a man to do at his own bloody sister's place, who he hasn't seen for bloody donkey's ages, and then you go and spoil the whole bloody day. You should be ashamed of yourselves. If Kaye says no then she means it. I knew it was a bloody mistake to bring you here in the first place and look at poor bloody June crying now because of your bloody awful behaviour. You can bloody-well get in the bloody car and not another word out of either of you.'

Then he downed the last of his beer, burped, kissed his sister on the cheek, saying: 'Thanks for the lunch, Kaye. Good to see you. Gotta go now. Sorry for the ruckus,' and he pushed Mum and Gran into the backseat of the wagon and slammed the doors after them.

'Come on love,' he said softly and picked me up in his arms and hugged me. Aunty Kaye discovered one more slice of beetroot between her boobs and flicked it out. Her nipple also flung itself out which made her and Dad kill themselves laughing. It broke his temper and he leaned over to kiss her again. 'Put it back in, love,' he said, 'or the dogs might think it's a snack.'

She hit him playfully on the shoulder and said, 'Come again, Kev, with little June here. Leave the old cows back home.'

I promised myself I was going to live with her when I was old enough to run away from home. I'd sit with her at the table that hugs the big old gum tree, eat my Rice Bubbles for breakfast, run around with the dogs, and have a perfect life.

But that was the first and last time I ever saw Aunty Kaye.

I cried my eyes out when Gran told me she'd died. It was only four days after the ram drowned Dad. I vaguely remember Gran saying it was a good thing he died first or he'd have grieved for his sister. Even though I'd not seen a lot of him, I always loved the times he came home and I'd follow him around like one of those sheep he sheared. I took his death hard on top of Aunty Kaye's.

'So you see,' I say, taking a sip of coffee, 'I only remember the house, not the address, and I never found out what she died of. Anyway, it was forbidden to talk about her after that visit.'

April sits cupping her mug for warmth. She didn't interrupt me as I described my memories of Aunty Kaye. 'What a bloody shame. Sounds like she was a terrific person. Imagine if you'd gone to live with her. You would have had a totally different life and met your real mother then.'

'If she was still alive,' I say, pulling a face.

'Or you'd at least have found out what happened to her.'

I sigh for what might have been.

'Any point asking your not-mum for some info? The address, for instance?'

'Not a hope in hell.' I pause. 'Actually, I didn't tell Mum what was in the letter.'

'What?'

'After her mute eyebrow-raising reaction to my new look, I thought, bugger you. I'm not telling you anything. Besides, she didn't ask.'

'What about that lovely sister of yours?' I shake my head. 'Or your wonderful brother?'

A thought occurs to me. 'I wonder if Little Malcolm would know something?'

Friday 3rd March

'Hello?' Same efficient secretary answering the phone.

'I'd like to speak with Malcolm Power.'

April and I are in Merv's office as I make the call. I don't want BBB or Mel listening in. I have it on loud speaker.

'June!' Little Malcolm is effusive. 'How are you feeling after your grandmother's awful letter?'

'Okay, actually, Malcolm.'

I tell him what I'm after.

I imagine him sitting behind the big oak desk that's been in the Power family forever. He's dwarfed by it. He probably has to ratchet his chair up so that his chin comes above the desk. Well, that's what it had looked like to me when I saw him last.

'I'm in the process at the moment, June, of sorting out a lot of old files. Leave it with me for a few days and I'll get back to you. I may be able to come up with something.'

April and I look at each other hopefully.

On my way home from work, I stop at a pet shop to buy a companion for Merv. I see her straightaway. She's got big eyes, a longish swishy tail and a mouth that could be singing. Hence, the name: Melba. I'm nervous as I undo the rubber band around the plastic bag from where she's inspecting her new world as it unfolds.

'Merv,' I whisper, 'I've got a surprise for you.' I hold up the bag in front of his tank. He looks at it with what I think is astonishment. 'Yes, I promised you,' I smile. 'Isn't she gorgeous?'

I slowly tip her into his world, his water. She whirls upon release in a slow but careful inspection of her new surroundings. Merv hides behind a coral. 'Come on, you silly boy,' I encourage. 'Say hello.'

Melba circles him in a dance both sensuous and glamorous. If I were a goldfish boy I'd go for her in a big way. They meet, blowing kisses, and I leave them to it.

I have 20 minutes to have a bite to eat and get changed into my gym gear. I decide upon a banana which, really, is a tube of glucose, so I figure it'll give me all the energy I need for this ordeal I'm not looking forward to. I didn't allow for the time it would take to wring, push, squeeze myself into the gym clothes April chose for me. I'm a colonial woman in her stays. I'm in a compression chamber. I'm being squashed between two buildings. Am I supposed to breathe?

I walk into the gym sucking in my breath so that my stomach doesn't ripple below the waist of my pants. My boobs are somewhere near my double chin. Don't ask me where my bum is.

I see April walking on a treadmill, earplugs in, oblivious to the world. I walk into her vision and she slows the machine. 'You made it,' she grins. 'Come and get on a treadmill to warm you up.'

She shows me how to work the thing and off I go.

Five minutes feels like I've walked 500 kilometres. How fast is this damned thing going? I look over at the other treadmills and they seem to be going at least twice as fast as mine. I'm beginning to perspire and my legs are screaming at me. Fortunately, the bunions are on holiday in my new gym shoes. April said to do 15 minutes. I don't know if I can make it. I've gone through my bottle of water already. She's nodding in time to whatever junk she's listening to, looking over at me occasionally. I will her to turn my way.

'What?' she yells, leaving her earplugs in.

'Is that enough?'

She rips her earplugs out. 'Already? You've gotta work at it. 15 minutes minimum.' She plugs herself in again and chortles as she turns up the speed of her treadmill.

I soldier on. I pretend I'm walking from my place to the station but I think I'm going around the block in circles because I don't get past my front door.

She puts me on a rowing machine. As I pull on the handle, my whole body shakes with the effort, fat and rolls wobbling in all directions. My heart's jumping out of my throat. Even though there's an almost satisfying feeling of drag against water when I manage to pull back with my arms and push with my legs, no amount of imagining I'm going up the Yarra River from Swanston Street would ever get me past Princes Bridge.

The dumbbells are no better. I can pick them up off the floor but, once they get to waist height, my arms won't cooperate. There's all this heavy machinery that you have to move in opposite directions with everything you've got. There's a thing called a chest press that you sit on and push like hell against some handles. You can feel your ribcage breaking and your shoulders dislocating. By the time April wants me to lie on the floor and try to lift up my torso, I'm a corpse. I lie there giggling with panic and exhaustion and am afraid if I close my eyes I'll start snoring. She has to help me up. I'm drenched with perspiration. My hair is dripping. There's got to be a better way to lose weight.

Ballroom dancing.

And sex.

Monday 6th March

Of course I'm on the earlier train because Merv's away, so I see Matt in the mornings. What a treat! On Monday the seat next to him is empty. He looks up at me expectantly. With all the grace I can muster, I plonk myself down beside him. His smile creeps into his eyes and I lose a heartbeat as I think of how he looks at me when we're making love.

'Sorry I haven't called,' he says quietly. 'Snowed under at work - you understand.'

'Of course,' I reply.

'Not that I haven't wanted to - every day, in fact. I've missed you like crazy,' he mumbles into my ear.

I say nothing, just look ahead and nod. People are all around us with their ears flapping.

'Your boss is away?'

I nod again but turn and smile at him. 'While the cat's away...'

'Exactly.'

He pulls out his mobile and sends a text. Work, I think. My mobile vibrates. I dig it out of my bag to find I have an SMS. It says: *Can I take you out and spoil you on Wednesday night?* I smother a laugh, then enter some text into my phone. His mobile sends a notification. Mine is already back in my bag. He reads his message and moves his leg against mine.

I open my book and get lost in another breathtaking romance imagining the main characters to be Matt and me. We're shipwrecked on a desert island where there's abundant fruit, fish and sunshine. We cavort naked in the deep blue lagoon that laps the shores of a palm-lined, pure white beach. Never mind that I'm not a swimmer and have never cavorted naked in the open. This is fiction that blissfully melts into my world. Ahhh, I'm transported from the packed train carriage to the heady perfume of frangipani strewn across a grass mat where I'm adored by my lover who's actually sitting next to me pretending to be reading *The Age* online. The secrecy is fun.

I'm in Merv's office watching him and Trish on Skype as he takes his iPad around the campervan. They show me every nook and cranny, how clever is this, how clever that, the road in front, the road behind them, where the toilet is tucked away - marvellous they don't have to use public toilets - and how the chemicals kill the odour. How they don't have to blunder around in the dark looking for a toilet out in the open or at camps. Trish shows me how it flushes.

Too much information, I think.

'We're taking lots of photos to show you when we get back,' Merv assures me.

'Can't wait,' I mumble.

'What's that? You're breaking up.'

'Can't wait,' I assure him. 'Take one of a kiwi for me.'

'Oh, we'll take heaps of them. Might even smuggle one home for you, June.'

I'm pleased to see Merv & Melba getting on *swimmingly* - hah! There they go again, side by side, on a path to romance in their own *Fantasia*. Well, I think the romance hit when she first arrived. They've been inseparable since she slipped into his world. His Queen of Sheba. His Helen of Troy. His Cleopatra. His Juliet. I wonder if she's pregnant yet? I don't feel jealous because Merv still greets me when I arrive home popping kisses at me (though I know it's probably: gimme gimme gimme food!) with Melba doing the same. It does my heart good to see how Merv's life has improved 100%. It must have been a lonely existence with only me for company before the love of his life arrived. Well, I'm glad I could do something about it.

I look down at my plate of rabbit food. I HATE this diet. I miss my cheese, my pasta, my chocolates. April assures me I'll lose weight soon. I bought some scales that are still shouting a horror story every time I step on them. I cover an eye in the hope it's wrong. I've lost only half a kilo so far. Just how much grated carrot can you pile onto rocket? Well, I add red onion, tomato, capsicum, canned tuna, canned 5 bean mix. Without the lemon juice and olive oil, it would taste like something someone dug up from a compost bin. Surprisingly, though, it fills me - physically, not mentally. It's not fair! Why can't I be fat and ugly without worrying how my neglected body will look to others? The thing is, I've never had that problem before. No Matt. No Rob. The pressure of trying to look different is so hard to live with but, when I'm with them, I feel every ounce of fat that's on exhibition. I'm embarrassed. Mortified. Want to stick my head in the sand. Humiliated. But if I want more wonderful sex, I have to do something about it. Even if just for me.

Have another forkful of carrot, June.

Tuesday 7th March

I'm in Merv's office writing replies to his Inbox when my mobile rings. It's Little Malcolm.

'I've got an address for you, June,' he says, obviously very happy with himself.

'Who's?'

'Kaye Cooper, your aunt.'

'Really?'

'Yes.' he says, 'As a matter of fact, I have more than just her address.' I can see him patting himself on the back, he's so pleased. 'It's a bequest.'

'A what?'

'Bequest. Inheritance. Gift.'

'Yes, yes, I know what a bequest is,' I reply tetchily. 'Who's it for?'

'You,' he says with a big smile in his voice.

'April,' I say sternly.

She looks up from her computer screen.

'Merv's office. Now.'

BBB and Mel follow us with their eyes wondering what the heck is going on.

I close the door behind her.

'Take a seat,' I order as I go around behind Merv's desk and sit.

'What ...?'

I can't help but break out in a grin. 'You'll never guess what.'

'Fucken hell, June,' she explodes. 'You scared the shit out of me.'

'Language, Miss Snowden.' I pretend a frown.

'Yeah, right,' she laughs, sucking air from between her front teeth. 'What's up?'

'I own a house.'

I can't hold it in - well, who the heck else would I tell? It turns out that Aunty Kaye left a will that got lost. I was her only beneficiary. She'd sent the will to Little Malcolm's father, when he was the big cheese in the legal circles of Beechworth, not long after our disastrous visit to her place in Mildura. Because Dad had died just before she did, no flag went up about her estate for some time. There was no one to care enough to ask about it.

Big Malcolm died within a few months of Kaye's death and, because Little Malcolm wasn't old enough to take over the practice for some years, it sort-of went into hibernation for a while. All the files were locked into a strong room where they were disturbed now and again by Big Malcolm's faithful secretary until she also kicked the bucket. The office was closed and left empty for decades, despite the local council's best efforts to rent it out. Businesses came and went on either side of the office, but it remained boarded up, an eyesore, the township said, but they could do nothing about it. You see, Big Malcolm's widow sat on her powerful throne distributing alms to the lunatic asylum on the hill and other worthy charities in the area, on the condition that the office remain untouched until Little Malcolm was old enough to take it over. There was a shortage of solicitors in the area at the time, so the locals mostly took their business to Wangaratta or Corowa.

Fresh out of uni, Little Malcolm dusted off his father's desk and occupied the office where his father had practised all of his working life. Some years later Gran died and I turned up to receive her letter. Little Malcolm had apparently been welcomed rather frostily by the township, no one believing he would be worth his salt but, surprisingly, he turned out to be pretty good in the law stakes. It was a relief to Beechworth's residents not to have to travel for their legal disputes and needs, and so business started to pick up for him. And that's when he had his ditsy secretary begin to sort through the old files in the strong room.

'The problem was, June,' Little Malcolm had told me, 'that the file the will was in hadn't been addressed or labelled correctly. Apparently your aunt had changed her name for a brief time when she married very young and then went back to her maiden name - Cooper - when she divorced. For some strange reason she used her married name when she made out her new will not long before she died. My father was becoming a bit senile before his heart attack and the surname wouldn't have meant anything to him. I think,' Little Malcolm admitted, 'it went into the too-hard basket and never surfaced.'

'So, the house ...' April says, 'it's not ... it's not *the* house in Mildura, is it? The one where you went?'

I nod.

'You're shittin' me!'

April and I frantically search for Aunty Kaye's place on Google Maps. Well, it's not really an address. It's a property. At least it was in the 1960s. The area looks pretty isolated, which is more or less what I remember, and we think we've found it but not quite sure.

'What did Little Malcolm say to do?'

'Well, he left it up to me, really,' I say, peering at the screen, hoping something will remind me of what my seven year-old self saw. 'I can leave it in his hands and he can arrange to sell it, or I go and have a look at it and see what I think.'

'Cool!' April jumps up and down excitedly beside me. 'Let's go and check it out!'

'Hmmm...' It hadn't occurred to me. Go there? But then I think of Merv. 'Oh, I couldn't ...'

'How long, Junee, since you had some leave? Took a holiday?'

'Well ...'

'Like never, I'll bet.'

'My recent trip to Beechworth to get Gran's letter.'

'Oh, sure. That counts - not.'

I rummage around my head for some previous time off. For the life of me, I can't.

'I knew it,' she says. 'When do Merv and Trish get back?'

'Next weekend.'

Wednesday 8ᵗʰ March

Tonight comes around so fast that April and I only have time to duck into *Myer* (!) after work for something for me to wear. Luckily - or, more likely due to April's shopping skills - we find a matching skirt and top that will do nicely. She reminds me that I should buy a new set of lingerie. This time it's a pale blue satin nightie that I could see Julia Roberts in - not me - but I'll do my best.

Matt picks me up in his dark green car at seven o'clock. This time he hands me a tiny spray of exotic orchids that he pins to my jacket. They're simply gorgeous. He drives to a restaurant overlooking the bay. The waiters obviously know him as they conduct us to a candle-lit table immediately we arrive. It's tucked away in a corner with an ornate screen shielding us from view.

'I hope you like seafood?' Matt asks as he consults the menu. At my nod, he orders oysters to begin. The only oysters I've ever had are in a tin and squashed onto a dry biscuit. I hope these fresh ones will be all right. The waiter brings us a gin martini with a lemon twist. I sip at it gingerly. It's nothing like I've had before and I'm not that keen, however, my education in alcohol is widening and I'm determined to drink it, if not like it.

Next, the waiter brings our slimy-looking oysters. Oh hell, they look like some disgusting obscene creature in a slate shell. They're a lot bigger than the ones in the tins. I hesitate as I watch Matt pick one up, actually sniff it, then tip it into his mouth. I see his jaw working, so he must be chewing the thing, and then swallows. I'm ready to duck if he vomits.

He smiles at me. 'They're so fresh, they're almost jumping out of their shells,' he comments, then reaches for another.

Hell, I hope not! Aren't they dead?

'Bring it to your nose and inhale.'

Bugger; despite my sophistication, he's guessed I don't know what to do.

'The aroma should be super-fresh, instantly transporting you to the sea. Slurp the meat with its juices and give it two or three good chews,' he encourages. 'Then tell me what you taste.'

Okay, here I go. I've got the shell up to my nose and sniff it. He's right! I smell the sea. I look at him in surprise. He smiles as he waits for me to put it in my mouth. I tip my head back and it slides in. Oh, hell, it's strange on my tongue. I want to spit it out but then I'm hit with a salty taste that's not unpleasant. Not like your fish and chips salt - more subtle.

'Salty,' I gurgle, hanging onto it, afraid to swallow.

'Chew,' he orders.

I tell my teeth to bite into the thing. I can't help but screw up my face.

Matt laughs. 'Go on, it won't bite you.'

I hold a serviette up to my face, just in case. I bite and my taste buds detect a creamy, buttery flavour that ends in a sweetness that is beyond my expectations. 'It's ... it's ... delicious!'

'You didn't mislead me,' he says. 'You *do* like seafood.'

We go to the same hotel as last time so I know what to expect. Almost. There's an ice bucket with a bottle of FRENCH champagne waiting for us, along with an arrangement of the most beautiful native flowers I've ever seen. I can't stop looking at them as champagne bubbles tickle my nostrils. But Matt's face, his eyes, and the rest of him, get in the way. In an M&B book, there'd be all of these things. Maybe Matt's read some of them. I mean, where does he get his ideas from?

I'm a little more confident this time as I'm more experienced now, aren't I? Matt's surprised when I initiate some moves.

'I've been studying,' I smile at him. 'Amazing where you can find tuition.'

'A library?' he asks as he's busy with my breasts.

'Something like that.'

We continue with my sex education in a huge spa, taking our champagne with us. This is just like the scene when Julia Roberts and Richard Gere are in the bath together, bubbles all around them. Even I feel like a *Pretty Woman* with this handsome man making love to me.

Friday 10ᵗʰ March

'Sorry, April,' I say. We're dishing out some Thai takeaway at my place and pouring a sauvignon blanc from New Zealand. This has become my favourite wine. The passionfruit aromas remind me of Passiona soft drink when I was a kid.

'What're you sorry about?'

'I know you were looking forward to a trip to Mildura, but there's no point now.'

And so I tell her about Little Malcolm's call late today. He's begun to delve into the matter and has discovered that Aunty Kaye's estate ended up with the Public Trust office because there was no one else to act as executor, given that they didn't know about the lost will. I explain to April about dying intestate. Apparently the Trust office had contacted Brenda to see if she'd like to organise the funeral and burial but she'd told them in no uncertain terms she didn't want anything to do with it.

Unbelievably, the person Little Malcolm spoke with at the (now) State Trustees office was about to retire, however; had been working there when this all happened. She remembered it clearly because Brenda had been such a difficult person to deal with. 'Very unpleasant', she'd told Little Malcolm. Actually, she behaved like a bloody cow until she found out that her *three* kids were next in line to inherit Aunty Kaye's estate given that Dad had been drowned by the ram four days before Aunty Kaye's death. Brenda had complained to the woman that she received two phone calls from the police within days of each other, firstly about the death of her husband, and secondly about her sister-in-law's death. Said she couldn't give a shit about Aunty Kaye. Charming. Then she told the woman that I wasn't her child, never would be, therefore, the estate would go to Wayne and Sandra.

So the estate ended up being administered by the Victorian Public Trust office until my half-siblings inherited at the age of eighteen. Of course, I was never told anything about this.

April looks at me with a dejected expression. 'So, no house?'

'No house.'

'Fuck!'

'April...'

'Yeah, I know - the neighbours. Well, fuck them, fuck Wayne and Sandra, fuck Brenda, and fuck that stupid solicitor for losing the file in the first place.'

I sigh. 'It would have been lovely to go and see the house, maybe even move there ...'

'What, to bloody Mildura?'

'Oh, I'm only pipe dreaming. A place of my own would have been nice.'

'Nice! Juneeeeee, it would have been fuckin' awesome!'

Somehow it doesn't bother me that she lengthens my name to Junee or longer. No one's ever done that before. It's like a term of endearment or, at least, that's how I see it.

'But, hang on,' April says hopefully, 'what about the rest of the money? Can't you get that back?'

I shrug. 'No. The estate would have been distributed according to the court order all those years ago and absorbed. It's too late.'

'Jesus.'

'Exactly.'

We sit for quite some minutes looking at each other over our wine glasses. I can see April's mind working, figuring it all out, trying to find a solution. She suddenly grins at me.

'I've got an idea.'

'I thought you might,' I say refilling our glasses.

'We could have a bit of fun with this.'

'Fun?'

'Yeah. Fun.'

I think I may have had a bit too much to drink because it takes some time for me to swim up from unconsciousness to answer the phone in the morning.

'Ummmm...?'

'June, is that you?'

I sit up to be knocked flat by a sledgehammer whacking my head. 'Oh god. Oh god,' I groan.

'Are you all right?'

I try to sit up again. Slowly. 'Who's this?'

'Rob.'

'Oh, Rob, I couldn't dance to save my life at the moment,' I almost weep into the phone.

'Nah, you don't need to dance today. We're going to the footy!'

Saturday 11th March

Having taken more than the advised dose of Panadol, and kept various appointments with the toilet bowl (head first), I'm feeling much lighter and slimmer by the time I meet Rob at Richmond Station. The roar in my head has subsided to a mere thud repeated at regular intervals. My stomach lurches threateningly as I sway in front of him. He bends his head to have a good look at me.

'If I didn't know better, I'd say you're hung over.'

'Right first guess.'

'Shit, June. I'm proud of you,' he says, belting me on the back in what I assume to be a male version of a hug, while my head snaps back and forth on a rusty spring.

Somehow, the scalding hot pie and beer at interval cure my hangover. Rob's enthusiasm and the infectious reaction of the crowd, all sweep me up into the moment and I find myself cheering with the best of them. I can understand mass hysteria now because this is it. Screaming and abusing fans on both sides make me feel like one of them, included, valued, because I'm wearing the colours of one of the sides playing. It's exhilarating. Fun. And I feel young again.

'Let's go to the pub to celebrate,' Rob yells at me over the crowd, even before the final siren. It's obvious the mighty Hawks are going to win.

'What - you want to leave now? Before the end?'

'Easier to get out,' he explains as he steers me out of the stands.

We race out of the ground and slow down to walk to a pub near the station. It's a fair enough day; clouds that refuse to squeeze any water out over thirsty gardens team up with a bashful sun poking out occasionally. We find somewhere to sit outside in a beer garden. The drinkers are rowdy but cheerful, obviously most of them on 'our' side.

'I can't believe how much better I feel.' I smile over the frothy head of my beer.

'Dog's eye and dead 'orse washed down with a beer cures most ills and chills,' he laughs, 'including a sod of a hangover. Geez, you looked like shit, June.'

'Well, thanks, Rob. I love you too.'

He tilts back in his chair, its front legs dangling in midair, obviously thinking about something. Suddenly he comes down with a thud, takes a swig of beer, then says, 'Well, how about it, June? You wanna go out for dinner?'

I look at him uncertainly. 'Well ... yes, that'd be lovely.'

'Good, then,' he smiles. 'I know a nice little restaurant not far from your place. I'll pick you up at 7:30.'

Back home, I race around having a shower and cleaning the place up. It looks like a hospital ward with towels everywhere, bucket, kidney bowl, tissue boxes, pain killers, bi-carb soda, ice packs - all mostly on the floor where I'd pitched them overnight, along with empty bottles, unwashed glasses, plates, cutlery and takeaway containers. It's truly disgusting. I think what a bad influence April's having on me, but I don't regret it a bit.

Rob arrives right on 7:30 with a bunch of those orchids they stain different colours. These are blue. I'm surprised at the gesture, as he doesn't seem the type. I'm happy I've bought some vases, because the first flowers Matt gave me ended up in a vinegar bottle. April had carted me off to the shops to buy vases - what I'd thought a waste of money at the time, but not anymore. Rob hovers around me as I arrange the orchids, looking a bit nervous. There's none of his former brashness, no closeness, not even a kiss. Hmmm, have I done something wrong? I feel myself blush and feel hot as I remember our night of wild sex. Maybe he's embarrassed now that he's sober? I'm confused and not a little hurt.

I turn and look up at him expectantly, inviting a kiss, but he looks at his watch. 'We'd better get going as it's a popular place. We don't want to lose our booking.'

It isn't until we arrive at the restaurant and are seated at a window table overlooking the street where his car is parked, that I realise it's a blue one and not the red one of the other night.

'You've bought a new car!'

'What ... oh, no, this one's a courtesy car while mine's getting fixed.'

I raise an eyebrow.

'Yes,' he goes on in a hurry, 'they're waiting on a part.'

'Oh, I see,' I say, but don't believe a word of it. I smell a rat.

The waiter places the menu in front of us. 'Would you like me to pour your wine?' Rob nods. She pours for us both, recites the specials for the evening, and then leaves us to read the menu.

'I'm going to have the steak,' he says.

'Gee, you can make your mind up quickly!'

'I always have steak.'

'Really? Doesn't that get boring?'

'No. I come here for the steak. You can't beat it.'

'Well, in that case, I'll take your recommendation.' I take a sip of my wine and watch him intently. 'No dancing tonight?'

He coughs as he brushes something from the table. 'Ah, no. It's up to me when I go, except for the private classes I book in myself.'

'Do you think I improved the second time?'

'Of course! We all improve with practice.'

'Even an uncoordinated clumsy person like me?'

'June,' he looks me in the eye as he leans towards me, 'I was clumsy the first time. And the second. And the third. And so on.'

'And what about the sex?'

'Eh?'

'That wild, wonderful time we had together the week before last?'

'Oh, that.'

'Yes, that.'

'I haven't stopped thinking about it.'

'Really?'

'It was ... fantastic.'

'Then why don't you want to kiss me?'

He looks around the restaurant before leaning over to plant a childlike kiss on my cheek.

'That's not what I had in mind,' I chide him.

'Sorry. It's the best I can do here.'

'Are you playing games with me?'

'Not at all.' He looks sooooo sincere. 'Wait until we have our dinner and go back to your place.'

'I'm looking forward to that,' I tell him equally sincerely.

What can I say? The new underwear is a hit.

Despite being tired, I enjoy every minute - no, second. And there are lots of them! This young man is certainly full of energy. Rob teases me about holding back with the kisses until we get home.

'A restaurant's a bit different from a bar,' he laughs as we come up for air. 'We'd have been thrown out if I'd been paying you the same attention there.'

True.

And, goodness me, he makes up for it. Twice - no, a couple of hundred times over.

We fall into an exhausted sleep. I look at the clock as I carefully get out of bed to go to the toilet. It's 3:35am. Rob is snoring softly as he lays on his back, arms over his head. He looks about twelve. I stare into the mirror and wonder what the hell I was doing. Eye makeup smudged all over my face. No lipstick to be seen - surprise, surprise. My hair looks as if it'd been tied in knots and then sprayed up into a point. I look haggard but oh so satisfied. Get that grin off your face, I chide myself. To hell with how you look. And I go back to bed, snuggle into Rob's back, and fall into a deep sleep.

'You wanna go for a drive?' he asks over the plate of eggs and bacon I've placed in front of him.

'Why not?'

'Let's have a shower first.'

Let us, that means. Both of us? Ahem. Yes.

I'll never look at my shower the same way again.

Sunday 12th March

The view from Arthur's Seat is spectacular from the newly-installed chairlift, especially as I've never been up there in my whole 62 years. Rob can't believe it. How can I tell him that I had no-one to go with, much less anyone who cared. As I look at the view, I realise how much I've been missing out on. Until April and I became friends, I'd never really had a close friend, one who I could talk and laugh with as I do with April. There'd been opportunities, of course, to go on bus tours but I'd never thought I'd have the courage to do it alone. Who would I talk with? Would the others on the bus want to talk with me? What would I do if not? It was safer to stay at home, talk to Merv & Melba, watch TV and curl up with a Mills & Boon. I lived other people's love lives between those pages and avoided being hurt myself.

We sit in the restaurant with Port Phillip Bay spread out in front of us. The day and weather are idyllic. Rob is excited, pointing out landmarks, talking about the many times he's been up here showing Melbourne off to interstate and overseas visitors. I realise how insular my life has been until now. I look at his young face and feel ashamed. Ashamed that he's here with me instead of someone his own age.

'Rob, why are we here?'

'What - did you want to go somewhere else?'

'No. No. That's not what I mean.' I take a sip of my wine as I study his face. 'I mean, why me? Why not someone your age?'

He looks startled, as if I've proposed a totally new idea. 'Well, why would I when you're the person I want to be with here, today, right now?'

'But what can I give you, apart from sex?'

He takes a deep breath as his face fills with colour. 'Is that what you think this is about? Is that all?'

'Well ...'

'I thought we were having a good time. I thought you liked going to the footy. Having a meal together. Having a chat. ...'

'Yes, but, why someone my age? I'm old enough to be your mother!'

He looks at me, his head cocked to one side. 'I have a mother,' he says quietly.

'I ... I ...'

'Look.' He leans over and grabs my hand. 'I don't really identify with women my age or younger. They're silly. They don't listen. They giggle all the time, or else they're career women and have balls bigger than mine. I HATE them! They give me the shits. They do nothing for me.'

'I'm ... sorry. I didn't mean to make you angry. I just ...'

'I'm not angry. Look ... I like being with you. The sex is just icing on the cake.'

'What about your friends?'

'Friends I've got and I get different things from them.' He studies my face, my lips, my neck. I feel a blush rising. 'But they don't have what you have.' I'm unconvinced. 'You know, I can't have a serious conversation with them other than the footy, the music and movies we like, the girls they fuck.' He notices my frown. 'Sorry. But you know what I mean?' He looks out the window as he gathers his thoughts. 'That first time on the train? When we started talking?' I nod. 'I had such a cool time with you and got off the train feeling good about myself for a change. You actually listened.'

'What about your family? Have you got any siblings?'

He takes a long gulp of his beer. 'A brother.'

'Older or younger?'

A pause. 'Older.'

'Are you close?'

He shrugs.

'Do you ...'

'What about you?' he interrupts. 'Have you got brothers and sisters?'

'I have a half-brother and half-sister.' I realise Rob has shifted the sibling conversation over to me and decide to go with that. It's his business if he wants to talk about his twin or not. 'Well, actually, they're my cousins - I think.'

'How does that work?'

And so I tell him about my childhood - not all of it - and the will turning up.

'Cool!'

'I suppose you could say that,' I concede, 'however, I did end up with nothing.'

'Can you contest it?'

'I don't think there's much point. It is, after all, 55 years later, so all of Aunty Kaye's estate has been absorbed by now.'

'That doesn't seem right.'

'I know,' I shrug, 'but I don't need the money ...'

'What about bloody Brenda?' Rob is furious. 'She got away with it, so did bloody Wayne and Sandra!'

'I doubt they knew ...'

'That's not the point, June.' He finishes off his beer in one go. 'We've got to do something about it.'

'What ...?'

'Yep. I've got some friends in the law. They can help us.'

'Rob. Rob.' I try to calm him. 'You remind me of my friend, April, who's also hot under the collar ...'

'Awesome! We'll get together. Figure out how to stick it up Brenda.'

'Of course I'd like to meet him,' April shrieks so loudly I have to hold the phone a good distance away from my ear. 'I think we're on the same page about your so-called inheritance.'

'April,' I sigh. 'There's nothing to be done.'

'Not bloody much ...'

'No, really. Little Malcolm explained it all to me and ...'

'Yes, but, if Rob's got some legal mates then why not make use of them?'

'Because, it doesn't matter how many solicitors I may have on my side, the estate is gone. Kaput. All soaked up by Wayne and Sandra.'

'Ah, ha!' she yells. 'I reckon Rob and me will stick it right up their ...'

'April, please talk softer,' I beg. 'It's too late.'

'But ...'

'And I don't really care.'

'You have to care,' she hisses into the phone. 'Even if it doesn't mean any monetary gain, then at least the big word: revenge.'

'Well, there's that about it.'

'Of course,' she says simply. 'Get your own back.'

Monday 13th March

Tonight the three of us meet for dinner at a Thai restaurant. I feel a bit nervous about bringing them together but they get on like a house on fire. They're equally furious about how Brenda excluded me from the inheritance, despite the fact that I really hadn't - at the time - any right to it. The reality of the will changed that - a bit too late.

Most of the conversation passes between the two of them making plans. I get in the occasional nod.

'So, we've got it right, eh?' Rob says, taking large gulps of his beer. Wine's not his thing. 'June hands her the ...'

'Hang on,' I say, a bit in the dark after watching the two of them together and thinking they suited each other far better than Rob and me, 'who am I handing what to?'

'The will, Juneeeee,' April chortles. 'The fuckin' - sorry - bloody will.'

'And to whom?'

They look at each other and laugh their heads off.

'Whom?' Rob asks April.

'Whom?' April asks Rob.

'Brenda!' they say at the same time, which results in more laughter. I can't help laughing along with them.

I have a great night. My friends like each other, we share a meal and drinks and make plans for a mythical happy ending to Aunty Kaye's wishes for her niece = me. It doesn't matter that it isn't practical but it's fun making plans together.

Rob wants me to get Little Malcolm on board but I'm not so sure about that. He's a Beechworth boy and Brenda's a Beechworth girl. He might not want to fight my case. Not that there's anything to fight. Just the scare factor.

The week flies by as I attend to Merv's business and keep up with his daily Skype sessions showing me how to pump up the tyres of the campervan, how to set up in a caravan park, where you get electricity and water from, the barbeques, the pools, the showers, and so on. I tell myself that I wouldn't ever want to go to New Zealand. It looks too stressful for my liking and, let's face it, I've been in every caravan park and on every road already!

Matt calls me to set up another night of dinner and sheer bliss. Rob calls to set up a night of sheer torture: another dancing lesson. I know which one I prefer, though it's a toss-up between the different styles of afterglow. If I had to, I couldn't give one up for the other, so I schedule them both in - Matt Wednesday, Rob Friday.

Wednesday 15th March

I twirl in front of the wardrobe mirror inspecting my new outfit, a dark green wrap-over dress almost the same green as Matt's car. I'm so pleased with my new figure. I've lost three kilos on my diet and I can feel the difference. My spare tyre has reduced from a mining truck tyre size to a 40-passenger bus tyre, and I feel that my double chin wobbles slightly less. Do I actually have a neck, I ask myself. Maybe the few sessions at the gym and the two dancing lessons have something to do with it as well. There's no doubt about it, something's working.

Matt's eyes light up as I open the door. 'You look gorgeous!'

I pat my hair as I hold my stomach in. 'You look pretty gorgeous yourself.'

His shirt is immaculate, as ever, and his suit, complementing his strong physic, screams dollars. He looks just like the gorgeous hunk on the cover of my latest M&B. White teeth lighting up a smile on a tanned face, startling blue eyes, shoulders and chest filling out a dark grey suit as he offers an open ring box to the lucky woman whose back is turned to the reader. I've borrowed that book just because of the cover - never mind the story - as I imagine myself to be that woman one day. Matt would leave his wife and whisk me away to ... oh, anywhere would do. Just away and being loved by him would make my dreams come true.

'We're going somewhere extra special tonight,' he remarks as he steers his car away from the gutter.

'Isn't it always?'

'I'm glad you feel that way.' He squeezes my hand holding onto it until he needs his on the wheel.

Our table overlooks the city lights from fifteen stories up. The view of the bay is breathtaking. The dinner an experience in itself - this time exquisite Japanese cuisine prepared by talented chefs. Each dish is served with calm reverence by the hushed waiters, the plating a work of art and such delicate flavours!

'Japanese chefs work with the best ingredients and do as little to the food as possible to bring out the colour and flavour,' Matt tells me as we sip on sake, an interesting flavour that I like. The waiter pours the sake until it spills over into a saucer as a token of appreciation for our visit. How lovely! Imagine an Aussie restaurant doing that with beer; the customer would probably complain and ask who was going to pay for it!

Matt goes on to tell me that to add contrast to the food, simple condiments are provided to enhance the flavours. This is my first experience with miso and wasabi. There is a small green ball on the side of my plate and, thinking it is a mere pea, I pop it into my mouth. A kimono-clad waitress throws her hands up in front of her face in horror and asks me if I am all right. I don't at first know what she's talking about until it hits me. The wave of agony that explodes into my sinuses reminds me of Gran's horseradish that she would get me to grate to go with the roast beef.

Other than the wasabi, the rest of the meal is delicious. It's served on antique ceramics and lacquer ware which makes it all look beautiful. I have awful problems with the chopsticks, however, until Matt teaches me how to hold them correctly (is there anything that man doesn't know?), which takes a long time, but we have all the time in the world.

We return to the same hotel afterwards where another stunning arrangement of flowers awaits us on a coffee table, along with a bucket of iced champagne. I think to myself that I could get used to this kind of spoiling. After I go into the bathroom to get ready for the rest of the night, I return to find a long red velvet box sitting beside my glass. I don't know whether to pick it up or not.

Matt smiles at me. 'Go on. Open it.'

It reminds me of my Mills & Boon book cover. The box is the wrong shape for a ring but I don't care. When I prise the lid open, I discover a string of flawless cultured pearls with matching earrings glowing with a radiance I've never seen. I don't know what to say but know I'll have to say something soon or I'll start dribbling. 'Are these for me?' I stammer.

'Of course, you funny creature,' he grins, watching every twitch of my face. 'Don't you like them?'

'I don't believe you,' I whisper, tears welling in my eyes.

'June?' He takes the box from me and gently cups my face in his hands. 'Have I done something wrong?'

I look at this beautiful, kind, loving man and wonder why on earth I'm there receiving this precious gift. Why not some model with a perfect figure and face? Why not some university-educated female brain that he could connect with and admire? Why not ...?

'June, for goodness sake, say something!'

'I just don't know how to express my thanks,' I blubber, knowing that my mascara is running down my face and my mouth screwing up in a most unlovely fashion, but I can't help it. 'Matt, I've never received anything like this. Never!'

'Well, it's about time, surely?'

'Oh, Matt! I don't deserve ...'

'Shhhh. Don't say that.'

'But ...'

But his mouth is on mine, tasting my tears of happiness and, well, the rest of the night passes by in a blur of feeling loved, valued, and for being sexy. Who, me? Yes, me. Pearls and all. Which I wear all night.

Thursday 16th March

I open the office early. It's so different walking across a few blocks to go to work instead of the whole public transport marathon. I'm sitting in Merv's office checking the emails when April arrives.

'Hi Boss,' she calls out from her desk.

'Hi yourself.'

I see her check to make sure no one else is within earshot as she enters the office. 'How was last night?'

I try to smother a yawn but just manage a distortion of my mouth which screws up my eyes.

'I saw that!' She chortles as she points her finger at me, then stops, mouth agape. 'What the hell is that?'

'What?'

'That on your neck?'

'Oh, these baubles,' I grin.

'Baubles. What the fu... hell are baubles?'

'Something superficially attractive but useless or worthless.'

'Bullshit!' She rounds the desk to grab hold of the pearls.

'Careful!'

'Jesus, June, these are real, aren't they?'

'Yep.' I manage to prise her hand away. 'I tried them when Matt wasn't looking.'

'How?'

'Run them over your teeth. If they're gritty, they're real.'

'What uni did you study that at?'

'I graduated from Gran's university. She had real pearls that had belonged to her grandmother. Can you imagine?' I stroke the pearls that sit on my neck - yes, that neck I discovered I had. 'She let me put them ever so carefully around my neck when I was very young. Under supervision, of course.'

'Did she wear them much?'

'The only time I ever saw them on her was at the Beechworth Ball one year. She wore a long blue gown that raised eyebrows. It stank of mothballs and some of the beads had fallen off, but she still looked like a million dollars to me. Never mind that she had a fag hanging out of her mouth and drank beer from a bottle.' I smile at the memory. 'And she danced like a queen.'

'Just like you, huh?'

That startles me out of my memories. 'Not quite,' I laugh. 'I've a long way to go yet.'

'Talking about which ...?'

Friday night,' I say. 'Dancing lesson number three.'

Friday 17th March

I go to a podiatrist during lunchtime to see if she can advise me on how best to look after my poor feet when I'm making an attempt to dance. 'Aside from bunion surgery, I'm afraid you're stuck with the problem,' she says.

I look down at my feet with a great degree of sympathy.

The samba is supposed to be a sexy dance. I decide that I need a hip replacement as I painfully try to bump with a hip this way, bump with the other that way. By the time my feet catch up my bunions are screaming.

'What about the *Evening 3 Step*?' I ask Rob.

'Nah, you need to learn more than a couple of dances, June,' he says as he pushes me this way and that. 'Challenge yourself.' And off we go in a different direction to what I expected and I stumble and twist my ankle. That's an effective way of ending a dancing lesson.

'I really want to learn to dance,' I blubber tearfully over my brandy and soda in the bar.

Rob sighs. 'Perhaps I need to take it a bit more slowly. Break you in ...'

'Like a horse?'

'I wouldn't go so far ...'

'It's all right, Rob. I know I'm a trial.' I look into my drink and speculate on how many it will take to dull the pain in my ankle. 'Why do you bother?'

He looks at me seriously, measuring me up. 'Because you're a nice person, June. I want to give you a skill that'll make a difference in your social life.'

'Here's another skill to add to your social life,' he says a little later. I no longer feel my ankle. I'm busy concentrating on other parts of my body that are working beautifully under his tuition. In this case I'm a quick learner.

When he takes me home, I notice he has the red car again. 'Got your car back okay, I see.'

'Huh?'

'Car.'

'What car?'

'Red car.'

'How many drinks have you had?'

Saturday 18th March

April and I catch up for a film at my place. I leave the film choice up to her, so she arrives with three to choose from: *Dunkirk*, *Avatar* or *The Dressmaker*. We watch the latter and love every minute of it. I wonder if someone from overseas would have appreciated it as much seeing as how it's so Australian. April came for a sleepover at my place, which means the couch. I feel a bit awful her sleeping on that but she assures me she can sleep anywhere. At least she doesn't have to get a taxi home.

We sit over hot chocolate before going to sleep. 'Have you told Merv both of us are taking time off?'

'I told him yesterday when he and Trish were showing me how to gut the fish they'd caught.' I pull a face. 'Disgusting!'

'You eat fish!'

'I know, but I'd rather not see their insides before eating them.'

'You eat sausages, don't you?'

'Hmmm ...' I'm getting bored with the guts conversation.

'Well?' She sucks her tongue between her teeth. 'I rest my case.'

'What do you mean?'

'Sausages are full of guts and stuff. Eyeballs, tendons, intestines ...'

'Remind me never to eat them again,' I say, shuddering.

'Black pudding?'

'April! No. No. No.'

'Anyway,' she says, knowing she's worn out the guts talk, 'what did he say about us both going?'

'He's fine with it. Said he'll get Mel to do a bit more around the place.'

'Oh, BBB's not gonna like that.'

Monday 20th March

This morning it's back to the twins on the train. Someone tries to beat Rob to the seat opposite me but he tells them to 'fuck off'. I wince. Why does everyone have to use foul language? It must be a generational thing.

'How're you travelling?' He looks at my face intently.

'Train.'

He laughs. 'Smart arse.' At my frown, he holds up his hands in surrender. 'Sorry, boss.'

'I'm fine,' I concede. 'And how about you?'

'If you mean have I recovered from Friday night then, yes, I have,' he grins. 'You up for more?'

I look around. 'Shhh!' You never know on a train. Ears are waggling in every direction trying to pick up some dirt. I open my latest M&B.

'What're you reading?'

'Something you probably wouldn't understand.'

'Try me.'

'It's a Mills & Boon romance,' I say seriously. 'Have you read any?'

'No. Have I been missing something?'

'Most definitely.' I hold out the book. 'Would you like to read it?'

He surprises me. 'Okay,' he says, taking it from me. 'Oh, it's a library book,' he notices. 'Is that a problem?'

'No. Just make sure you get it back to me as soon as you've read it.' I watch him leafing through it. 'How long does it take you to read a book?'

'I don't know,' he shrugs. 'I don't read books.'

'Well, I think it's about time you started.'

I look up to see his twin studying us from where he leans against a seat. As our eyes meet, he grins and then slowly looks the other way.

After a couple of hour's catch-up, Merv leans back in his chair, front legs off the floor, with a flatulent explosion that would have rivalled Vesuvius.

'Sorry, June,' he shrugs, covering his mouth. 'Never bloody lets up.'

'I'm used to it,' I mumble.

'What?'

'Glad you're back,' I say more loudly.

'Oh.' He looks at his calendar. 'So you and April are off exactly when and for how long?'

'Tomorrow, for the rest of this week and next.'

'So ... you're both off for exactly the same time?'

I nod.

'What - are you going away together?'

I nod again.

His chair thuds back to earth. 'Are you lezzos or something?'

'Hell, Merv. Of course not!'

'Oh,' he says, sitting back in his chair. 'Well, that's a relief.'

'Why would that be, Merv?'

'Well, we couldn't have those goings-on in the office, could we?'

'Jesus, Merv. What's wrong with you?'

'Well, I dunno. Being back in Melbourne. Culture shock, you know?'

Tuesday 21st March

Southern Cross Station, for the early hour, is crowded. We board our train and open the thermos I've packed, along with egg and bacon sandwiches April made.

'Tell me again why we're up at this fuckin' hour,' April whines.

'Because we're going to Beechworth.'

At Wangaratta we board a bus.

'Tell me again why we're on a bloody bus when we should be at work?'

'Because we're going to Beechworth.'

Nearly two hours later.

'We're at Beechworth.'

'Thank Christ for that,' she cries, looking at me through bloodshot eyes. 'Now can we go and have breakfast ...'

'We've had that.'

'No,' she insists. 'Real breakfast. And then some bloody sleep.'

'I know just the place,' I say, heading for the Beechworth Bakery.

With full bellies, we check into our hotel accommodation. April bounces up and down on the bed she claims and then collapses in a heap, fully-clothed onto the bed and falls asleep immediately. I cover her with a blanket and leave her snoring as I have a quick shower and make my way to Little Malcolm's office just in time for my appointment.

The secretary can't find me in her appointment book. 'Cooper,' I say again. 'June Cooper.'

'I just ...'

'I arranged it with you last week,' I tell her firmly. 'You said you were writing it in as we spoke.'

'Yes, well ...'

'I came up from Melbourne just for this appointment.' I look up at the wall clock. 'And I'm here on time, so I don't expect to be waiting.'

'Just a moment,' she says, pressing a button on the switchboard. 'Mr Malcolm? It's Ms Cooper here to see you.'

Within seconds the door to his office slams open to his short frame darting through the doorway. 'June! So good to see you. Come in. Come in,' he invites. 'Susie, make us a cuppa will you, love?'

I sit in front of his desk, crossing my stockinged legs casually. 'Good staff hard to find?'

He looks up at me, startled. 'What? Oh, yes,' he shrugs. 'Not exactly rich pickings around here.'

'Lucky your dad's old secretary still had it up here,' I say, pointing to my head, 'otherwise what on earth would have happened to the will?'

'I know. I know.' He shakes his head in supposed sympathy with me. Embarrassment, more like it.

'Anyway, I've done my homework back in Melbourne and realise,' I say, 'that it's all too late for me to claim anything from my aunt's estate. All gobbled up.'

'Afraid so,' he agrees.

'Though, there's the paternity in question. Well, who the hell was my father?'

He opens his mouth but shuts it again.

'That's what I thought. I haven't a clue either,' I shrug. 'And what happened to my mother?'

Silence.

'I doubt Brenda will tell me.'

'Probably not.'

'Can we coerce her?'

'Legally?'

I nod.

'No.'

Susie enters the office wobbling a silver tray. She just manages to land it on Little Malcolm's desk without losing anything.

'Would you like me to pour?'

'Thanks,' he nods.

'Sugar and milk?' she asks me as she pours the coffee which smells surprisingly good.

'One of each,' I say.

She looks puzzled.

'One sugar and one serve of milk,' I explain.

'Oh!'

Little Malcolm rolls his eyes in unison with mine.

I find April in exactly the same position that I left her two hours ago. I've strolled along the shops, getting to know Beechworth again: who's closed shop, what new businesses there are. No one recognises me, though I sure know some of the faces that look uncertainly at me. Faces that had sneered at me and my so-called family. Faces that had rebutted me. Laughed at me. Called me names. I look at them defiantly and think, who the hell are you today? No better than me, that's for sure.

As I sit down wearily on the bed opposite April, she looks up at me through bleary eyes.

'Are we there yet?'

I have fun showing my childhood surroundings to April. We explore the shops and then make our way up the hill to the asylum. I'd never been game enough to go there when a child, so it's through older eyes I discover the immense grounds, beautiful gardens, and careworn buildings that had housed some of the most tortured minds this side of the Black Stump. I wonder aloud if any of my family had been inmates there.

April looks sideways at me as we sit on the grass overlooking the township and surrounds. 'Wouldn't you know, though? I mean, they'd have talked about a loony amongst the rellies.'

'No. Not in those days. It was covered up. Mental illness wasn't admitted to, much less understood.'

'Shit, that'd be tough.'

'I imagine so,' I say, looking at the retaining ha-ha wall.

April's rummaging around in her head, I can tell. It's all a bit beyond her experience. She looks back at the historic asylum buildings and then over to some trees where we'd stopped. 'I reckon those dogwood trees would've softened their days when those big white flowers decorated the dogwoods like butterflies. That's if they'd been allowed out.'

'I'm sure they were because why would they have the ha-ha wall? They couldn't escape but at least they had this magnificent garden to admire.'

'That's if they cared about gardens.'

'Even if they didn't when they arrived here, I think they might have eventually.'

'While we're on the subject, what's the plan?'

'Which plan might that be?'

'Firstly, dinner,' she grins. 'Then the Brenda plan.'
'Oh, that plan.'

I think about what Little Malcolm advised. 'Tread carefully,' he'd said.
I'm paying him for that?
'You don't want to upset her - or the rest of the family.'
'Malcolm, I don't care if I upset them or not.'
His eyes and mouth had widened with surprise.
'As a matter of fact, I think I'd enjoy doing just that.'
His mouth's 'O' shape turned up into a grin. 'Serve them bloody right.'

April gasps at what I've just said. I can see a lump of steak in her mouth.
'That's disgusting!'
'I know,' she says, snapping her mouth shut, chewing furiously. She swallows, her eyes protruding in the effort to get it down. 'But you said...'
'Never mind what I said. I think going to see Brenda first would be a mistake. We have to find as much ammunition that we can beforehand.'
She's digging at her teeth with her tongue as she tosses the thought over in her mind. 'Well, I'm up for it. Why not?'
'Good on you.' I look at her fondly. 'You're a great friend, you know.'
'Don't get all soppy on me.' She pulls a face at me. 'Do I have to worry about sleeping in the same room as you?'
'Oh, shut up, you twit!'
'Imagine what Merv would say,' she snorts.

Back in our hotel, we pour over my notes and maps. Then we check Google Maps. It's a while since we looked up Aunty Kaye's house.
'There it is,' April says, pointing at a property in First Street, Mildura.
There's a house still standing there with what looks like a tin roof. A lot of them have tin roofs. It's close to a bend in the Murray River. There are a lot of what could be orange or citrus groves, certainly a lot of trees. We can see a property to the left of what was Aunty Kaye's property.
'I wonder if that's the property where the friendly neighbour was?'
'Possibly,' says April, 'but would he still be there?'
'Only one way to find out.'

Wednesday 22ⁿᵈ March

'This is my friend April Snowden,' I say to Little Malcolm as we sit before his desk after a big breakfast. 'She's helping me discover who I am.'

He studies her closely. A little too closely. I look from him to her and notice her blush.

'It's okay,' I add. 'You can trust her.'

And so we discuss my next move. He's surprised but supportive.

'We've had a look at how to get from Beechworth to Mildura...'

'It's just a seven-hour drive,' he interrupts.

'We know that,' says April, 'but neither of us drive.'

His eyebrows shoot up. 'You don't drive?' He looks at us both. 'Neither of you?'

'Never needed to. We live in the big smoke,' she adds rather sarcastically. 'Public transport and all that.'

He has that funny habit of forming a perfect 'O' with his mouth. A fly could make a landing in there with ease.

'Soooo,' April continues, 'we've found out that there are no direct flights from Albury to Mildura, so it seems the best option is a bloody f-ing bus that goes via Wangaratta and Swan Hill and takes ten hours plus. As if we haven't been on our arses long enough.'

'Well, if you drove...'

'But we don't, Malcolm,' she says, thudding the desk. 'We don't.'

'April,' he says, eyeballing her. 'There is another option.'

'Oh, really? Broomstick?'

'Shut up, April,' I hiss at her.

'No. No. It's all right,' he says with a bit of a grin. 'I wouldn't want to be sitting on my arse for ten plus hours either.'

April sits back in surprise.

So do I.

Little Malcolm said 'arse'.

'The Beechworth Community often sends out feelers to let people know someone is travelling to such-and-such-a place. Passengers are welcome.' He taps his keyboard and squints over his glasses at his monitor. 'Ah, here ... Jean McCready's going to Swan Hill on Tuesday ... Ted Hudson's driving to Wang tomorrow ... hang on ... John Appleby's taking his daughter to Mildura for something-or-other this afternoon.' He turns to us. 'Would that suit?'

We're into the fifth hour of our journey to Mildura. We haven't had to worry about how we'd get along with John Appleby as he's not stopped talking since his 'Gidday there' as he pulled up at our hotel. His daughter, Pauline, hasn't contributed more than three sentences to his conversation, punctuated by an occasional 'Hmmm' or 'Ahhh' from either of us. Not that it matters. John's an amiable fellow who's happy to disclose every skeleton in his family's cupboard, along with those of the future. Pauline's getting married to a Mildura farmer in a month's time and she's going there to sort out the reception arrangements. John thinks her fiancée is 'a dickhead of the first degree'. Pauline remains evasive about her own opinion.

Driving along the Sturt Highway, we eventually pull up outside our motel right near the Murray River.

'Let's know if you want a hitch back on Friday,' John says. 'We'll pick you up at sparrow's fart.'

That gives us two nights here. April and I think it's enough.

We take a walk down to the river. The air is lovely. Pure and fragrant. Birds are going nuts in the trees as they settle down for the night. We find a restaurant and make short work of a bottle of riesling with a Chinese meal. We're tired but enthusiastic about what we might find tomorrow.

Thursday 23rd March

We get a taxi to where we think Aunty Kaye's house might be. Not that we expect it to still be standing after fifty-five years or so. Everything looks different from what I expected. The land is mostly cleared with orange groves everywhere around it. I remember bushland. Gum trees. Wild landscape. Red dust. Heat. Instead, there are modern farm houses, organised agriculture, sealed roads, contemporary life layered over history.

'You want me to wait?' the taxi driver asks as we slide out of the back seat.

I shake my head. 'No, thanks.'

I stumble towards a house that has an enormous gum tree standing over it. I can't speak for emotion. This is it! I would know that tree with the table surrounding it anywhere. I would know the front door (minus the beaded curtain), the windows on either side, the shape of the house, the verandah on three sides. I run my hands over the table surface, surprised at its clean and smooth state. I can almost see Aunty Kaye, skirts swirling around her, hair caught up in a comb, beetroot juice dripping from her cleavage. I look at the front door foolishly willing her to open it.

Hold me. Kiss my cheeks. Tell me over and over you love me.

Tears roll down my face as I sit at the table, wishing, oh wishing things could have been different. If only she'd lived. If only my dad had lived. If only. If only.

I feel a hand lightly touch my shoulder. 'Junee?'

I look up at April. Tears are running down her face too.

'This is it, isn't it?'

I nod as I grope for a tissue in my bag.

'Here,' she pushes one under my nose. 'It's just like you described it.'

I look around me, memories colliding with the certainty that Aunty Kaye is dead, that she's not going to walk through that door, that my dad isn't going to sweep me up in his arms and tell me everything's going to be all right. I try to push out the image of Brenda and Gran throwing food at Aunty Kaye, their faces full of hate and spite.

'Oh, God. I had no idea I'd feel this ... emotional. It's stupid but ...'

'There's nothing stupid about it. Geez, June, this is your history, your lovely Aunty Kaye - at least her house. That's something, isn't it?' She gives her nose a resounding honk and I follow suit. 'Do you think we should knock?'

'Well, we might be charged for trespassing if we stay here unannounced.'

I feel trapped by the table, though, and the overarching presence of the eucalypt. We look around us in case we're about to be chased off the property at gunpoint. A tractor mumbles erratically in the distance. A truck and three cars sweep past and disappear. Insects buzz, hum and lunge. Birds chatter, swoop and sing, their busy lives contributing to their survival.

'Gidday there,' says a voice full of gravel and years. 'You girlies lost?'

We turn as one to see a tall old farmer walking across from a farmhouse not far from Aunty Kaye's. I notice that he's walking along a well-trod path through trees that separate the properties.

'Well, we're not exactly lost,' I tell him, 'just lost in memories.'

He cocks his head to one side then winces. He grabs his neck with his left hand. 'Now, that's an interesting statement,' he says. 'The sound of you, you could be a hundred years old like me - all lost in memories.'

'Get out with you,' April hoots. 'You're not a hundred!'

'Eighty-seven, to be exact.'

'Well, you might look a hundred, sound like a hundred, but you walk like an eighty-seven year-old,' she laughs.

He looks at me, an eyebrow up inside his forehead. 'Is she always this charming?'

'Always.'

'And you might be ...?'

'June. June Cooper.'

He catches his breath and grabs at his neck again. 'June? June? June...?'

'Cooper.'

His sits down beside me with a thud.

'And you are ...?' April asks with a shake in her voice.

'Charlie. Charlie Dixon.'

'You can't be,' I gasp. 'Can't possibly be.'

A short time later, we're sitting around the eucalypt tree, hugging mugs of steaming hot tea that Charlie makes in Aunty Kaye's kitchen. Actually, it's his kitchen. The whole property is his. He bought it when Aunty Kaye died. He was, and still is, the neighbour. The one who found her dead after the snake bit her. When he talks about her his grey/green eyes mist over and his voice shakes.

'So you're little June,' he keeps saying.

April and I nod agreement.

'I know all about you. About your ...'

And then he stops.

'It's okay,' I say gently. 'I know about it. The woman I thought was my mother wasn't. Her sister was my mother. Helen. Helen Rivers.'

He looks at me sideways.

'She stayed here to give birth to me. Did you know her?'

'Well ... yes,' he says.

'Did you ever meet Brenda and my grandmother?'

'Oh, struth, yes!'

'Can't forget those two, eh?'

'Kaye told me about the time you came and they threw beetroot at her.'

The three of us laugh.

'That was the last time they had any contact with her until ... until ... she died.' He takes a sip of his tea and puts the mug down carefully on the table. 'That Brenda was a piece of work. Didn't want anything to do with Kaye's funeral arrangements. Anything.'

'Until she found out about the estate?'

He nods. 'You know, she didn't even have the decency to go to the funeral.'

We sit in silence for a while, busy with our own thoughts.

'I read in some paperwork that you did everything: called the police, organised the funeral, helped the State Trustees with Aunty Kaye's effects, found documents, and so on.'

He's quiet, reliving that traumatic time, eyes focused behind the present.

'And you bought this place,' April asks. 'Why?'

'I couldn't bear the thought of someone else living here.'

April and I look at each other over his bowed head.

'You see, I loved her. Always loved her.' His voiced cracks as he whispers, 'Love her still.'

We follow Charlie along the short track to his place which is showing its age, like he is at the moment. It's easy to see how bringing up all these memories has made him very tired, but he insists that we go to his place for a BBQ lunch.

'That's my specialty,' he smiles, 'snags and onions.'

And he's not kidding. We wrap delicious sausages up in bread with lashings of tomato sauce, topped with sliced barbecued onions, and get it all over our faces and into our laps.

April wants to know where he got the sausages and tomato sauce. 'Never tasted anything like them.'

'I should hope not,' he says, washing a mouthful down with icy cold beer. 'I make 'em.'

He shows us his veggie patch brimming with tomatoes, lettuce, onions, cucumbers, herbs and every other vegetable you can imagine that's in season. He's got kitchen shelves stacked with tomato sauce in bottles, pickles, chutneys and jams, and a freezer full of sausages that he's made - pork, beef, chicken.

'You're quite the cook,' April remarks, inspecting the labels he's neatly written for each jar.

'Kaye taught me.' He takes a deep breath as memories invade his kitchen. He looks over at the bench beside the sink. 'She stood right there and taught me how to sterilise the jars, how to make the stuff, label it, and then eat it.'

My mobile intrudes upon the stillness of the kitchen. I see it's Rob and cut off the call. April lifts an eyebrow. 'Rob,' I tell her. 'I'll call him back later.'

'One of the boyfriends,' April says out of the corner of her mouth at Charlie.

He lifts his own eyebrow.

'Don't ask.' She rolls her eyes. 'It's a long story and you're probably too young for it.'

He cracks another stubby for each of us with a grin on his face. We take them out to sit under his verandah which has at least a dozen wicker armchairs waiting for our bums and goodness knows who else's. There's also a table surrounded by more chairs out on the burnt lawn.

'Who're you expecting?' April indicates the chairs.

'You,' he says looking at me.

We remain for hours sitting under Charlie's rusted tin roof which is framed by grape vines. We watch the sun dip behind the orange groves, the breeze wafting the scent of the fruit past our noses. He's been asleep, slumped in his chair, for some time now. Neither April nor I want to disturb him so we sit in the pleasant quiet fumbling around in our minds' past and trying to make sense of what Charlie's told us.

Kaye moved from Beechworth to Mildura in the early 50s when Kevin and Brenda were married. She couldn't stand Brenda and the feeling was mutual. Kaye was a promising artist who made a modest living from her art, however, it was her half of her parents estate that enabled her to buy the house on First Street, Mildura. She'd been thrifty ever since she earned her first pay packet, saving every penny she could. By the time she took off for Mildura, she had a sizeable balance in her savings account to add to her inheritance.

Kaye and Kevin's parents died together on the way to Melbourne when their ute hit a truck just as they were turning onto the Hume Highway. Mercifully, they died upon impact, but it left their traumatised teenage children in the care of an aunt and uncle who they hardly knew. Kevin left school immediately to become a shearer and Kaye got a job working at the local newsagency in Beechworth. The siblings hardly saw each other after that. Kevin met Brenda at a local dance and, after a drunken session of heavy petting, she told him she was pregnant and they'd have to get married. That was nonsense but Kevin, who wasn't blessed with much in the brain department, believed her. A hurried wedding took place and Kaye left for good.

Kevin and Kaye kept in touch by letter - hers, newsy pages full of enthusiasm for her artistic life in Mildura; his, mostly a half-page of illegible scrawl about nothing in particular that she had trouble deciphering. But he made an occasional effort to drive over to Mildura to reconnect with Kaye and in the hope of bringing the little one who never eventuated. 'Where's my bloody niece or nephew?' she'd taunt Brenda, knowing full well that the cow had trapped her brother into a loveless marriage. 'Longest bloody pregnancy I ever heard of,' Kaye had said.

And then Helen, Brenda's younger sister, had fallen pregnant. Gran was livid as smoke literally chugged from her ears and nostrils. 'You can't have the brat,' she'd ranted. 'The whole of bloody Beechworth'll turn it's backs on us. You've brought disgrace upon our family!' The story goes that Gran had grabbed Helen by the ear and marched her off to the local midwife who performed abortions on her kitchen table after dark. The 16 year-old had squirmed as Gran held her legs and the midwife attempted to push something into her. Helen leaned over and bit Gran on an arm, who let go shouting curses that most soldiers wouldn't even have heard of. The girl grabbed her underpants, broke through the kitchen door flywire and disappeared into the night. Before Gran could get home, Helen had packed a bag and was running down the street when Kevin almost ran her over. And so Kevin brought Helen to Mildura where Kaye looked after her until I was born.

No one except Kevin knew where Helen was until she gave birth. He'd gone up to Kaye's on the pretext of helping her with some fencing and returned to Beechworth with a baby stuffed inside a basket. He insisted that he'd found it on the front doorstep - never mind that he came in the back door - and, of course, no one believed him. He finally admitted it was Helen's baby and that he and Brenda were going to bring it up as their own.

Gran and Brenda were incensed that Kevin had never told them of Helen's whereabouts and that he'd had the cheek to return with the baby. They accused him of being the father, saying why would he want to bring her up as his own if she wasn't. But, because the baby was there and they didn't know what else to do with her - and considering the fact that Brenda looked pregnant most of the time anyway - they agreed to pretend she was theirs, providing that Kevin had to feed her, wash her dirty nappies and generally be responsible for 'his brat'.

When it came to naming the baby, Brenda didn't want a bar of it. Gran wouldn't even talk about it. Kevin had no idea. So, when they had to register the birth, Brenda was forced into making the decision. As the baby had arrived in their house on the 6th of June, she decided that would be the birth date and I would be called June. How original.

'Why didn't Brenda and Gran want to take the baby back to Helen?' I ask Charlie when he wakes up.

'Kev told them she'd cleared out. No point trying to find her as Kaye didn't know where she was either, or at least that's what Kev said.'

April looks puzzled. 'But surely they knew where she was.'

'None of us did,' he says, elbows on his knees, head hanging down.

'But why would she leave Aunty Kaye? Wasn't she happy here?'

Charlie looks up at me. 'She used to come here and visit, mostly in the school holidays. Loved it here. She and Kaye had a close relationship. Very close.' He takes a breath. 'She had no life with your grandmother and her sister. She wanted to come up here and live with Kaye when she finished school.'

'But she got pregnant,' I say.

'Yeah.'

'Was Kevin my father ... my real father?'

'Helen wouldn't tell anyone who the father was, not even Kaye.'

'Did she have any boyfriends in Beechworth?' April asks.

Charlie shrugs. 'Who knows? Apparently she was the life of the party on weekends. Went to dances. Had a bit to drink.' He shifts in his seat and takes a sip from his stubby. 'Oh, Christ!' He throws the contents in a wide arc across the dry grass.

'Flat?' April grins.

'You could say that,' he pulls a face, then gets up holding out his hands for our bottles. 'Refill?'

When he settles back down in his creaky chair and massages his neck, he looks at us both with a wry smile on his face. 'Cat got your tongues?'

'Well,' I say, 'aren't you a bit tired? I mean, it's getting late ...'

'Getting late for who? Are you feeling your age, girlie?'

'Cheeky!' I laugh, liking this old man who loves to talk.

'I'm starved!'

'April's always starved,' I grin.

Charlie regards the sky. 'The local pub puts on a good counter tea.' He looks at us both hopefully.

Charlie takes us to the local in his dusty ute where April knocks back the biggest steak I've ever seen and Charlie's not far behind her. We leave the family history alone for the rest of the night, asking him about his life in Mildura. We learn that he never married and his two brothers have been long gone. He has cousins on the Gold Coast but they're not in touch. That might make him a lonely man, though he's well known in the pub with just about everyone raising a hand in his direction or coming over to check us out. Apparently he's very active in the local men's shed and the senior citizens club, which he says keep him busy.

'Never enough hours in the day,' he smiles, 'though you wouldn't think it me chinwagging with you two all day. Just as well I don't have the oranges anymore.' He looks up at a group of men playing pool. 'The young ones look after that side of it now.'

Charlie's one of those people who you feel you've known forever. You feel comfortable with him, the conversation going from one thing to another. He doesn't just focus on himself. He asks us about our lives in Melbourne, how we met and where April came from. She's a bit evasive about her past but is practised in changing the subject. He asks us how long we're staying. 'Two more nights,' I say. Then he wants to know where we're staying.

'Well, come on girlies. Time to check you out and settle you in Kaye's place.'

He won't hear of us staying anywhere where we 'don't belong'.

'The place is just as she left it, minus the dust.' He laughs. 'She wasn't big on housework.'

'But ...'

'But nothing,' he insists. 'If you two don't mind sharing a bloody big bed, we can make it up in no time.'

April hoots with laughter and I know what she's thinking. 'Don't tell Merv,' we say at the same time.

'Who's Merv?' Charlie looks from one to the other.

It's late by the time we settle down in the enormous bed. Aunty Kaye had had it custom made - the mattress too. Apparently, she'd had to sleep on a tiny mattress out on the verandah of her aunt's house up until she left Beechworth, hence the big bed. It's strange to lie in her bed and see what she saw: a dressing table with a framed photo of herself and her brother when they were young; a large lacquered jewellery box with necklaces falling out of its drawers; a silver trinket box; a tortoise shell comb; a worn dog collar. An oval cheval mirror. A round willow bin. And, with the curtains open, a view of that magnificent gum tree.

'I feel like I'm trespassing and she'll walk in the door and tell us off,' April says.

'Me too.'

'And it's so bloody clean!'

'That's what's lovely about Charlie. He's kept this place like a shrine to Aunty Kaye, almost like he's waiting for her to come back to life.'

'Do you think he might be bonkers?'

'Not a chance. He's sharper than you and me put together.'

'Ahh,' April sighs. 'Wouldn't it be lovely to be loved by a man as much as he loved her?'

'Still does.'

Friday 24ᵗʰ March

It's strange waking here to a raucous bird chorus instead of the traffic din as it rumbles past my flat back in Melbourne. April doesn't move as I get up to go to the toilet so I tiptoe to the bathroom where there are clean towels, fragrant soaps, even a maidenhair fern hanging over the bath. I look at myself in the mirror over the basin wondering if there's any trace of Helen left in my face. Strange not to know what your mother looks like.

Do I look like Kevin? Our mouths are different. His was wide with even teeth. Mine aren't bad either but I don't think I smile so widely as he did. My cupid's bow is more pronounced. He had faded green eyes; mine are hazel. We have similar textured, wavy hair, mine a bit lighter. But it's hard to draw comparisons when I'm looking at a fat, 62 year-old frumpy woman and I'm remembering with my child's eye a vital 27 year-old man.

As I stand under the shower, I think about how Kevin and Helen, his sister-in-law, could have got themselves into the position where she ended up pregnant with me. She was younger than Brenda by three years and, from what Charlie told us, a bit of a party girl. Maybe she was more fun than her sour-faced sister. Maybe she and Kevin got on well. Maybe Kevin realised Brenda had tricked him into marriage and he was pissed off. Maybe Helen provided a sympathetic ear, a shoulder to cry on. Maybe they had a few drinks when Brenda wasn't around and things got out of hand. Who knows?

I try to put myself in my mother's place. She'd found herself pregnant by, most probably, her brother-in-law. Didn't tell him. Waited until the aborted abortion and he spirited her away to his sister. Maybe he was going to leave Brenda and look after Helen and her baby. Maybe Charlie can tell me more today. His memory seems reliable. I'm sure he's got a lot more to say.

As I get dressed, there's a knock on the back door. 'Yoo hoo! Are you girls awake?'

'Yes, in here.'

April rolls over and opens one eye. 'Huh?'

'She's not a morning person,' I tell Charlie.

'That's obvious.' He grins as he shows me six eggs cushioned in his hands. 'They're yours?'

'Well, I didn't lay them myself,' he laughs.

And then he makes himself at home in the kitchen, tossing a frying pan around like a pro. In no time at all, we have fried eggs on toast with bacon and tomatoes and onions. I make the tea.

We sit outside at the gum tree table, which makes me feel all warm and fuzzy inside. We're settling down over our second cuppa when April makes an appearance.

'What sort of time is this,' she groans as she looks up at the sky. 'Shit, the sun hasn't even come up yet.'

'It's behind the trees, you idiot,' I laugh. 'You want breakfast?'

'Ask me again when the sun's over the horizon.' And she goes back to bed.

Charlie raises an eyebrow that disappears under his white hair into his forehead. It's an interesting knack he has. Along with grabbing his neck from time to time.

'What's that about,' I ask him next time he does that.

'Arthur Ritis.'

'Bad?'

'Bad enough,' he shrugs. 'What can you expect for an old fellow?'

'Anything else?'

'Nah. Just the ticker's a bit dodgy now and then but nothing to write home to Mother about. It's under control.'

I feel a stab of concern. I'd hate to see anything happen to this lovely man.

He picks up the dirty plates and we clean up in the kitchen.

'Would you like a tour?'

I'd not ventured into Aunty Kaye's studio, feeling as if I was intruding upon Charlie's territory, so I'm glad of the offer.

I remember a room full of light and paintings. I remember the smell of turps and oil paint. Although it's a jumble of paintings, they follow a theme from one place to the next. It's a wild splash of colour, the whole studio, with one painting still to be completed on its easel. I recognise a kelpie/Queensland healer dog emerging from the canvas.

'Was that one of Aunty Kaye's dogs? The time I came here?'

Charlie nods, reaching out to run his finger lightly over the dog's mussel captured on the canvas. 'Yep, that was old Rover. I had him and old Jessie after Kaye died. They missed her like crazy but we got along all right. Rover was around thirteen when he died, and Jessie went a month after. She couldn't handle his absence.'

He rummages around a stack of animal paintings. 'Here's Jessie,' he says, holding up the painting.

I recognise her too, even after all these years.

'You got a dog or a cat?'

'No, I've got a goldfish,' I smile. 'Two, actually.'

'I suppose you take 'em out for a walk every day.'

I'm glad to see his eyes clear of sadness again.

He pulls out a painting from a stack of portraits. 'Here,' he says, putting it up on an easel. 'This is your mother.'

I gasp. My breath sucks inward, staying there. I can hear my heart thud in my ears. I look from Charlie to the portrait. 'My ...'

'Sorry, girlie. A bit of a shock, eh?'

I shake my head as my eyes collide with her features. 'I know her. I've seen her!'

'I thought you didn't have any photos?'

'I don't.'

'Then ...?'

I close my eyes. I'm at primary school. In the playground. I'm sitting on a tree branch with my lunchbox on my lap. There's a lady on the other side of the wire fence. She's looking at me with tears rolling down her face.

'Are you hungry?' I ask her, offering half of my sandwich.

'No, darling,' she says with a catch in her throat.

No one's ever called me darling before.

'Are you sad?'

She nods.

'Who made you sad?'

'Life,' she cries.

I don't understand.

She swipes at her tears. 'Are you happy?'

I nod. 'I got eight out of ten for arithmetic.'

'Do your mummy and daddy love you?'

I look at her, unable to answer.

The bell rings. 'I have to go.' And she disappears.

Sometime after, when I've sat on the same tree branch looking for her, she's there! I hold out a piece of my sandwich and pass it, folded over, through the wire.

'Thank you, my darling,' she cries.

'Did you like it?'

She smiles through her tears. 'All the more because you gave it to me.'

'Really?' Can I really make someone *that* happy?

I'm in the second year of high school. I see her leaning against a yellow car as I begin my ride home. I brake. I walk the bike over to her.

'Do I know you?'

'A long time ago,' she says, through misted vocal chords.

'Are you a friend of the family?'

'You could say ...'

But we're interrupted by my brother, Wayne, on his bike.

'Stop stuffing around and get on home. Mum wants you to ...'

I turn around and she's behind the wheel of her yellow car. I raise my arm to her and she waves back.

'Stupid cow,' Wayne says, as her car turns away. Was he referring to me ... or her?

April sticks her head around the studio door. 'Have I missed anything?'

We're sitting around the gum tree, arms leaning on the circular table.

'I've got something to show you girls,' Charlie says, as he magically removes some of the tree bark to reveal a cavity. 'This is where Kaye kept her secrets.'

We're transfixed as he removes an old tin from the tree. He places it reverently on the table and gently opens the lid. He takes out a package wrapped in greaseproof paper. As he opens the flaps, old photos spill out with folded letters, postcards, certificates.

'Here,' he says, offering the contents to me. 'All of this belongs to you.'

I look at him with gratitude and - yes - love. He's kept these secrets all this time for me.

I pick up a photo of a teenage Helen sitting at this very table, Kaye putting rollers in her hair. 'That was during a school holiday. Helen was going to a kids dance that night.'

Another with Kaye and Helen sitting up in *that* bed reading magazines. 'They loved reading all that rubbish. Goodness knows what they got from it.'

A photo of Helen with a prominent belly, Kaye rubbing it. They're both laughing. 'Yeah, I took that one too.'

Helen *very* pregnant, holding her belly up, Kaye and Charlie helping her. 'Kev took that one.'

Now here's one of Helen holding a baby. Me.

There's a photo of a very young me between Kaye and Kevin. 'I took that one,' Charlie says. 'You were here for a holiday too young, we thought, but it worked out real good. You loved every moment, and so did we.'

I look at him in surprise. 'You mean I was here before I was seven, what I thought was the only time I'd been here?'

'Oh, yeah,' he says, 'you came two or three times.'

I look at him, this man who holds so many secrets that mean so much to me.

'Did you know Kaye left her house to me?'

'Oh, sure,' he nods. 'I helped her write up her will.'

April shuffles through the photos.

She holds one up. 'You and Kaye had a thing going, didn't you?'

Charlie takes the photo from her and I lean over his shoulder to see. He and Kaye are dancing in the lounge room. He's holding her bent over backwards and they're laughing. You can see how much he loves her, the way he's looking at her.

'Who took that one?' I ask.

'Kev. This was not long before Helen gave birth to you. He came up to see how she was.'

'So ... you had a thing?'

Charlie looks at her with a grin on his face. 'You could say that.'

'I knew it!'

Charlie laughs. 'You want to know the ins and outs of a duck's bum, don't you?'

I open a document. It's a copy of the will.

'Yep, that's it,' Charlie confirms.

'Fat lot of good that did,' April snorts.

I look at Charlie. 'I didn't come up here looking for anything material. I just want to know the truth - who I am.'

'Can I open this?' April's got her hands on a letter addressed to Kaye in beautiful handwriting. My hair stands up on end. I have goose bumps on my arms.

'Oh, I forgot,' Charlie says, taking it from her. 'This letter came after Helen left. And there are more.'

Dear Kaye, I've settled in okay. The milk has finally stopped dripping from my nipples. God, that's been awful! So embarrassing at times! I'm so grateful for the money you gave me. I'll pay you back one day. Promise!

After I left Melbourne the bus went up the Princes Highway and when it went past Merimbula Lake I thought it looked so pretty and asked the driver to stop at the turnoff to Merimbula. The driver was a bit worried and asked if I had someone to meet me. I said sure I did my aunty and uncle would be along shortly and so he let me off. After the bus was out of sight I looked for a bus to Merimbula but couldn't see any so I hitchhiked. I know you and Charlie told me not to do that but heck I was out in the middle of nowhere and had to do something. A nice man in a ute gave me a lift and dropped me in front of a church here.

The reverend and Mrs Reverend are really nice Kaye. They looked after me, gave me a bed to sleep in, found me a job and then I've got a little flat of my own. I'm working at a milk bar. The owner and his wife are okay but his brother is a bit of a problem with Roman hands and Russian fingers. I can hold him off though.

I will write again when I have something more to tell you. At the moment I really like the town and so far the people (except for Roman Hands) are nice.

Have you heard anything about my baby? I think of her all the time and wish I didn't have to give her up to bloody Brenda. Of course it's fine that Kevin is with her but Brenda and Gran won't love her like I do. If you get the chance, would you hold her for me and whisper to her that her real mummy loves her and misses her. Even if she doesn't understand.

You can write to me at this address.

Thank you for all your help. I just don't know how I could have managed without you.

I miss you and your cooking and your painting.

Love and kisses, Helen.

PS - please say gidday to Charlie for me.

'She missed me,' I whisper into Charlie's armpit.

'Of course she did. Just read the others,' he says.

And there's more from Merimbula and then her departure when Mr Roman Hands became too much to handle. She spent two years in Sydney and then made for Port Macquarie. She said it reminded her of Merimbula. During that time she wrote a brief post card.

I did the most daring thing! I travelled down to Beechworth and saw June through the fence at her school. We talked and she, dear thing, offered me her sandwich. She had no idea of course. My heart broke.

So I didn't dream that encounter. I really did talk with her. If only I'd known. Tears pour down my face; April dabs at them ineffectually. 'They keep coming!,' she complains. That makes me laugh.

Later, from Port Macquarie, where she'd gone back to studying.

I've finished high school as a mature aged student. Can you imagine that? Me - mature aged! At least it makes me more employable. I've gone for an interview to be a receptionist at a doctor's surgery. Wouldn't that be great? Keep your fingers crossed.

She worked at the surgery for a year before this came:

I went again to see June. She was sitting on the same tree branch as if she'd been waiting for me all that time. She passed me a scrunched up bit of squashed, sweaty Vegemite sandwich and I ate it and it was the best thing I've ever eaten! She looked sad. I just wanted to grab her and take her with me but what could I hope to give her? Maybe when I've saved a bit more.

I hold the letters and cards and sniff them, trying to take in her essence. But there's nothing left there except the smell of the tree and the musty box.

I'm going out with someone. I'm not game enough to tell him about June just yet. He's the doctor I've been working for these past years. His wife just died.

A wedding invitation.

'Did you go?'

Charlie looks at me with that mist back in his eyes.

'Oh,' I murmur. 'Aunty Kaye had gone?'

'I had to write and tell Helen the awful news. It took me a few goes to write it because I knew it would be a hard letter to read, especially before she got married.' Charlie looks from April to me. 'I couldn't ignore the invitation, could I? I had to tell her why we couldn't go.' He sorts through the other cards and letters until a photo falls out of a thick envelope. 'This is it. Your mother's wedding photo.'

Helen - my mother - looks like a princess in a long dress gathered at the waist with some sort of sash and a whole lot of lace over the top and sleeves. Her long hair's pulled up at the sides and she's got a short veil somehow tied into some flowers at the top of her head. I can't see me there at all. She's too pretty. Her husband is a lot older, has some grey at his temples, but he's really good looking and tall. They're posing outside of a small church. The wedding party isn't that big but the rest of the guests might have been in other photos.

'Here she goes again,' April groans as she mops me up with more tissues.

'I can't help it,' I cry. 'It's just that ...'

'Hey, girlie,' Charlie's quick to say, 'don't apologise for being human. Finding your real mother after all this time must be a bit of a kick in the guts.'

'You could say that,' I smile through watery eyes. 'In a good way, though.'

'Go on,' he rumbles in his chest, 'have a bloody good cry.'

And I do.

'There's one last letter,' Charlie says later, his rough fingers shuffling through the rest of the pile. 'After this one, I lost touch with her.' He hands me a bulky envelope. There are about a dozen colour photos of a baby boy. All dark eyes, dark hair, chubby cheeks, his father's eyebrows. Lots of expensive-looking clothes and toys. Helen, sparkling eyes, holding him, changing his nappy, kissing him, loving him. The doctor proudly holding him up to the camera, holding a stethoscope to his son's heart, smiling face.

Charlie, I thought you'd like to know that I've become a mother again, this time legitimately.

I catch my breath.

Little Eric was born on the 16th of October at a good weight of 8 lbs 10 ozs. Ian, of course, wouldn't be allowed to be the delivering doctor but, as fate would have it, we didn't make it in time to get to hospital so Ian delivered Eric on the back seat of our car (never mind the mess!). Our boy was in such a hurry!!!

I study the photos of my half-brother. I have a new brother! I do the sums. Helen was 22 when she married Dr Ian Temple, so she was 23 when she gave birth to Eric in 1962. That makes him around 55 years old. Only 7 years younger than me. I wonder what he looks like now.

'That was the last time she wrote?' April asks.

Charlie nods.

'Did you write to her again?'

'A couple of times but there was no answer. I figured she was in her new life and had said goodbye to the old.'

'What about this?' I'd turned over her letter to find a few scribbled words overleaf.

If you ever see June would you tell her I always loved her, Charlie.

<u>Loved</u> - past tense. And I hear a door shut firmly in my head.

'How about some lunch?' Charlie asks, rubbing his hands together, getting up from the gum tree table and stretching. We've been here for hours.

April looks at him expectantly. 'Sausages, tomato sauce and onions?'

'Girlie, all you bloody want.'

'Now you're talking,' she hoots.

'We just had breakfast,' I complain half-heartedly, my traitorous tongue already watering.

I stand up with a tremble in my body. It's been a harrowing, if enlightening, morning. I now know what my mother looks like, have discovered what happened to her, where she went, that she married, that she gave birth to a boy. I'm stunned. I need some time to digest all this. I think Charlie's home-made sausages are just what I need. Probably a beer or two as well.

We return to the same seats on Charlie's verandah, the wicker chairs groaning under our weight. We each have a very full plate of sausages wrapped in bread, fried onions spilling out, dripping with his killer tomato sauce. In the other hand, a stubby. We're not on ceremony here. We begin to eat in companionable silence.

I sink my teeth into the sausage and close my eyes savouring the flavours. Oh, hell, this is gastronomic heaven. I wonder if Matt would like this? Or Rob? Yes, I'm sure he would.

Sulphur-crested cockatoos scream in alarm at something in their world that upsets them. They rise in a snowy-white cloud and veer off over the roof.

'What do you girls want to do this arvo?' Charlie says, as he wipes his mouth with his arm. 'I could show you around Mildura?'

'Geez, that'd be great, Charlie.' April's all smiles.

'A mate's got a boat. We could take a ride on the river.'

'The Murray?'

'Is there any other?' he grins.

The rest of the afternoon is taken up with a walk around Jaycee Park and a paddle steamer which follows the twists and turns of the mighty river. What a busy place it is with boats going back and forth, people walking around the parks and streets. I like it here.

Over dinner at the same pub, we discuss tomorrow. Charlie's insisted he drive us back to Beechworth. 'You're kidding,' I say as I watch him and April sawing into their huge steaks. 'That's a long drive.'

'Don't I know it, girlie, but I'm not seeing you get on any bus in the morning. You'll go with me.'

'What about Whatshisname who brought us here?'

'You mean John Appleby?' I say, pushing the food around my plate. 'It's probably too late to ring him.'

Charlie's watching me. 'Not hungry?'

'Not really.'

They both put their fork and knife down.

'What's wrong?' they both say in unison.

I look at them both, tears streaming down my cheeks.

'Oh, shit, she's doing it again!'

'What?' asks April as she tries to clean me up, snotty nose and all. She hands me a bunch of tissues and I blow my nose.

'It's just that ...'

'You don't want to go back, do you?'

'No,' I tell her.

'You've fallen in love with him?'

'Sort of.'

'What's that, girlie?' he asks from the other side of the table. 'Speak up.'

'She's feeling a bit emotional. All the family history stuff. She'll be right.' April pats me on the back.

Saturday 25th March

We're up at sparrow's fart, ready to go after tidying up Aunty Kaye's place. I run my hand over the table top under the gum tree. I look up into its canopy. *I'll be back sometime soon I hope*, I tell it.

'Yoo hoo. You two ready?' Charlie calls as he walks along the track from his place.

'As ready as we'll ever be,' April calls back. 'Come on Juneeee. Stop bloody crying, will you?'

Charlie goes into the house and comes out with a large flat parcel wrapped in a blanket and tied with string. 'This is yours,' he says to me as he stows it in the back of the truck.

I look at him, twist my neck to look at the parcel again, then back at him. 'Is that what I think it is?'

He grins at me. 'It's been waiting for you a long time.'

April groans. 'Okay, get it out,' she complains handing me a bunch of tissues. 'Anyone'd think it was a portrait of the bloody Queen.'

'Same thing,' I blubber, 'but better.' I lean over to give Charlie a kiss on the cheek.

'I reckon your mum – and Kaye – would be happy you've got it.'

'Now can we go?' April splutters. 'The way we're going, it'll be midnight by the time we arrive in Beechworth.'

Charlie laughs as he turns the ignition on. 'We'll stop for a cuppa at Balranald, then have another stop at Deniliquin. That should be enough to get us into Beechworth in the arvo. What do you girls reckon?'

'Sounds good to me,' April says fiddling with the radio.

'None of that head banging stuff, girlie. Just something nice and relaxing.'

She fiddles for a while until she finds Dolly Parton singing *Nine to Five*.

... Working Nine to Five, What a Way to Make a Living ...

The three of us sing along with Dolly as if we've been singing all our lives together. Charlie's got a lovely baritone voice.

We pull up in front of Brenda's house at exactly four o'clock. 'Struth, it hasn't changed a bit,' Charlie says, turning the radio off. 'Same bloody garden gnomes out the front; just a bit faded.' His ute sits ticking as it cools down after the long drive.

'We going to do this now?' April asks, looking a bit apprehensive.

'Just like we said,' I say.

April points at a black Mercedes in the driveway. 'Who's is that?'

'Sandra's.'

'Should we come back when she's not here?'

'I don't see why we should. Let's drop the bombs where they hurt most.'

'In that case we're missing Wayne.'

'Doesn't matter,' I tell April. 'He'll hear about it soon enough.'

'Come on you two.' Charlie gets out of the ute. 'No time like the present.' He turns to me. 'You right?'

'Yep.'

Instead of going round the back, I knock on the front door.

Sandra opens it with a look of surprise on her face. 'What'd you knock for, you stupid cow?' Then she notices April and Charlie.

'Her name's June, not Stupid Cow,' Charlie says firmly.

Her mouth opens and closes making a popping sound.

'And this here's April. I'm Charlie,' he adds.

I force my way past her and go through to the kitchen where I can hear Brenda banging pots around.

'Who's at the door?'

'June pretending to be the bloody Queen,' Sandra says loudly.

'Charming,' April comments, looking daggers at Sandra.

'Who the bloody hell are you?' Sandra spits back.

'April,' Charlie says as we stop outside the kitchen. 'I already introduced you.'

'Well,' Brenda says when she catches sight of me, 'look who the cat dragged in.'

'This is gunna be fun,' April mutters.

We three enter the kitchen. Brenda's wrist goes limp when she catches sight of Charlie. 'Jesus Christ.' Whatever she's cooking ends up on the floor.

'Charlie Dixon, actually,' he says. 'Remember me, Brenda?'

'Mum! Look at the bloody floor,' Sandra says in a flap, not knowing what's going on.

Brenda's gone a pasty colour. 'Never mind the bloody floor.' Colour gradually returns to her face. 'What're you doing here?'

'You might ask June that.'

She looks from him to me, her eyes narrowing, her lips a thin line. I can almost hear her brain churning over. Charlie + June = Trouble. She focuses on April. 'What do you want?!'

'I'm here as a witness.'

'To what?'

'Depends on you,' April says, cool as a cucumber.

'Well?' Brenda glares at me.

Sandra's given up on the floor as, after a quick welcome lick on my ankle, an exploratory sniff at April and Charlie, Barry the Beagle has zoned in on the stew and makes short work of it, the sound of his housework cracking the silence.

'I know you're not my mother.'

Sandra stares at the two of us. 'What's she on about, Mum?'

'Shoosh,' Brenda says, giving her a pat on the arm.

'I know how you and Dad - Kevin - covered up the fact that I'm your sister's daughter.'

'Whaaaaaat?!'

'Sandra, go and get your brother,' Brenda says.

'But he's ...'

'Now!'

'Yes, Sandra,' I say calmly. 'That would be a good idea. I have a few things to tell the two of you.'

'In the meantime,' I continue 'we're going to check in at our hotel. We'll be back at five-thirty.' I pause for good effect. 'On the dot. We have a family meeting to hold.'

This time we go around the back after noting Wayne's BMW parked up on the grass. As we round the house we can hear Sandra screaming at Brenda, Wayne following her at a few less decibels.

'Why the bloody hell didn't you tell us before that bitch came here with a smirk on her face?'

'How was I to know she knew?'

'Doesn't matter whether she knew or not,' Wayne yells. 'We had a right to know she's not our sister.'

'No wonder she's nothing like us. No brains,' Sandra sniggers, 'and no looks.'

'Downright ugly,' Wayne agrees.

I hear April's intake of breath but silence her with a frown. Charlie's face is black as thunder.

'Why didn't you get rid of her when Dad died?'

Sandra's got a point.

'How do you think I could have done that?'

'An orphanage?' Wayne offers.

'Or the asylum up there,' my half-sister laughs. 'She'd have been right at home.'

Charlie can't stop himself. He charges around the corner. 'That's enough!'

We follow him to see Brenda sitting at the outdoor setting, wringing a tea towel between her hands. Wayne and Sandra stand over her, each holding a glass of wine. Sandra's face is bright red, as is Brenda's.

Wayne whirls around and sees me. 'What are you up to?'

'I'm on a mission,' I tell him calmly.

'Who are they?'

'Haven't they,' I indicate Brenda and Sandra, 'told you yet?'

'She's brought her bodyguards,' Sandra spits. 'Probably too scared to ...'

'Scared of what, dear half-sister?' I look at the three of them slowly. 'The truth?'

'The truth!' Brenda glares at me. 'I'm glad it's out at last. I've had to raise you, see your ugly face every day, having to pretend you're my daughter, wanting to kill you. Yes,' she yells right in my face, spit flying. 'Smother you. Throw you in a river. Drop you from a cliff. Throttle you, you bastard!'

'My. My,' I say with exaggerated surprise. 'Charlie. April. What do you think of that?'

'Doesn't surprise me.' Charlie shakes his head.

'Well, it does me,' April says, more serious than I've seen her for ages. 'She's just admitted to wanting to murder you.'

'Hmmm,' I say. 'I wonder if that's an offence: intent to murder? Historically, I mean.'

'Just what do you want?' Wayne grinds between his teeth. 'What are you and these two doing here?'

'Well, Wayne,' I say, 'it's like this ...'

And I go on to explain the whole bloody mess that was my life - the early part that I shared with them, and then Charlie filled them in on Aunty Kaye's side of it.

'As if we care,' Sandra sniffs as she refills her glass for the third time (not that I'm counting). 'Get to the bloody point and then piss off. Get out of our lives for good.'

'Gladly. When this is all finished, I want nothing further to do with any of you.'

'When what's finished?' Brenda's looking uncomfortable.

'The matter of my paternity.'

Then I explain what I want.

'You're fucking crazy!' Brenda and I both wince at Sandra's language. 'I'm not having anything to do with it. You can get DNA from the Pope, for all I care, but you won't get it from me.'

Wayne considers me over the rim of his glass - his fourth. 'So, if I give you my DNA, you'll leave us alone?'

I nod.

'You'll put that in writing?'

'I don't see why not.' Then I look at Brenda. 'I want yours too.'

'What the blazes for?'

'A sample of a known mother gives stronger results. If we can supply it, they remove your share of genetic inheritance in the DNA of us siblings and work solely with the DNA inherited from our father.'

'Who told you all that shit?'

'It's not shit Mu ... Brenda. It's how it works.'

'I still don't ...'

'Mum, just say yes,' Sandra sighs in defeat.

'What do you want to know who your bloody father was anyway? It's all in the past.' Brenda's scowling enough to break all the plates and glasses in sight. Who needs a soprano?

'Makes no difference,' she sniffs. 'That little slut of a sister of mine had a go at any and all of the boys at school. Right little town bike.'

'Steady on,' Charlie protests.

I ignore her insults of my mother. 'How do you know that your husband wasn't my dad?'

Brenda gets off her seat so quickly, it slaps back onto poor old Barry the Beagle who runs off yelping. 'How dare you! My husband ...'

'... was a terrific dad to me,' I interrupt. 'He always treated me like his daughter, whether we were connected by blood or not.'

Brenda's blood pressure's about to hit the top of the scale.

I step up to Wayne. 'Did you know he changed my nappies? Bathed me? Dressed me? Took me to school when he was in town? Signed my reports? Taught me how to tie my shoelaces? Showed me love?'

Wayne is looking very uncomfortable. Reaches for the wine bottle.

'Would a step or foster parent do all that? Your mother wouldn't. Wouldn't even bathe a little baby who, through no fault of her own, made a mess in her nappies that stung and ate at her skin for days until her dad came home because her aunt hated her?'

Wayne turns to Brenda, his mouth hanging open. She looks daggers at me. 'Really?' he asks. 'Really?'

'She wasn't mine.'

Sandra's sitting facing the fence looking at the weeds.

Wayne has a jaw grinding dust. Skeletons, more like it. He looks at me differently than he's ever done. 'How do we do this?'

'I get a kit. It has mouth swabs and tells you where to send them.'

'Sandra?' he asks her back. She shrugs.

'Mum?'

'No!'

Wayne puts his arm around her shoulder. 'Why don't we just get this over with?'

'No.'

He looks at me and nods, which I take to mean that he's going to talk her into it.

'Do you think she will?' April takes a sip of her wine, regarding me seriously.

I run my finger around the rim of my glass. 'Well, if anyone can persuade her, it'll be Wayne.'

'What if she won't?'

'Then I'll keep at her.'

'Piece of work like that won't be shifted easily,' Charlie observes.

'I can always threaten to put it in the local paper.'

'You wouldn't!' April's impressed, her tongue darting in and out betweeen her teeth.

I smile at her.

'Cool!'

'I'll drink to that,' says Charlie, making for the bar.

Sunday 26th March

It's 7:30 when Matt calls me. Thank goodness I have my mobile on silent. April wouldn't have been impressed. I take Matt into the bathroom and sit on the toilet trying not to sound like I'm peeing.

'How'd it go?'

'Like I thought it would. Brenda's not budging about the DNA sample, but I think I've got Wayne and Sandra convinced. I hope they'll be able to talk her around.' I wipe myself and lower the lid carefully. I'll flush it later.

'I can hear water,' he says.

'Oh, just washing the sleep out of my eyes,' I say as I wash my hands. How can I be embarrassed at having a pee when he knows every part of my body?

'When are you coming back? I miss you.'

'Same here. I'm going to see Little Malcolm tomorrow morning if I can get an appointment. I want to bring him up with the latest. I should be back by next weekend.'

I tell him I'm afraid to leave without getting the DNA samples in case Wayne changes his mind. Matt asks where I'm getting the DNA kits from and I tell him I have to jump on the internet to find out. There's a split second silence and then he says: 'I'll get them to you via courier, latest Tuesday.'

'What? How ...'

'Never mind.' Then he says some pretty romantic things that get my hormones tickling me.

We meet Charlie for breakfast where he and April eat an ENORMOUS plateful each, despite last night's dinner: 2 eggs, bacon, tomatoes, onions, sausages, chips, toast, washed down by a huge pot of tea! I feel sick thinking of it.

We go up to the asylum again and lie back on the grass tossing ideas around as we look over Beechworth.

Charlie's pretty impressed that Matt's going to send the kits. 'Is he serious about you, this Matt?'

April snorts. 'Not likely.' Even though she says it under her breath, there's nothing wrong with Charlie's hearing.

'Why not?'

'Ahh, early days yet, Charlie. Early days.'

'Where're we gonna have lunch?' April's good at deflecting the conversation.

April's sitting in front of her laptop in our hotel room. Charlie and I are sitting either side of her. She consults our notes.

'So ... we're looking in Port Macquarie for Dr Ian Temple and Helen Temple and Eric Temple. Right?'

None of that results in anything.

'She'd be around 79 or 80,' says Charlie. 'He was quite a bit older, so they might be in a retirement village or a nursing home.'

Quick as a flash, April's searching for retirement villages. 'Heaps of them!'

We note down the phone numbers and each of us begins calling the villages. We don't have much hope as we begin crossing them off. I'm down to the second last number.

'Shoreline Retirement Village,' answers a bright voice.

I go through my spiel yet again. '... so do you have anyone by the surname of Temple - Doctor Ian and Mrs Helen?'

'Oh, Helen Temple. She's been here for many years ...' I punch the air. '... a pity Doctor Temple left us so suddenly last year.'

I feel weak and collapse back on my chair. My mother's alive. Almost within reach.

'Hello? Are you still there?'

'Yes. Yes. I'm sorry.' I put my mobile on loud speaker. 'So, she's living there now?' April and Charlie whirl around staring at the phone.

'Oh, most certainly. She's in unit 11 with a beautiful view of the river.'

I shut my mouth which has been hanging open for more than a decent time.

'You're family or friend?'

I splutter something unintelligible.

'Would you like me to give her a message?'

'Ah, no thanks. I'd like to surprise her.'

'Oh, how exciting.' The voice lowers to a conspiratorial level. 'She's been a bit poorly since her ...'

'She's ill?'

'Oh, no.' She sighs. 'Fit as a fiddle. But she's down. You know how it is?'

'Yes, I do. But Eric ...?'

'Visits when he can. It's a bit of a hike for him and the family.'

'Family?' I say weakly.

'Well, not all of them live around here, do they? I believe his second daughter's in the UK now, isn't she?' This woman is a fount of information.

'Yes, of course,' I manage to squeak out. 'I'd forgotten.'

Liar, April mouths, stifling a hoot.

Charlie's mouth has dropped open (it's catchy). April leans over and pushes his chin up which closes his mouth with a snap, his teeth causing an earthquake in his head. He leans to the left and clutches his neck, poor thing.

'Are you sure you don't want me to let her know you called?'

'No, thanks. Her heart's okay?'

'Yes, as far as I know.'

'Then I'll surprise her with a visit soon. It'll knock her socks off.'

Monday 27th March

I'm sitting in front of Little Malcolm's desk with April and Charlie flanking me. A convincing line-up, I think. I tell him what I'm proposing with the DNA samples and our plans to visit my real mother.

'I must say, June, I'm impressed.' Little Malcolm sits back in his father's huge winged leather chair. (He obviously has problems relinquishing his father's presence in the office.) He turns his upper lip, nose and left shoulder in sync with a complimentary grimace. 'Who would have thought?'

'Thought what?' I ask testily.

His chair thuds back into position. 'Oh,' he says, employing his diplomatic attitude, 'just how you've ...'

'Changed?' I challenge. 'Different from the loser at school? Dressed suitably? Able to think?'

'Easy on, June.' Charlie admonishes. 'He means well.'

'Sorry,' I scowl, appropriately chastised. 'Beechworth doesn't hold many happy memories.'

'I don't suppose so,' Little Malcolm says sympathetically, actually looking at me. 'You got a raw deal.'

'Well, we're hoping to turn the tables,' April offers. 'Give 'em a taste of their own shit.'

I laugh at her straightforward view of the world.

Actually, Little Malcolm and Charlie are laughing along with us. It's such a nice feeling.

'Hello Wayne,' I say as he picks up on the fourth ring.

He sighs. 'I was expecting you'd call.'

'Any progress with your mother?'

'Not yet.'

'I hope ...' Then I'm interrupted with a notification that Matt's sent a message. 'Sorry, I'll have to call you back.'

DNA kit on the way. Arriving tomorrow. Please confirm arrival.

No nonsense Matt. Totally different from how he is tucked away in a hotel room.

I call Wayne back and arrange for us to meet the three of them at Brenda's place tomorrow at four o'clock. 'Talk with her, will you?'

He hangs up without replying.

My mobile rings. It's Rob!

'Hey June! Any dancing up there?'

'Not likely,' I smile into the phone.

'Unfriendly natives?'

'You could say that.'

'Progress?'

'Some. Trying to get the family to agree to give DNA samples.'

'You need some strong arm support?'

I laugh. 'I'll let you know if I need any help.'

'Well, come back soon. I could do with a bit more after-tango torso tangling between the sheets.'

'Did you rehearse that?'

'No, but it was pretty good, huh?'

April's eyebrows are requiring an answer. 'Rob,' I say.

'Who's Rob?'

'A friend.'

'Another one?

April chortles.

'And the joke is?' ' Charlie wants to know the ins and outs of a duck's bum.

Tuesday 28th March

We look at the instructions again, making sure there are 4 colour-coded swabs each along with the consent forms.

'We already did this,' April complains.

'I just want to make sure. I think we've only got one go at this.'

Charlie touches me on the shoulder. 'That's all right, girlie. You take all the time you need.'

'Okay,' I say, putting it all back in the envelope after another glance. 'Let's get this over and done with.'

'You need to rub it inside your mouth and under your tongue for about a minute,' I tell Sandra. 'Now let it dry in these glasses the hotel loaned me.'

Charlie's doing the same with Wayne. 'You haven't had anything to eat or drink for a half hour or so?'

Wayne shakes his head as he swabs around his mouth.

April's holding out the first swab to Brenda who's got her arms crossed over her chest and her mouth firmly shut.

'Come on,' April whines loudly. 'We're not asking for blood, are we?'

'Same thing,' Brenda grinds out between her teeth.

April rolls her eyes around in her head, which wasn't missed by the others who are done, consent forms signed.

I turn to her calmly and say: '*The News Weekly* has, conservatively, around forty to fifty thousand readers, distributed widely from Albury all over the place, including Beechworth. I've got an article written ready to email to the editor. They wouldn't have had a story like this for a while: baby dropped on doorstep; kindly Beechworth couple take in the baby as their own; turns out the baby is the bastard child of the wife's sister; wife's sister has buggered off to God knows where; the baby's brought up in Beechworth until she leaves the region; and who the hell is the father???'

Brenda's gone white like your toothpaste (unless you use striped). 'You wouldn't dare!'

I meet her eyeball to eyeball. 'Try me.'

She glares at me with such hatred in her eyes that it takes all my willpower to resist looking away.

'Your neighbours'll love it and it'll be a juicy bit of gossip at the footy club.' I pause a few beats. 'Won't it?'

'You fucking bitch!'

'Brenda,' I smile at her, 'nothing you can say or do can ever hurt me again.'

Wednesday 29th March

We leave Charlie's ute next morning at Albury Airport's long term parking. I'm worried about my mother's portrait so we stow it in a locker inside the airport before checking in our luggage. He's still a bit miffed that I wouldn't hear of him driving us all the way up to Port Macquarie and back within a few days. Miffed again about my footing the bill for the flights.

'Charlie, I've never had anything to spend my salary on, except,' I smile at April, 'when April's racking up bills for a new wardrobe on my behalf.'

'Oh?' He swivels towards me, then clutches his neck, wincing in pain.

April shakes her finger at him. 'You have to do something about that neck of yours, Charlie.'

'One day,' he says unconvincingly.

'I might have to drag you to a doctor myself,' she scolds.

'Where?' he laughs.

'Oh ...' She looks around her. 'Here in Albury. Up in Port Macquarie. Beechworth. Mildura. I'm going to stick with you until you do.'

'That makes two of us.'

'Don't you start on me,' he says, holding up his hands in surrender. 'Besides, don't change the subject.'

Oh, oh. Here it comes ...

'The new wardrobe. What's that about?'

'Well, it's like this,' April says in a mock whisper. 'June's got all these boyfriends and she has to come up with different outfits all the time.'

I look at her in horror.

'Trouble is, she's got no dress sense, so someone's gotta get her wardrobe in order. Don't you reckon, Charlie?'

He looks at me with his right eyebrow doing the disappearing trick under his hair again. Bugger April. I'm annoyed with her. Why would she tell him that? I guess my feelings are showing.

But Charlie turns it all around, laughing. 'Well, so she should have plenty of clothes! Gotta make a good impression. June's lucky to have you as an advisor, like. And what about your boyfriends, April?'

As soon as we check into our hotel at Port Macquarie, I round on April. 'What'd you tell Charlie about my wardrobe for and Matt & Rob?'

'Well, you brought it up.'

'Did I?' I'm surprised as I backtrack on the conversation. 'So I did!'

'So?'

'Sorry.' I think hard. 'You know, I feel so comfortable around him that I feel I can tell him just about anything. Well, not quite *everything*,' I concede.

'I feel the same. He's a bit like a big brother tagging along.'

'Exactly! I can understand why Aunty Kaye loved him. It's so sad she died that young, not only for me, but more for him. They had such a close relationship.'

There was a knock on the door.

'Come in!' we call out in unison.

'You girls want a cuppa before we go or a drink?'

'Maybe a quick cuppa,' I say. 'We don't want to go there smelling like a winery.'

Charlie sits on one of the beds. 'You thought any more about how you want to do it?'

I sit beside him while April makes the cuppa. 'I'm still not sure. If we all front up, she'll get a shock when she sees you and wonder who we are and maybe feel threatened. If I turn up alone and say, hi Mum, it's me, she'll probably have a fit. If April goes in as our representative and breaks the news to her, she might tell us to go to hell. If you go alone, she might refuse to meet me.'

We drink our cuppa in silence. April looks up from hers. 'I reckon the last option because, Charlie, you're the familiar face. You represent the past, Aunty Kaye, the birth, June's early childhood. Probably mostly good memories because she got away from that cow, Brenda, and her bloody mother.'

'Yes, but what about the fact that she didn't stay in touch with Charlie after Aunty Kaye died?'

'A lot of water under the bridge since then.' April shrugs. 'Shit happens.'

The taxi takes us the five kilometres or so to the ferry and then over the Hastings River to Shoreline Drive. It's such a beautiful afternoon that we wonder if we could walk it back. Depends what happens.

I'm as edgy as a trapeze artist walking a tightrope. What if this? What if that? April and I take a walk around the grounds of the village. It's very nicely laid out with the units in an arc surrounding a community building, all pointing towards the river. What a terrific location with a wooded area behind and, beyond that, a short walk eastwards, is the ocean. No wonder Helen didn't want to leave here.

Charlie checks into the office and then we watch him make his way to Unit 11. We clutch each other's hands as we see him at the front door, a pause, and then we see the figure of a woman outlined in the doorframe. She opens the door and they disappear inside.

'I can't stand this,' I gasp as we walk out of the village. I feel sick. What if she doesn't want to see me? What if there's a horrible scene? What if I'm back on my own again. No one to love me - as usual. Worse off than I was before. At least I had Brenda and Wayne and Sandra to hate me. But then I hear April struggling to keep up with me and I turn and I burst into tears.

'Juneeeee! Not again!'

And then I think that even if Helen, my mother, wants nothing to do with me, at least - and probably the best - I have April and Charlie. I also have Matt and Rob, don't I? Don't I? And isn't that more than I've had all my miserable life? So shut up, June, and deal with it.

April offers me her limitless supply of tissues and hugs me. 'Jesus, June, if you keep this up, the Hastings River will rise.'

And I laugh. She always makes me feel better. I hug her back.

'Okay, chill,' she snorts. 'I'll have to tell Merv about you if you do that again.'

And we laugh together.

We walk along North Shore Drive until we reach a T-intersection and can see the ocean.

'Why's it taking so long?' I'm close to tears. Again.

'She's stabbed Charlie and burying him in her backyard.'

'Oh stop it!' But I can't help laughing a little.

'The two of them are having it off on the kitchen table.'

'Heavens, April, that's disgusting!'

My mobile rings. It's Charlie.

'You girls want to come and meet Helen?'

She's standing there in the doorway watching us walk - well, almost run - to her unit. I feel conscious of my rolls of fat, my thick ankles, my messy hair. Hold your stomach in, I scold myself. Stand up straight. And for heaven's sake, don't cry! But she's got tears pouring down her face and I start up again.

'For crying out loud, June. I'm running out of tissues,' April complains.

'Come in. Come in,' Helen says breathlessly.

We enter a charming light-filled lounge area that opens out to an expansive view of the river.

'Wow!' April's impressed. 'How'd you get this place?'

Helen smiles. April's broken the ice without even trying. 'My husband pulled a few arms and legs.'

Charlie takes my hand. 'This is June.'

'I can tell,' Helen says. Her tears have begun again, so I follow suit.

I look at a face not dissimilar to mine, though she's aged better, even though she's 17 years older than me. I study her face, as she's doing mine. Our eyebrows are the same, and our eyes are the same shape and almost the same colour. Our chins and double chins have the same roundness, though her face isn't as fat as mine. Her cupid's bow is a bit more pointed than mine and my bottom lip more full. She wears her hair cut short and messy with highlights in it, whereas mine's longer and tinted. She's not wearing glasses where I do all the time.

'I had my cataracts done,' she laughs. 'That's why I don't wear glasses most of the time.'

'You read my mind!'

'You both cry a lot,' April observes.

Helen turns towards her. 'Charlie told me about you.' She takes April's hands in hers and studies her face too. 'You're a good friend to June. She's lucky.'

'Oh, don't go all gooey on me,' April swallows.

'Please,' Helen indicates the sofa and chairs. 'Sit. Sit.'

There's a tray on a coffee table already holding a large teapot, a plate of biscuits, and the rest of it. She was ready for us. That seems encouraging to me. We sit facing each other. I'm holding my breath.

'June,' she breathes, 'I don't know where to begin.'

April takes over the tea making, pours, takes hers, Charlie takes his, and they step outside.

And then my mother tells me about her rotten childhood with Gran and Brenda. She tells me about her school years. About the dances, the boys, the drinking. But I'm hungry to know more about Aunty Kaye.

'I had my happiest times with her,' my mother says. 'She had a certain grace about her, you know?' I nod. 'And she treated me like I was *her* daughter, like she enjoyed having me there, like there was room in her big big heart for me - and plenty more!'

I smile as I remember that day when we visited her. 'She talked with me. She listened. No one else, except Dad, ever did that.' I feel a stab in my heart. 'I fell in love with her. I wanted to be like her and live with her and put my shitty childhood away.'

'Me too.'

We look at each other with understanding. We've been through similar childhoods, it seems.

'And then you fell pregnant.' I look at her expectantly.

She looks down at her hands and nods. She takes a deep breath before looking up at me. 'Yes.'

I wait. She pauses.

'You want to know who your father is.'

I look at her in mute appeal.

'It's not what you think.'

'I don't know what to think.'

'I'm not sure who he is.'

My mouth drops open in shock.

'That makes me sound cheap. A slut ...'

'No ...'

'It's all right,' she stops me, putting her hand over mine. 'I'd think that if I were you.'

And then she tells me of a visit to Aunty Kaye's when she turned sixteen. There was no party for her in Beechworth so Aunty Kaye invited her to Mildura to celebrate and '... bugger 'em all, especially that bitch, Brenda ...' Aunty Kaye had said. Helen recounts the journey to Mildura in Dad's station wagon. They sang most of the way and laughed 'till they cried. They stuffed their faces with apples and slices of bread slathered thickly with butter and Vegemite, and washed it all down with cordial. By the time they got there they just about needed a bath because they were sticky from everything they'd had to eat and drink.

They arrived to the gum tree festooned with Chinese lanterns, streamers, balloons and a big banner that said *Happy Birthday 16*. The circular table was covered with party plates and serviettes and coloured glasses and flowers and presents and new cushions on the bench seats. It looked like a fairy land and music was blaring from speakers up in the branches of the gum tree. Helen had never seen anything so beautiful. Charlie and Aunty Kaye welcomed them with jumpers and rugs and scarves, saying that the bloody winter wasn't going to spoil their fun. Even the dogs were decorated with festive collars and stars painted on their fur and they, too, wore party hats, though they didn't last long on their heads.

Some neighbours arrived with kids around the same age as Helen. They danced under the stars, whirling around and around as they drank a potent punch that Aunty Kaye had made. Despite the fact that Helen had been drinking a bit after school with the local Beechworth kids, she didn't have a good head for it, so the punch kicked her in the head and she passed out for a while. She woke up on the couch, raced into the bathroom and threw up, then joined the party again, as sixteen-year-olds can do. Aunty Kaye was also under the weather. Charlie carried her to her bed and took over as host. Helen remembers Charlie and Dad dancing with her, laughing with her, drinking with her, until the rest of the guests left. They made a cursory effort at cleaning up the mess as they giggled in the starlight, falling over each other, dancing around the house as the dogs put down their heads in sleep.

Helen frowns as she tries to remember. 'I've gone over this a thousand times,' she sighs, 'but it's all jumbled up - with alcohol I suppose.'

I wait for her to continue, afraid that she'll stop.

'I sort of remember looking into your dad's eyes as his face lowers onto mine.' She looks at me anxiously.

'Go on,' I urge.

'It's just that ... oh, I don't know, I feel so cheap. The sister-in-law being kissed by her brother-in-law. You know ... well, I don't suppose you do ... but it was so unexpected. I never thought of Kevin that way. He was Brenda's. And then he was kissing me and I was kissing him back. And then I woke up propped up against the back of the house and Charlie was leaning over me with a concerned look on his face. And then he was kissing me and I was kissing him back. And then I woke up and Kevin was kissing my breasts and I was arching up to him and then it was Charlie's face that was looking up at me from my chest and I was arching up to him, wanting him to go further. And then Kevin was going further. And then it was Charlie and then it was Kevin.'

She returns her gaze to me from her lap. 'I woke up at dawn under the gum tree with my pants off and semen oozing out of my vagina. I've had sex, I thought to my 16 year-old self, and I felt so grown up and surprised I wasn't sore. I wanted more but I didn't know who'd done it, if it was a dream even.

And then I was overwhelmed with grief and shame. What if it was your dad? I'd have had sex with my sister's husband who'd protected me. What if it was Charlie? I'd have had sex with the boyfriend of the most wonderful woman on this earth who'd looked after me and loved me. I couldn't bear to think of either.'

She sighs and looks down at her hands that are shaking. I want to take them in mine but am afraid of disturbing her recollections. Her face is flushed as tears slowly make their way down to the corners of her mouth and splash off her chin.

'I got up to see if Kaye was awake but all was quiet in the house. The dogs looked up at me hopefully for some breakfast so we padded softly into the kitchen and I fed them. Kevin was snoring on the couch and Charlie was sound asleep across Kaye's legs on her bed. I didn't know what to do. I had a shower and got dressed. Had something to eat. Looked at myself in the mirror to see if I looked more grownup.'

She stops, gathering her memories up like pegs in an apron, and then continues.

'The three of them woke up with giant hangovers and one-by-one they joined me outside around the gum tree. I'd squeezed some oranges, made a huge pot of tea, toast with Vegemite. None of them said much, except to acknowledge my presence. It was all rather civilized, you could say. And that's how it remained. No one said anything about it. Kevin and Charlie looked a bit sheepish but perplexed as well, like as if they thought they'd had a dream. Because I didn't know what to say, I didn't broach the subject. Kaye slung her arm around my shoulders and asked me how it felt to be sixteen, to which I burst into tears and she laughed her head off and the dogs barked and ran around and around the gum tree. I ended up laughing too and thought it would all go away and I wouldn't have to deal with it. Until my periods stopped.'

She gets up and looks out the window at Charlie and April sitting on the grass nattering. 'He's such a good man. Hasn't changed a bit,' she says onto the glass that I see fogging up. Her fingers touch his image, leaving streaks on the window.

She comes over to sit next to me. Touches my face, as no one ever has, her eyes brimming with tears. 'You know, Charlie could be your dad, or the man who you always thought was your dad could be your dad after all.'

'You never asked either of them?'

'How could I?'

'I suppose not,' I say, putting myself in her younger skin. 'Either way, I wouldn't mind.' I look out at his strong back and shoulders that belie his age. 'Actually, I'd love him to be my dad.'

Helen (Mum) drives us back to our hotel (there goes the exercise) and we change for a meal in a seafood restaurant close by. I'm not sure when she's going to have THAT conversation with Charlie to see what their collective memories can come up with but she's a smart cookie and arranges to have a drink with him before dinner. April and I go for a walk around town and I fill her in.

'Cool!'

'It is, isn't it?'

'So did you ask her to do a DNA test?'

'What for?'

'You may as well, seeing the cow in Beechworth has done it. It'll prove Helen's your mum.'

'Well ...'

She rounds on me and I walk into her. 'Of course!'

'What?'

'Charlie! He has to do the DNA test!'

I look at my friend in wonderment. 'You really are the ant's pants.'

'Don't go fuckin' gooey on me or I'll tell Merv.'

'The fish?'

Helen and Charlie are already seated opposite each other at a table overlooking the water. Their backs are stiff and they're not talking as they gaze at the view.

'Oh, oh.' April pulls up before we get close. 'Doesn't look good, does it?'

We hesitate for some moments before a waiter decides his main aim in life is to accompany us to the table. April and I slide onto our chairs, which melts the ice in the wall between them, and they both start talking at the same time.

'The menu's ...' Helen gasps.

'Did you find the ...' Charlie tries.

'Geez, ace view, eh?' April says over them. 'You come here often, Helen?'

I watch their bodies sink into their seats and expect them to melt into blobs and spill on the floor but they hold whatever's bothering them inside their skin and manage to grin maniacally and fake a semblance of having a great time.

'For special occasions,' Helen answers, 'and to simply enjoy the food.' She turns to me. 'Do you like oysters, June?'

'I like them very much,' I say, trying to stifle a giggle thinking of Matt. 'As a matter of fact, I've only recently acquired a taste for them. They surprised me.'

'They look like something out of a sewer.' Charlie screws his face up in disgust. 'Give me a steak anytime.'

'I'm with you, Charlie,' April agrees, clinking her glass against his.

And then the table descends into silence which is difficult to break. It's a relief when our waiter brings the food and we busy ourselves with the business of getting it into our mouths. Fish and shellfish don't take all that long to chew, but it seems ages before anyone's mouth is empty enough to speak. Reluctantly.

Helen looks at me. 'How did you enjoy your walk around town?'

'Lovely place,' I say, taking a sip of wine. 'I can see why you'd want to live here.'

She smiles. Her mouth is lying because her eyes have been infected by a sadness that I didn't see earlier today.

The rest of the dinner goes in awkward fits and starts. It's a relief to say goodnight to Helen and walk back to our hotel. Charlie walks slowly with his hands in his pockets, jiggling some coins in there which gets on my nerves.

'So, what's up?' April doesn't muck around.

'Eh?' Charlie's head jerks up from studying the footpath intently.

'What's with the cardboard cut-outs in there?'

'What do you mean?'

'You and Helen. You were as stiff as boards.' She stands in front of him so he has to stop walking.

Charlie looks at me for help.

I shrug. 'You weren't exactly thrilled to be in each other's company.'

'Ah, just let it go, girls.'

I put my arms around him. 'What happened, Charlie?'

He looks down at me and I see that his eyes are misty and his mouth is twisting. God, he really is upset.

'Let's leave it until tomorrow, eh?' I say softly.

He looks at me gratefully and nods. We walk back to the hotel in silence but it's not quite as thick as before. We kiss him goodnight as he unlocks his door.

'What the fuck is that about?' April demands.

I shake my head in confusion. 'Helen said she was going to talk with him about the night I was conceived.'

'So?'

'Exactly. I wouldn't have dreamed it would upset him.'

'He's pretty open-minded about most things.'

I look at the clock. It's 10:15. 'Do you think it's too late to ring Helen?'

'Nah. She'll still be scraping her makeup off.'

I look at my mobile doubtfully. I guess the old rule of not ringing anyone after 9:00 pm is still ingrained in me.

It rings until I think it's going to message bank when she answers.

She tells me about the two of them sitting over their drinks, swapping stories enthusiastically about the intervening years, laughing, grieving, their impressions of April and me and the whole mystery about my paternity. Charlie had pressed her to own up about Kevin. She hedged a bit. Opened and closed her mouth like a fish until he told her to spit it out. And she did. He was shocked. The whole idea was so distasteful to him, the thought that he would be unfaithful to his beloved Kaye, that he stood suddenly and knocked his chair over as a woman, passing the table, fell and broke a tooth and split her lip.

'June, it was a total bloody disaster. There was pandemonium in the bar. The poor woman was distraught about her tooth and bleeding mouth. Charlie was horrified and insisted upon accompanying her in a taxi to the hospital to make sure she was all right. He was apologising, she was crying, people were gawking, Charlie was supporting her and almost carried her outside without so much as a bye your leave to me. We both arrived at the restaurant not long before you two showed up and I only had time to ask him how the woman was.'

'Oh, hell. That's awful,' I gasp.

'What? What?' April's busting to know and I only now remember to put the phone on speaker so she's missed it all so far.

I mouth that I'll tell her later.

'So, where do we go from here?'

'I don't know, love,' Helen sighs. 'I feel even more cheap after Charlie's reaction. The way he looked at me ... like I'd betrayed Kaye ...'

'But you were young, drunk, and passing out. Surely ...'

'That's what I tell myself, over and over, but when I saw his disgust I realise I've been kidding myself. I was a cheap little ...'

'Hey, Helen, that could've happened to anyone,' April chimes in. 'Geez, you should see your daughter drunk!'

And so on. Helen says she doesn't think it a good idea for her to see Charlie again. Says she thinks he wouldn't want to anyway. And what about tomorrow's lunch with Eric and his family that Helen's organised? Would Charlie go now? Oh, what a mess! We decide to sleep on it.

Thursday 30th March

Here we are in the dining room waiting for Charlie to show up. He's normally first. April's already into her eggs, bacon, sausages, tomatoes, mushrooms, hash browns, toast, etc. Honestly, where that girl puts it is beyond me. She must have hollow legs because it doesn't show in her stomach.

'Sorry girls,' he apologises when he arrives. 'I'll just get some brekky.' He queues up for his usual, piles it on his plate, brings it over and plonks it on the table. He looks at it as if it's something out of the rubbish bin and pushes it around the plate with his fork. I notice he's cut himself shaving; he's got torn bits of toilet paper drying on four spots around his face. He looks like he hasn't slept a wink.

'Not hungry, tiger,' April observes.

He sits back in his chair and rubs his belly. 'Nah, not much.'

'Well,' she says, leaning over the table, 'if you don't want that sausage I'll have it,' and she stabs it with her fork and it's on her plate in a flash.

'Help yourself,' he mumbles pushing the plate towards her.

'Charlie,' I say, 'are you going to tell us why you're so different and what happened yesterday?'

'Look, girlie, it's just that Helen and I had a disagreement, like. It's all right. You don't need to worry.' (To which April rolls her eyes.) 'It's probably best kept between her and me. A bit delicate, the subject.'

'What, you think we're too young for *the subject*, that you might corrupt us little city gals?'

'April,' I stab a warning with my laser eyes, 'leave it.'

Despite Charlie's absence, April and I have a lovely time at Mum's place with my new brother and his family - well, most of it. There's Eric and his wife Susan (both 55). They have 3 children:

Jenny (32) and husband John (he couldn't make it as he was sorting out a drainage problem on their farm) and they have a son, Jet, (8) who they call Blackie. And he's blonde.

Next in line is Tricia (30), the daughter who lives in the UK doing some high-pressure executive job in animal welfare. We saw her on Skype with her two dogs. She's living with a guy she's known forever but no kids, just the dogs.

Last is Roger, (24) who's studying oceanography at the University of New South Wales (smart kid). He's rushed down here to meet us.

He and April have their heads together over Mum's record and CD collection. I can hear the words 'crap' and 'shit' and the occasional whispered 'f' word which I'm sure not only I can pick up. I frown at April's back. I don't know who's worse, Roger or April.

Mum's put on an impressive lunch of cold meats and salads and Jenny's brought bread and cheeses. Thank goodness we picked up a couple of bottles of wine on the way. Even so, there's a bottle of champagne sitting in a cooler in the centre of the table. Eric looks at his mother who gives him the nod and he pours the champagne. The buzz of conversation mutes as we raise our glasses to this amazing celebration.

'To my sister,' Eric smiles as he touches my glass with his. 'May your absence from my life be a thing of the past and all our tomorrows be enriched by our new sibling relationship.'

I'm speechless. April looks at me in horror as tears, happy tears, run down my face. I notice Mum doing the same. In the temporary hush as Eric's words sink in, I look into his eyes trying to fathom the generosity of his soul. His reaction could have been one of rejection. I'd have understood that. But, instead, this lovely lovely man is claiming me as his sister, no matter how I may have upset his family life.

Suddenly, there's a blast of music from the CD player and Cliff Richard sings:

Congratulations and celebrations...

April and Roger have a look of triumph on their faces, giggling their heads off.

When I tell everyone that you're in love with me...

And then those of us who remember the song join in:

Congratulations and jubilations

I want the world to know I'm happy as can be.

April and I stand outside Charlie's room not getting any reply to our knocking.

'Maybe he's left Port Macquarie already?'

'Don't be silly,' I say. 'Charlie wouldn't leave without us or at least without saying goodbye.'

'You think he's on the floor unconscious, had a stroke, heart attack, his bloody neck broke ...?'

'Stop it!' I'm scared. 'Let's go down to the bar.'

And that's where he is, sitting with an untouched beer in front of him, staring out of the window. I lean over to give him a kiss on the cheek.

'Ah, girlie,' he sighs. 'Good to see the two of you.'

April gives him a gentle cuff on the shoulder with a fist. 'You too, big boy.'

He turns his chair to face us as we sit at his table. 'A drink?'

'Is the Pope a Catholic?' April says as she gets up to go to the bar.

'You had a good time?' His voice and face are flat.

I take his hand. It feels so big around mine. 'We did, Charlie, though we missed you.' He shrugs. 'Really.' I squeeze his thumb. 'You've been such an important and huge part of my life this past week and to go anywhere without you seems strange. My heart ached,' I say touching my chest where I think I have a heart. I look at his misty eyes full of sadness. 'I love you, you know.'

Friday 31st March

We've flown back to Albury, a quieter group of three than when we arrived there only days ago. Charlie's ute starts up first time. He's reluctant to leave us and the feeling's mutual. We explore Albury for a bit then grab some sandwiches and have a late lunch parked right beside the Murray watching the boats go by.

He sees us off at Albury Station a bit after 5:00 pm. April and I have decided to go back to Melbourne by train. See a bit of the country even though it'll be dark in a few hours. We'll get home late - after 10:00 but who cares? It's a pity there are no trains on Saturdays, otherwise we could have spent another day with Charlie.

I cry my eyes out when we say goodbye to him. April's going crook at me but her nose is dripping and she's ducking her head. Charlie has a silent tear or two tracing their way down his face.

'Don't cry, girlie,' he rumbles from his chest as he holds me and pats my head. 'You'll have to come up and visit me again real soon.' He grabs hold of April. 'You too.'

'Just try and keep me away,' she sniffs. 'I'll be hanging out for your snags.'

That makes the three of us laugh and we blow our noses in unison, which makes us laugh harder until I start crying again.

'Jesus, June,' she complains. 'I've got no bloody tissues left. You'll have to use your sleeve.'

To which Charlie and I groan. I get the hiccups.

We have to get on the train. April opens our window and we lean out to take Charlie's hand. He looks smaller from here and just a bit older.

'Call me when you get home,' he says, 'so I know you're home safe.'

'It'll be too late,' I say as our train begins to move.

'Doesn't matter. Just call me.'

It feels strange walking back into my flat after what seems like months instead of ten days. Merv and Melba give me a joyous welcome. Pat, next door, has been in and fed them; they seem in good shape. I make up a bed for April on the couch and she's asleep before I have time to unpack my toothbrush.

I call Charlie. He picks up on the second ring.

'That you, girlie?'

It's so good to hear his voice.

'Who else rings you at this time?' I laugh. 'Have you got a woman friend you haven't told us about?'

'Beating them off with a stick,' he chuckles. 'You two okay?'

'April's snoring on my couch along with Merv and Melba.'

'Who're they?'

I call Helen (Mum) who also insisted on a call when we got back. She, too, picks up on the second ring sounding very alert.

'June!' Her warmth travels through the line. 'You're home finally, then?'

'Yes, Mum.' It seems so strange to be calling her Mum but she wants me to. I'm okay with that. 'Sorry to keep you up.'

'No. No. Don't be sorry. I couldn't have slept a wink until I knew you'd arrived safely.'

'Thanks for caring,' I gulp, tears at the ready.

'I always did.'

I'm sitting up in bed thinking about those two phone calls. Calls that these people had requested I make because they care about me. For the first time in my life. I can't get over it. I flop back and look up at the ceiling which has water stains all over it and mould in the corners. But that's not what I'm seeing. I'm seeing the face of my real mother and her family - my family - and the man who might be my real father.

Monday 3ʳᵈ April

April stayed on for the rest of the weekend so my routine is out of sorts as we get ready to catch my normal train.

'Come on,' I call through the bathroom door, 'We'll be late.'

'Juneee,' she groans between her toothbrush and teeth, 'who cares?'

'I do,' I say. 'I've been late three times in all the years I've worked at Danks and I don't want this to be the fourth.'

'Only three? What happened?'

'The first time there was an accident on the railway line. A car had got stuck on the tracks trying to dodge the boom gates and the train couldn't stop in time.'

April sticks her head around the door. 'Shit! Did the car driver die?'

'No - he was lucky. The train running times were all over the place, though.'

'And the second time?'

'Oh, that,' I laugh. 'It's a bit embarrassing, really.'

'What? What?'

'I had food poisoning and couldn't get off the toilet.'

'So you took the day off?'

'I couldn't. It was end of the month and Merv would have been ropable if I hadn't shown, not that I was much use that day,' I say remembering the struggle to hold my insides together and not disgrace myself.

'He would've understood, though.'

'I didn't tell him.'

'Geez, June, you're a bloody hero.' She pretends to bow. 'Now, for the third time you were late.'

I shake my head. 'It doesn't matter.'

April's pulling a jumper over her head which pops out of the neckline, just like a jack in the box. 'Yes, it does.'

I'm busy with the contents of my handbag. 'Let it go, April.'

She pulls my hand out of the bag. 'Why? What's wrong?'

'It's nothing.'

'No, it's not.'

'Look,' I say sharply. 'We're going to be late - or at least you are. I'm going right now. There's just ten minutes to get to the station.'

We're catching our breath after running up to the platform as the train pulls in. My heart's threatening to jump into my throat. I'm perspiring everywhere. I dab at my forehead with a tissue while my hair's sticking to the back of my neck. April's in better shape than me, though I'm satisfied to see she's perspiring too.

I'm cross with myself because I mentioned the three times I've been late for work, the third time particularly. I don't want to think about it as we run for the station but those memories spiral through my head like cyclonic winds gathering up moments and spitting them out to torment me again.

Philip, who moved in next door to my flat two years ago. How we'd smile at each other as we put our rubbish bins out. How we'd comment on the weather. How his blonde hair flopped over his left eye. How I'd catch a whiff of his aftershave. How he'd stand rocking back and forth with his hands in his back pockets, cupping his buttocks. How he'd invite me into his flat for a cuppa. How I'd blush. How I couldn't find things to say. How his knee would touch mine as we sat on his sofa together. How his hand ran up my leg. How he pushed my legs apart, explored my private parts, not looking at me but at the TV, talking all the time. His fingers exciting me. The two of us looking at the TV, not acknowledging what was happening. The doorbell ringing. The tall, blonde, young girl arriving. Kissing him, pushing herself against him. Saying something to him. Both laughing looking at me. Me stumbling out and into my flat. Feeling cheap. Looking in the mirror. Hating what I see. Crying. Crying. Crying. Trying to read a Mills & Boon to forget. But romance is not mine. Taking a sleeping pill. Waking at nine o'clock. Late for work.

And I'm cross because we have to get onto a different carriage, the one behind the driver. He gets out of his cabin to put a ramp out for a person on a scooter. As he retrieves the ramp he looks back along the train, back into the carriage, and our eyes lock. They are the darkest, blackest eyes I've ever seen, hooded by bushy eyebrows. He turns, disappears into his cabin and the doors close with a gulp.

'You see,' I hiss. 'We almost missed it.'

She shrugs then looks around the carriage.

'Is this Matt's week on the train?'

'No, but even if it was, he wouldn't be in this carriage.'

'Is he a stick-in-the-mud like you?'

'No,' I shake my head, 'but he knows where to find me.'

'Where do the twins get on?'

'Moorabbin.'

'Good,' she says as we pull out of the station. 'Let's change over to your normal carriage next stop.'

'Only if you promise to behave yourself.'

She rolls her eyes as she places her hand over her heart.

We change carriages in the nick of time and settle down amongst some familiar faces. Funny, but it feels like a year since I was last on the train. So much has happened since discovering my family history.

April nudges me and hisses, 'There they are!'

As they usually do, Rob gets in and comes over to us while his twin props himself up against the door at the end of the carriage.

'April, mate,' he says, 'what are you doing here?'

She grins at him. 'Checking you out, big boy.'

His eyebrows shoot up over a huge grin.

'Good morning, Rob,' I say in my most dignified manner.

'Sorry - gidday, June. How'd it all turn out up there?'

'Terrific,' I say as images of my new family flash across the screen of my mind.

'Complicated, though,' April adds.

And so we put our heads together catching up, April and me watching the twin out of the corners of our eyes, Rob seemingly oblivious. We make arrangements to go to the footy next Saturday, all three of us. As April would say: that's cool!

'About time you turned up,' Merv says trying to look grim. 'The place has gone to rack and ruin.'

'What, Merv, are you saying you missed me?'

'What - miss you?'

'I love you too, Merv.'

And so I'm catching up on everything Merv has left for me. Most of it, actually, as he's planning their next holiday - another attempt at the Amsterdam/Budapest cruise. Trish doesn't know and, of course, neither does Marj. I hope he gets away with it this time.

Friday 7th April

Did I mention Wednesday night? Dinner and the night with Matt? Utter bliss? Oh, heavens, each time with Matt drives me crazy when I look back on it. He's more romantic than any Mills & Boon story. And he's mine. Well ... when he's not with his wife. I've no illusions about that. Strangely enough, it's doesn't bother me. There's Rob in the meantime ...

Tonight is a return to suffering of the feet variety. Not to mention the knees, hips and back. My balance is all over the place and I step on my own feet numerous times, once catching the instep of my left foot with the heel of my right. Down I go straight on my bum. Fortunately I don't drag Rob with me. He holds out his hands to get me back up and I try to do it gracefully but somehow my right foot slides under me and I end up on my back with my skirt around my waist. Thank goodness no one else is there and Rob's seen more of me than is on display right now, so I shrug it off, turn over onto my knees and claw my way back to a vertical position.

'Okay,' he says, 'back right, left, right ...' That man has the patience of Job.

We're having a go at a waltz. I fancy it will be easy. Wrong. Dead wrong.

'Under my arm ... no, the other way. No, don't drift off to the wall. Back here June. Over here,' he calls as I bounce off the wall and end up supported by the bathroom doorframe. At least I've stopped.

He explains about going under his arm and back the other way. Simple. For him, yes. I feel the walls whirling around me, threatening to pull me over. I narrow my eyes and look at the floor next time. I actually manage to go under and back again.

'Now kick your left foot up. Not there!' he gasps as I neatly catch his groin with my foot. At least it's the left one. I can get something right. No - left.

It takes Rob a few minutes to get his breath back and not look like he needs an ambulance. He assures me he'll live. I'm not sure my feet will.

'How about we give it a miss tonight?'

'Not yet,' he grinds out between clenched teeth. 'You're going to waltz to-night if it kills me.'

One, two, three. One, two three ...

We're at my place in an advanced state of undress on the couch.

'What're they looking at?'

'They haven't seen me being ravaged before.'

'What - they've got brains?' Rob cackles. 'I thought they forgot everything after so many seconds.'

'No, these are very intelligent goldfish,' I boast.

'Well, if we keep at it all night, they'll have a new experience every time you go off your rocker.'

I pull his head down. 'Well, come on. What are you waiting for?'

Saturday 8th April

I meet April and Rob on Richmond platform before the match. They're in animated conversation waving their arms and hands around. They turn to give me a hug and kiss. I try to catch his eye. I even wink at him but he looks at me quizzically as if last night didn't happen. He looks far fresher than I feel. Actually, I'm having trouble walking straight and planting my feet flat on the ground. Utter exhaustion is weighing me down. Today I feel my age. I look at him and, for the umpteenth time, wonder why he wants to spend time with me. Maybe a mother complex? But you wouldn't want to have sex with your mother, would you? I know some people are sick and depraved but I don't think Rob is. April's far more suited to him but, then again, I don't know that I'm ready to give up the perks of a 'friendship' with him.

I'm a bit numb (all over) but somehow get through the afternoon yelling and jumping up and down in my seat along with the two of them. It's infectious, football. And there are all those gorgeous men on the field showing off their biceps and leg muscles. The noise is deafening, the excitement enthralling, the crowd hypnotic. I could do with a damned good sleep though. A couple of days would help. And no exercise.

Monday 10th April

I slept nearly all day yesterday, so I'm feeling much recovered as I walk to the station. The morning's overcast but not too cold. I'm expecting a busy time before Merv and Trish leave for Europe and then I'll be boss cocky for three weeks. The extra work never worried me before but now I'm wondering how I'll fit in the longer hours and carry on my social life as well.

I'm smiling to myself as I think of Matt's warmth and feel my heart pounding in expectation as I wait for the train door to align with my spot on the platform. I see him through the windows. His face is turned towards me and I swear he winks at me. God, he's so handsome.

He's managed to spread himself across two seats while the carriage isn't full. He moves his briefcase to the floor between his legs and I sit down beside him with just a nod. He pretends to be reading *The Age* on his tablet and I open up a Mills & Boon. We move closer surreptitiously; I can feel the heat of his left leg and arm against me which travels to my breasts and groin. It's almost pain, this exquisite lust, but I'm glad I have it. I'm struggling to breathe as my heart threatens to burst out of my chest. I feel a slight jiggling beside me and realise Matt's trying not to laugh.

I go over the same sentences again:

This was the moment she'd been waiting for all these weeks and months. She observed her hand shaking as she opened the door to find him standing there holding a single blood-red rose. She opened her mouth to speak but no words invaded the charged tension between them. He followed her inside,. His eyes caressed her outline, observing how she moved, the hang of her blue-black hair, and his nostrils flared with the hint of the perfume she ...

Oh, how I wish we didn't have to hide our relationship but it's too risky. Some of his staff travel on this line.

... his lips brushed hers so lightly that every nerve ending screamed for the release she desperately wanted, needed ...

I can feel myself flushing. It reminds me of Matt, how he first kissed me, how he still kisses me.

... his hot breath on her neck ...

My mobile tells me there's an SMS:

> I'm reading it out of the corner of my eye. No wonder you're panting like a dog in heat :) How about we meet for a long lunch and I take over where he leaves off?

I smother a laugh in my hand. A few people look up from their screens. He coughs when he reads my reply:

Bring it on, Romeo!

'June, I thought we'd go over these figures at lunchtime,' Merv protests, 'share sandwiches ...'

'Sorry, Merv. I've got a long appointment,' I say over my shoulder as I leave his office. 'I could be a bit late back.'

'But ...'

April's relieving on the reception desk. She's trying to stifle a smirk as she points at the clock.

'Don't say a thing.' I struggle with my own laughter as I sail past her.

'Don't have to. It's frickin' obvious.' Then she bends over killing herself laughing.

BBB stands near my desk tapping his foot with a bundle of folders up to his chin.

'Not now, Bob.' I walk right past him and lock myself in the bathroom grinning from ear to ear in the mirror.

Merv and Melba greet me ecstatically when I open the door and switch on the light. They swirl in circles, tails undulating in a most sensuous manner. I think of *Fantasia* again and how Waltz Disney's cartoonists captured a fish dance so perfectly. I reward my babies with flakes that are clearly a gourmet delight to them.

I open the pizza box from Tony's Pizzeria. He was surprised to see me on a Monday and I surprised him further by ordering a Gran Supremo. His mouth dropped open at least a foot and he made a show of landing on a stool clutching his chest. 'June Cooper,' he said, 'I never thought I'd see the day!' And so I smile to myself as I bite into a really delicious slice that he would take no money for. 'Go on. Enjoy,' he said.

I decide to check my emails as I tuck into another slice and pour myself a glass of red. Not that I get many emails and they're mostly rubbish. My eyes lock onto the sender of an email. It's the DNA test lab! Oh, hell, is this it? Is this the result of the sibling test and genetic reconstruction? My heart's pounding as much as it does after Matt or Rob has given me an orgasm that shakes the earth or at least the bed. I'm half afraid to open it. I'm surprised it's only taken a week after the delay in getting Mum's DNA. Matt was so kind to express post a kit to her.

I can hardly believe what I'm reading.

Based on testing results obtained from analyses of the DNA loci listed, the probability of paternity is ...

I call April.

'What?' she screams so loudly that I have to hold my mobile at least a hundred metres from my ear - well, that's a bit of an exaggeration. 'You're fucking kidding!'

'I feel a trip back to Beechworth happening,' I say sipping on my third glass of red. I've finished the whole pizza and feel quite tipsy. 'You want to go?'

'Is the Pope a Catholic?'

I call Charlie.

His deep voice rumbles from his chest to my ear.

'Well, I'll be damned.'

'April and I are going up to Beechworth again as soon as possible,' I tell him. 'Do you want to meet us there?'

'Wild horses couldn't stop me. Just let me know when.'

I call Mum/Helen.

'Oh, June. No!'

I feel bad for having upset her.

'I can let you know what happens ...'

'I'd go to support you but the thought of seeing Brenda again ...'

'You don't need her in your life again, after everything.'

'No. I don't.' She's quiet for a moment. 'I feel it'd be so awkward, so ...'

'With Charlie there?'

'Yes,' she says. 'I don't know that I could face him.'

I'm not going to have time to go before Merv and Trish leave - and they're going to be away for three weeks - so I guess we'll all have to sit on it until they get back. Well, these secrets have lain dormant for so long, I guess another couple of months won't make any difference.

Friday 14th April

Matt's had to go over to Perth to sort out a problem there so I won't see him for the rest of the week. That doesn't stop him from calling me, though, and sending me a huge arrangement of native flowers that looks beautiful on my desk. It's raised eyebrows but I don't bite. April sniggers every chance she gets and I could just hit her. I don't, though, because she's laughing with me, not at me. Big difference.

Matt's amazed at the results of the DNA tests. So is Rob. They both want to go to Beechworth too. Now, wouldn't that be just fine with everyone there? I could sell tickets to the Greatest Show on Earth!

I almost miss my train because Melba jumped out of the fish bowl as I was leaving and I had trouble picking her up without hurting her and getting her back to Merv. I waited some minutes to see if she was swimming properly. Oh, Hell, I hope she's all right.

As a result, I arrive on the platform with moments to spare and jump in the front carriage just as a scooter drives up on a ramp and almost knocks me off my feet. The driver tells the scooter man to be more careful of his passengers and asks me if I'm okay. I turn and see it's the driver with the coal black eyes and wild eyebrows. He smiles at me and my heart thuds to a stop. He's ... gorgeous in an earthy, solid, very masculine way. I can feel sex oozing from his every pore. Oh, Hell.

'Yes, thank you,' I smile back.

He nods, reclaims the ramp, jumps back into his cabin and the doors close with a shush.

Hmmm.

Interesting.

Very interesting.

'So far so good,' Merv comments between two burps. 'Trish has no idea. I even let her buy tickets for that Abba musical which'll happen while we're away.'

'Ummm,' I murmur, thinking of the train driver with the black curly hair protruding from his collar.

'You can have the tickets if you want.'

'Sure.'

Merv looks at me suspiciously. 'What do you mean, sure?'

'What?'

'Sure. You said sure.'

'Did I?'

He clicks his fingers in front of my face. 'Hello, anyone home?'

I look at him crossly. 'What's the matter with you this morning, Merv?'

'What's the matter with me,' he explodes. 'I really wonder about you sometimes, June. Are you going to be able to run the office when we're gone?'

'Well, why the hell wouldn't I?'

'I just offered you tickets!'

'Tickets to what, for goodness sake?'

'I give up!' He throws his hands in the air and slumps back in his chair with an enormous burp.

I glide out of his office on a huge puff of huff and stop at April's desk.

'Do you know what's wrong with Merv this morning?'

'No, do you?

When I leave work, I have time to dawdle inside the station. I look along the perches (that rail thing where I've seen train drivers sit looking out over the tracks, along with passengers looking at their phones) in case I see Mr Coal Black Eyes but, of course, he's not here. Why would he be? My mobile rings.

'What're you doing tonight?'

It's Rob. My heart sinks because I'm afraid he's going to insist I have another go at dancing. I just don't think I'm made for it.

'Nothing really.'

'Wanna dance?'

'I ...'

He laughs. 'Don't worry, June. I know you hate it.'

Oh, oh, I'm so relieved.

'Are you still in the city?'

I tell him yes.

'Then why don't we have a bite at Southbank and go back to my place for some hot sex?'

'Gee, Rob, you're so romantic.'

'Aren't I just?'

He ties my wrists to his bed head. I feel uncomfortable and vulnerable.

'No, untie me, Rob. I don't like this.'

'Just a bit longer,' he grunts as he grinds into me. His face loses its boyish appearance, taking on a cruel aspect.

'You're hurting me!

'Nah, you like it rough, don't you,' he thrusts. 'Don't you? Don't you?'

He collapses onto his orgasm and gasps between my breasts, his body heavy on top of me.

'Rob,' I say with as much authority as I can muster. 'Untie me now.'

He rolls off me to lean on his elbow, looking at me critically from my toes to my head.

'Not bad for an old girl.'

'Gee, thanks. I love you too.' I try to still the wobble in my voice. 'Untie me I said.'

He pulls my left nipple. Hard.

'Owww!'

Then he leans over and sucks and sucks and sucks on my neck until I realise he's marking me. I shove my knee into his stomach. He gasps and retches.

'What'd you do that for?'

Then he slaps my face. Hard.

Against my will my eyes begin to overflow down the sides of my face and onto the pillow, soaking my hair on the way. I can't stop and my nose runs and I'm dribbling out the sides of my mouth.

'For fuck's sake, June,' he whines. Then he undoes the ties.

I rub my wrists as I sit up, then scramble around the room to find my underwear. I'm scared. I just want to get out and go home.

'You going?' He looks surprised.

I stand over him on the bed. 'Of course I'm going.'

'It's only 10:45! We can ...'

'You've got to be kidding.' My shoes won't go on and I realise I'm trying to put the wrong shoe on each foot. I hop around until I get it right. 'I don't want to do anything with you ever again.'

'But ... but ...'

I slam the door and then realise I've left my bag inside. Fortunately, the door didn't lock so I go back in and scoop it off the table.

'I'll drive you ...'

But I'm gone.

Saturday 15th April

April's incredulous. 'What're you going to do about it?'

'Nothing,' I shrug. 'I don't want to see him again.'

'But he's such a nice guy ...'

'Nice!' I explode, pointing to the bruises on my neck and wrists. 'You call that nice?'

'I'd never pick him for ...'

'An abuser?'

'It's just that...'

And then she stops, frowning. She's looking at me with her tongue protruding between her front teeth. Her eyes are on mine but I can see she's somewhere else. I don't interrupt her thoughts, though I'm getting a bit uncomfortable with the deep gazing thing. Finally I blink. So does she.

'Well?'

'Have you ever wondered,' she says slowly, 'about the other twin?'

'Of course,' I say testily.

'What if you had sex with the other one?'

I can feel my eyes poking out of their sockets. 'You mean they switched?'

She nods.

I sit back in my chair stunned. No, that hadn't occurred to me.

'In fact,' she continues, 'you may have been having a relationship with the two of them without knowing it.' She takes in my shocked expression. 'Yes,' she nods,' I think you've been having dancing lessons with the other twin and going to the footy with Rob.' She focuses on Merv and Melba. 'I've had dinner and gone to the footy with Rob and you. He showed no signs of cruelty.' She looks up from the goldfish bowl. 'But you'd know. Think about the times you've had sex with Rob. Were there times he was rougher than others?'

I feel sick to my stomach as I go back over my relationship with Rob. I nod. 'Dancing Rob is more rough than footy Rob.'

'There you go,' she says.

'Oh, hell. But Rob's...'

'Not like that? Too nice? Whatever?'

I begin to cry. April passes me a fistful of tissues.

'I feel ... dirty,' I sob. 'Used.' I blow my nose. 'They're making fun of me!'

April blows her own nose, though she looks angry. 'Fuckin' bastards.'

I don't disagree.

I wake April with a coffee. She surfaces from wherever her dreams had her on the couch. Melba blows kisses at her. I blow my nose.

'You're not still crying over those shitheads, are you?'

'No, I've just got a runny nose.'

'Okay, then,' she says searching my face for a lie. I'm not lying, though. I'm angry and disgusted.

'Have you got a plan, then?'

I nod.

Tuesday 18th April

It's Tuesday and I haven't heard from Rob or his twin or seen them on the train. Just now, though, he sends a text from his work mobile:

Hey June yor not still pissed off r u? We could do a lesson and a bit of u no what Fri night. How about it?

I walk over to April's desk and hold my mobile out to her. An eyebrow disappears into her fringe, then abruptly dives into a frown. She hands the mobile back.

'Plan A or B?'

'A ... I'm ignoring it.'

She nods. 'Good stuff.'

Merv and Melba give me a rapturous welcome so I reward them with a good shake of flakes. She blows some bubbles at me as she swirls in a graceful circle. My mobile blurts in my handbag. A text:

Come on June. Cut me some slack here will u? U need to go over the waltz again. I'll be yor prize later on.

It suddenly dawns on me that the 'work' number is probably dancing Rob's mobile and the 'home' one is footy Rob's. How could I have been so gullible? I drop my mobile back into my bag.

Wednesday 19ᵗʰ April

Rob's back on the train today without his twin. No – there he is in the other carriage. Rob falls onto the seat next to me like a bag of bones.

'Shit, I'm stuffed.'

He looks it.

'What've you been up to?' I ask, cool as a cucumber.

'Too many people off work sick and I'm having to cover their arses.'

I study his face trying to remember each detail of dancing Rob's. I can't tell the difference.

Plan B is about to begin.

'Sorry I didn't reply to your messages.'

'Huh?'

'I'm still uneasy about the other night.' I tap him on a knee. 'Very uneasy.'

He looks at me with panic in his eyes. Then a flicker towards the other carriage which carries his alter ego.

'In fact,' I carry on, 'I don't want to do any more dancing classes with you. Or go back to your place.'

'Wha......t?''

'Well, don't look so surprised. How would you feel if I did the same to you? It was degrading.' I lower my voice as I lean into his ear. 'You had no right. You didn't ask my permission or consider how I felt about it. It was like something out of a horror film. And what's more – it hurt!' I sit back and say loudly: 'I don't trust you anymore.'

He just stares at me, obviously without a clue as to what I'm talking about. The passengers surrounding us are lapping it up hoping for more. I turn to each of them smiling. 'Show's over, folks.' They shuffle their papers, return to their screens/books, look out the windows. Anything but look at this mad woman who's sporting a huge love bite.

'June, I ...'

'Don't,' I say, holding up my hand in front of his face. 'Don't say anything. Unless you want to tell me the truth.'

I sense a leaning-in of the passengers and grin at them. They turn away hurriedly.

'Truth?' he asks weakly.

'About him,' I nod towards his twin looking at us between carriages.

'So what'd he say?' April's all eyes as we make coffee in the kitchen at work.

I lean back against the bench with my mug which says: *Shit faced at 60* Someone thought it clever to give me that at our Kris Kringle Christmas break up a couple of years ago and I thought it meant I had a face like shit so I kept using it to give them the shits (April language).

'He didn't know what to say. Denied it until he had to get off the train.' I shrug. 'I'm pretty sure he's footy Rob. He really did look like he hadn't any idea what I was talking about.'

'There you go!' April punches the air. 'I did some research on the net last night and it seems that some twins hate each other. They compete. It might be they're operating separately without communicating.'

'That could explain why they never sit together.'

We study the contents of our mugs.

'Plan C?' April asks.

I nod.

'When?'

'Saturday. Hawthorn plays St. Kilda. You're invited.'

Friday 21ˢᵗ April

'What've you told Marj this time?' I ask Merv as we go over his calendar.

He sits back so far on his chair that I'm sure it'll topple and I'll have to call OOO.

'You'll never believe it, June,' he says with a silly grin on his face. 'Last night I owned up to Trish and we told Marj the truth, that we're going away and nothing, nothing, nothing can stop us, including her.'

He laughs at my expression.

'Yep,' he burps sedately for a change, 'we read her the Riot Act and said if anything happened, then Trish's brother would have to take care of it.'

'I'm proud of you, Merv.'

He nods sagely. 'I'll tell you the truth, June, I'm sick of all the fart arsing around trying to get away and Marj spoiling everything. No more, I told Trish. This time we're off, free as birds, without having to skulk away like rats in a sewer looking for a sandwich.'

I'm not really sure about the simile but I get his meaning.

'Well, that's a relief,' I sigh. 'Save me having to lie my head off every time Marj calls.'

'You can still have the tickets.'

'What tickets?'

I've waved Merv off at lunchtime so that he can help Trish pack. We have a quiet afternoon in the office before the usual chaos of getting home on public transport. I see predictions of a Hawthorn win tomorrow on the newsstands as I climb the steps under the clocks at Flinders Street Station. I hold my Myki card up to the reader and the barrier opens for me to pass through. As I do, someone pushes me in the back so that I stumble to my knees and he jumps over me to avoid paying. The contents of my bag scatter all over the place in front of me. I try to get up with some dignity as a hand extends to help me up.

'Thank you,' I gasp, as I pat at my knees, noting the holes and runs that have appeared in my panty hose. My right knee is bleeding.

'Here,' says a deep voice in my ear as I'm offered a clean blue handkerchief. 'Are you all right?'

I look up to see coal black eyes scanning my face. Bushy, dark, curly eyebrows scatter across a wide forehead, almost joining in the middle, matching the thick wavy hair that curls down to his collar and below. I suck in my breath. It's him! The train driver. I feel the thrill of his touch on my arm.

'You're bleeding,' he says inspecting my knees.

'Oh,' I say, 'it's nothing.'

'No,' he insists. 'I'll take you to the ...'

'Really,' I breathe, 'I'm not hurt. It's just a graze.'

'Well, let me take you to your train.'

And this wonderful man accompanies me on the escalator and waits with me on the platform until my train pulls in.

'I've seen you before, haven't I?' he asks inspecting my face for the umpteenth time.

'Yes, you drive my train in the morning sometimes. The Frankston line.'

'Ah ha! I knew it. I could never forget a pretty lady like you.'

I feel a blush rising up my neck and into my cheeks.

He laughs. 'You don't see a blush like yours much these days. It's nice.'

I touch my neck to make sure the love bite's still hidden under my scarf.

'I'm on early shift on the Frankston line next week,' he says looking along the track as my train pulls in. 'Hopefully I'll see you.'

'I hope so too,' I say as he steps back for me to board the train.

Saturday 22nd April

I catch sight of April and Rob at the end of the Richmond Station platform as I'm jostled by the crowd surging towards the ramp. They're in deep conversation.

'I don't know,' April says. 'That's up to June.'

'What's up to me?' I ask, interrupting them.

They turn to give me a hug.

'About going to Beechworth.'

'Oh, that,' I smile, relieved that the conversation isn't about the twin mystery. 'I have to wait until our boss comes back from holiday.'

'I don't see that I'd be able to get the time off,' Rob says with his arm around my shoulder, 'the way things are at the moment.'

'Don't worry,' I tell him, 'we'll give you a blow-by-blow description when we get back.'

And then we're swept down the ramp and off to the G.

We have a great time cursing the umpires, screaming *Ball!* at the opposition for holding onto the ball, yelling at the Hawks to *Come on, kick it!* Rising to our feet each time we get a goal. *Yeah!* Arms lifted, fists clenched, scarves flying, *Come on Hawks! Yeah! Yeah!* Smiling faces, boos from the Saints supporters. It's a close, suspenseful game which we win by one point.

I'm exhausted as my elbows prop me up on the table in the beer garden. I'm afraid I'll fall asleep and slump my aching limbs and muscles onto the floor. I'm hoarse and can only talk in faint squeaks. I've given up and leave the others to go over each point and goal of the game.

'So,' April says suddenly, 'where's your twin today?'

I wake up.

Rob looks at some point above my head.

April leans towards him. 'Dancing?'

It takes some time (and lots to drink) for us to get Rob to open up about his twin, at least that's after he insists on knowing what I was carrying on about the other morning on the train. Something hurting in a horror film and that I don't trust him anymore. April and I exchange looks. We realise he really has no idea. I take a deep breath and tell him about the tying up of my hands, about the painful sex, about my not wanting to see his brother again.

Rob's face goes bright red and then sickly white. His hands shake as he tries to get his beer glass up to his lips. He looks terrible. 'I knew it,' he says into his beer. 'Bastard.' He looks up at me with a hint of tears in his eyes. 'I'm so sorry, June. I should have stopped him before this.'

I take the wobbling glass from his hand and put mine around his. 'What do you mean?'

'He just doesn't get it ... relationships. He's always after what I have. My job, my car, my achievements, my friends, our parents.' He shudders as he looks up at us. 'Exactly two minutes and forty seconds after he was born, his main rival showed up: me. He can't stand the fact that I might be as good – if not better – than him. We might have been close, you know, like other twins, but he's hated me from birth. He resents that I get half of the love our parents have for us. I'm a threat to his position in the family.'

He takes a gulp of his beer, wipes his mouth with the back of his free hand (I haven't let go the other) and continues. 'He started beating me up since we were walking. He'd grab me by a foot, a hand, and drag me down the stairs, then laugh his head off. Mum used to go off at him but he wouldn't stop. As we got older, the beatings got worse. I was covered in bruises, which Mum tried to cover up she was so embarrassed. Her darling little twins were supposed to be closer than close. All the books said so. It was easier for him when we went to kindergarten because our parents couldn't keep an eye on him. Apparently I came home on different occasions with a broken wrist, bruises on my back, a broken nose, broken arm, twisted ankle and black eyes, none of which could be proven that he'd done it.'

I'm sure April's heart is hammering like mine. Tears are streaming down my cheeks. I dig in my bag for some tissues.

'Secondary school was no different,' he shrugs, 'only the injuries got worse, despite the counselling our parents forced him to attend. He was outraged by that and refused to cooperate with the psychologist – or should I say, psychologists, plural. In the end, I was transferred to a different school and the beatings stopped. By that time I had a lock on my bedroom door and became pretty good at avoiding him the rest of the time.'

'You're shittin' me,' April splutters.

'I wish I was.'

'But ... but ... what about your parents? What the fuck were they doing about it?'

'Everything they possibly could,' he shrugs, 'but he was too clever for them. For anyone.'

'And after school?' I ask.

'Same. Same. I get a job. He muscles in without them realising, making me sick and absent so that he creates havoc too hard for me to fix. Screws everything in sight and I have to leave because it's all too hard. Then I get another job. I'm sick again – even though I inspect everything I eat – and he's there in my place taking over. I can't go back and explain what he's fucked up – the work and the girls. Pinches my phones, copies my contacts – everything – without me even realising. So I left home and got myself a place so that he doesn't know what I'm doing or where I'm working.'

I stare at him in horror. 'But what about his presence on the train? He gets on and off with you, even though you're not together.'

'Stalking. Simple as that.'

April gets up to buy another round. Rob and I are silent as he considers his horrific relationship with his twin and I try to make sense of it which, of course, I can't.

She puts a tray in front of us and distributes the drinks. I'm feeling very tipsy but don't care.

'So,' April says slowly, 'your twin ... what's his fuckin' name, by the way?'

'Marty.'

'... Marty the madman,' she continues, 'follows you onto the train to see where you go?'

'Yep.'

'And watches you talking with June and latches onto her?'

'Yep.'

'Oh, Jesus.'

His breath, hot in my ear, has me climbing again. This time, though, his hands encircle my neck and squeeze tightly. This time his hands are too tight. It's no longer any fun.

I gasp as I surface from the nightmare. I sit up to drink some water. I'm aroused, yet scared out of my wits as I relive the dream. *Marty, whirling me across a dance floor. I make a mistake and collapse at his feet, staring up at him from the polished floor, its rigidity digging into my shoulder blades. He lunges with hot lips, panting as he devours me. Everywhere. Then his hands on my neck.*

My eyes swivel to the fishbowl where Merv and Melba swirl in their erotic dance now that I've disturbed them. I push myself up from the couch and stagger to my bedroom. I fall onto the bed unable to pull the cover back.

That's the last time I drink so much, I tell myself.

Monday 24th April

I position myself on the platform where the first carriage will stop. I see the train rushing towards me, the driver's cabin filling my eyes. I try not to look eager, though my pounding heart surely gives me away. The whole world must hear it. Our eyes lock as he smoothes the train into the station. The doors exhale as passengers board but I hesitate a moment – just in case. And then the driver's cabin door opens and there he is. He extends his hand to open the door for me. I take his hand and feel something pass from his palm to mine. My fingers close over it as I smile at him and nod.

'Thank you,' I murmur.

'Most welcome,' he replies.

And then he's gone, back into his role as train driver, dark eyes on the tracks ahead as he takes us passengers safely to our destination.

I take a seat inside the carriage and open my hand to reveal a neatly folded piece of paper.

> I like to have coffee with you. Please call or sms my fone.
> Respectfully yours, Yannis.

I note his number in my contacts and decide to wait until I get to work to reply.

Yannis. I like that.

Wednesday 26th April

We sit opposite each other at a table in Degraves Street, people rushing past us to get home. He's been telling me about his childhood in a village on the east coast of Greece. His eleven brothers and sisters!! His mother's death some five years ago (I like that he has tears running down his face) and how he's been trying to convince his father to come to Melbourne to live with him.

I'm studying his face, his open shirt at the neck where I can see the hair protruding. I find it very sexy. He catches me looking and stops mid-sentence. We clutch our cups, finger knuckles white with tension. He's looking at my mouth, my eyes, and slowly lowers his gaze to my neckline, hovers at my breasts which tingle. He's sporting a 5 o'clock shadow, giving me an idea of what he'd look like with a moustache and beard. His nose is straight and finely shaped. His earlobes peep from under his curly hair. I want to touch them, suck them. My breath shudders as I watch his mouth break into a slow smile. I know he knows what I'm feeling and I'm thinking it's mutual.

'June,' he says, rasping my name up from his chest, 'I want to take you to my brother's restaurant.'

'Your brother?' I'm surprised. 'You have brothers here?'

'Well, yes,' he spreads his hands and shrugs, 'and sisters.'

Friday 28th April

Yannis has a hand on my back guiding me into Giorgos & Katerina's Restaurant, a homely place decked out in blues and whites: tablecloths, flags (I assume they're the Greek one), chairs, balloons (must be someone's birthday). It's noisy and laughter-filled. My nose detects astonishing aromas.

A carbon copy of Yannis comes towards us, arms spread wide. They slap each other violently on the shoulders and hug with loud greetings. Yannis includes me in the embrace. 'This is June, I told you about.'

'Ahhh,' his brother smiles expansively, 'you didn't exaggerate. She's beautiful.'

I blush. *His sight's not the best*, I think.

'This is (*blah blah blah* sounding like nothing I've heard before) – George.'

'How do you say your name in Greek, George?'

'Blah blah blah (*like he's eating an oyster that's off*).'

He looks at my blank expression.

'It spells like G-I-O-R-G-O-S.'

I think that over and decide the English equivalent much easier.

'Call me George,' he laughs. They both laugh.

Our table is just about groaning with the weight of food. George (and his staff) brings plate after plate of food for me to try. Yannis is attentive and eager that I like everything, including the ouzo.

'This is Greece's national drink,' George tells me as he pours it into a glass and adds water. I'm surprised to see it turn cloudy and can smell something familiar. 'Can you smell aniseed?' he asks.

'Yes, yes, I can,' I say with surprise as it explodes amongst my tastebuds.

'Cinnamon, cloves, fennel?'

I'm not sure I know what he's talking about. Are they people's names? Regions? Towns in Greece?'

He thumps down on a chair next to me and waves my glass under my nose, eyebrows raised. 'Close your eyes and sniff gently, June.' I obey. 'Now ... can you smell any spices?'

Oh, spices! I try to remember the ones he said. I'm sure I don't know any of them. 'I'm sorry ... I ...'

'Don't put her on the spot,' Yannis says, squeezing my arm reassuringly. 'This is new to her.'

'Well,' George shouts. I jump, not knowing if I'm going to be punished or not. 'We have to teach her!'

They laugh as George pours another drink for the three of us. 'June will learn,' George toasts. 'She will learn about Greece.'

We drink to that as an enormous woman spreads a platter of dips, fried zucchini and dolmades (leaves rolled up and filled with rice and minced meat) in front of us. I'm surprised when George grabs her by the waist and pulls her onto his lap. 'This,' he announces, 'is Katerina, my wife.'

I love this night with Yannis and his family (kids included, who are lined up and named in front of me). They are roudy and spontaneous and joyful. They are generous with their hospitality, their food, their ouzo (which I'm determined to like), their sense of fun. We eat octopus and marinated anchovies, spicy pickled peppers – and then follow it with more ouzo.

'Moussaka,' Katerina announces, as she plonks down a huge bowl. 'Aubergines, potatoes, mince, sauce.' She gives me a generous portion. 'You try,' she urges.

Meatballs are next. She tells me they are beef with mint and I must wash them down with more ouzo. 'Dolmadakia, June.' Katerina is very keen that I put back all the weight I've lost on the dance floor. 'Rice, dill, fennel, spearmint, spring onion, vine leaves.' At least I recognise some of the names. The ingredients are rolled up in the leaves and have a tasty sauce which Yannis tells me is egg and lemon. Yum! He writes down the name of the dish for me on a serviette.

'Souvlaki,' says Katerina as she makes room on the table. Now, that one I've heard of. Never tried it, of course, but it's delicious. She takes me into the kitchen and shows me how they cook meat on a vertical grill and then shave it off and fill some pita bread with that, along with whatever filling you'd like. She tops it off with a yoghurt, garlic and cucumber dip. I'm converted, if not completely ruined on ouzo. The front of my outfit is stained with food and dripping souvlaki which has also run down my arm. My chin feels crusted with god-knows-what. Yannis dabs at it. I must look a fright.

My head spins as I look at myself in the bathroom mirror. That ouzo has an oomph to it. I feel like I may vomit but I burp instead and feel much better.

We say goodbye as if we are long lost friends/relatives. I feel a genuine loss in leaving. His family is wonderful. 'Come back soon, June,' George and Katerina say in unison. 'Plenty food. Plenty ouzo.'

Yannis takes me home. He walks me to my door and stands there like he doesn't know what to do. I can feel the heat of his breath, the curl of his hair, the breadth of his back as he embraces me. His arms drop as he backs away.

'Thank you for the beautiful hours with you, June,' he says formally.

'No, it's me who's grateful,' I smile. 'I had a lovely time with you and your family. The food was delicious.'

'You eat with your heart and mind. I like that you eat a lot.'

I can feel a blush rising. *Oh, he must think me a pig!*

He laughs. Touches my arm. 'To share food and enjoy is a very good thing.' He hesitates. 'Would you like to eat dinner with me again sometime?'

I try not to look too eager but I say yes in the next breath. He takes my hand briefly and then leaves.

Monday 1ˢᵗ May

I can't think about anything or anyone except him. I'm exhausted, but in the best possible way. The past weekend has been a blur. My body tingles at the thought of him and I break out in a sweat of desire.

'Are you … you know … going through menopause?' Amy asks as she returns to reception after her lunch break.

'What!'

'Oh, sorry,' she says, waving her hands in apology in front of me. 'It's not my business … but I was just thinking that you … you …'

'Spit it out, girl,' I say crossly.

'… you seem to be having a lot of hot flushes lately.'

April drops a pile of envelopes on the desk. She coughs and splutters violently.

'Oh, April,' Amy cries with concern, tapping April on the back with her long fingernails. 'Are you okay? Have you got a cold?'

'April's fine,' I say. 'She's got a touch of the collywobbles.'

'The colly whats?'

To which April breaks out in a fresh bout of coughing and hurries to the bathroom.

'I think she wet her pants,' I observe seriously.

'Oh! Oh!' Amy looks in alarm from me to the bathroom door. 'Is it contagious?'

Matt rings to invite me for a night of bliss which I reluctantly turn down. He seems surprised but I tell him I've got a touch of gastro and hope to be over it next week. It's not that I wouldn't like to see him; I need time to think about the impact Yannis is having on my life and how that fits with Matt and Rob.

Rob wants April and me to go to the footy on the weekend but I tell him the same lie but to enjoy the footy with April. He asks if I'm mad at him and/or his darling twin but I assure him I'm not, at least with him. Marty's another kettle of fish.

Marty sends one text after another with apologies and silly promises I know he can't keep – about never hurting me again and resuming my dance lessons so I can dance 'with the best of them' – which I ignore.

Charlie rings from time to time just for a chat. I love that. He asks me about the DNA results again and, surprise surprise, he offers to do the test. I ask him what changed his mind.

'I can't stick it in the sand and forget about it. It's not going to go away, is it?' I tell him no. 'I slept in Kaye's bed last night and woke up feeling she'd want me to.'

I'm taken aback. 'Do you sleep there often?'

He chuckles softly. 'When I need to sleep on a problem. She usually gives me the answer.' He pauses. 'And you know what, girlie? I'd like to be your dad, despite what it means.'

Mum and I ring each other often. She tells me about Eric's 'doings' and the rest of the family. They send their love to me and ask when I'm going back to see them again. I wish. Maybe after the triumphal return to Beechworth. Mum asks after Charlie but he doesn't mention her. I feel sad about that but I suppose he feels he's betrayed Aunty Kaye by possibly having sex with Mum and feels guilty.

Merv and Trish get me at work on Skype when their chaotic schedule allows. The last time, they both dropped their lycra to show me their 'muscled' legs from bike riding along the banks of the Danube. Aside from squinting away Merv's way-too-tight underpants, I couldn't see any real muscle on either of them. White lies are such a tactful skill, I think, as I pretend to be impressed.

Wednesday 3ʳᵈ May

I open the door to drop-dead-gorgeous Matt who's holding a gift-wrapped pot containing a stunning white orchid with six yellow-centred blooms running along a central stalk. Guilt hits me as I gush something appropriate. My telltale blush makes him smile.

The car ride to our dinner destination is mostly taken up with Matt's account of his time in Perth. He tells me how much he's missed me and that he's looking forward to a romantic dinner together. Tonight we're at a French restaurant where I pretend enthusiasm over the dishes he chooses and depend too heavily on the wine to calm my nerves. He notices me fingering the pearl necklace he gave me as he asks about my work while Merv is away, about the DNA report, about my life in general.

I'm in the ladies looking at myself in the mirror. I look like something the cat dragged in: sweat dripping through my hair, eye liner smudged, lipstick all over the place. *Honestly, June, what does this man see in you?*

He stands as I return to the table. 'Are you okay?' Concern wrinkles his forehead.

'Yes, yes,' I say, as the waitress brings our dessert. Something to do with a bomb in Alaska. I get such a fright when she lights a blowtorch and sets fire to it! I put my hands up to my ears waiting for an explosion.

'It's okay, June. She's supposed to,' Matt laughs. 'It's theatre.'

I always thought theatre was about people on a stage.

He's looking at me closely. 'There's something different about you.'

'Oh, really?'

'Yes, I can't quite put my finger on it, aside from the fact that you're very unsettled tonight.'

I'm busy with the bomb thing, which is delicious, by the way.

'Do you want to talk about it?'

I look up and nod. 'Not here.'

We finish our meal and, as Matt settles the bill, I make my third trip to the toilet. I lean against the cubicle wall trying to get my breathing under control. My heart's going at a hundred miles an hour. I don't want to do this but I know I have to. I take a deep breath, practise a smile in front of the mirror and exit the ladies with it glued onto my gums, probably looking like the Joker.

An hour later we're still sitting in his car in the restaurant's parking area. Matt has run out of tissues, so have I, and now I'm dabbing at my eyes with his handkerchief.

'It's all right,' he assures me. 'Really.'

I see his eyes caught in the streetlight that angles into the car and realise he means it.

'I just can't lie to you ...'

'I appreciate that,' he says, stroking my face. 'I don't have any rights to you anyway, because of my ... home situation.' He shrugs. 'I knew it couldn't last, that you'd find someone more worthy of you, someone who can offer you the future I can't.'

'Oh, Matt ...'

'Shhh,' he smiles, touching my lips. 'It was wonderful while we had it, though, wasn't it?'

Thursday 4ᵗʰ May

April tears off some paper towels in the kitchen at work. 'Here,' she says, 'mop yourself up before anyone sees you.'

I blow my nose and turn back to the huge flower arrangement that Matt has sent, giving it some water.

'Did he ask for the pearls back?'

'I offered but he wouldn't hear of it. Said that's what friends are for.'

'Don't expect me to give you any.'

Saturday 6ᵗʰ May

The crowd surges to its feet, the roar deafening as the player lines up in front of the goalposts. It was an extraordinary mark, as if he jumped on pogo sticks over everyone's head, so he deserves this kick unopposed. There's a momentary collective intake of breath as the ball sails high and straight and another roar erupts. It's so thrilling and contagious. I'm hoarse from shouting, part of the Romans-roaring-for-blood mentality. I wonder if the audience in the Coliseum was as passionate about lions vs gladiators as we are over two teams playing footy. Different outcome, of course, though some of our players are injured and bloody – not mauled to death.

We fight our way to a table in the beer garden where we learned about Rob's twin, Marty. That was pretty traumatic, as is this for me now. I tell Rob about Yannis and how happy I am with him, and about the need to end my relationship with Rob. His mouth hangs open for a minute before he takes a long gulp of beer.

'So, June,' he says, frowning at me, 'I'm redundant now, eh?'

'Oh, don't put it like that ...'

'You're giving me the flick, the piss-off, the fuck-off, in fact.'

'I suppose I am,' I say miserably. 'I'm so sorry. It's ...'

April shares a glance with Rob and then they both burst out laughing. And that's it. Rob wants to remain friends. Can you do that after you've had sex with someone? I guess only time will tell.

Sunday 7ᵗʰ May

Yannis and George are deep in conversation about a soccer game on TV last night.

Two of the children are on my lap as I try not to spill more food down my clothes. Each time I've been here I'm filthy. Yannis says it shows that I've appreciated the food.

Katerina is telling me about Yannis's wife who left him for another man, an Aussie. Yannis has said very little about her and I don't like to ask. I know she existed, because he has children and grandchildren.

'She ... she was never happy, you know? Always with her head up there,' she points. I look up at the ceiling wondering why her head was up there. 'Always in the sky, you know?' I nod. 'Even back in our village she dreamed big, big dreams.' Her arms take in the whole restaurant. 'Always wanting more, more.'

'Who wants more?' chirps in one of the children on my lap.

'Never you mind,' Katerina playfully slaps her. 'You get down. Let Aunty June have a rest.'

Aunty June?

'And when they come here to Melbourne, she talked nothing but diet. She come here, sit where you sit and eat a leaf, a tomato, a glass of water!'

'No ouzo?'

'No ouzo. Can you imagine?'

Not really. Not with all this delicious food and drink in front of me.

'She became like stick.' She holds up her index finger. 'No curves. No woman. Hah!' Her mouth curls in contempt as she leans towards me. 'I know my brother-in-law. He doesn't like to be married to a stick. And then ... then she has hanky panky with her boss. He likes sticks.' She looks around as Yannis comes back to the table. 'You are no stick. You are real woman!'

'What are you girls so serious about?'

'Secret woman's business,' she laughs. 'None of your business.'

'Well, that's okay then,' he smiles, as he fills his plate again as well as mine.

I toss and turn every night thinking about Yannis and wonder why he hasn't made any advances. This is so different from Matt and Rob/Marty. They wasted no time with the sex thing. Yannis, on the other hand, takes me to the restaurant, the pictures – even a picnic – but stays at a respectful distance. Maybe he doesn't fancy me. Maybe I'm reading too much into this new friendship. When he holds my hand as we cross a road, I feel a sense of belonging and desire rips through me. Sometimes I catch him looking at my mouth and then he breaks into a smile and looks away. When we sit together at George & Katerina's, our shoulders touch, he puts his arm on the back of my chair, he pops morsels into my mouth and watches closely for a reaction, he hugs me at the end of a date, but nothing more. And all the time my body is a quivering, melting, yearning mess waiting, just waiting for him to touch me, tell me he wants me, make love to me.

I'd never have imagined feeling this way before my relationship with Matt began. My Mills & Boon books gave me a glimpse into other people's lives, but I never thought it could happen to me. Besides, I thought it was all made up. I'd look up from a steamy page on a train, look at people seated around me and never thought they'd get up to *those* things. Not in a million years. But they do. I do.

Yannis makes me laugh, really laugh, like I've never laughed before. He's so cute, the way words pour out of his mouth like gifts for me to savour and remember. So many of them and they all matter, even if they're not correct. That's part of his charm, along with his enthusiasm for everything and everyone.

And his family! Yannis has taken me to George & Katerina's restaurant nearly every time we have together and I feel almost like *family* with them. It's weird how quickly they've taken me into their hearts – and they into mine – kids and all. The younger ones compete to scramble up on my knees and babble earnestly in a mixture of Greek and English about anything and everything. Somehow I get the gist of it. The two younger ones – a boy and a girl – like to touch my face, pull on my ears, look down my neckline (everyone laughs how much I blush) and play with my bra straps. In contrast Sandra and Wayne's kids have never even spoken to me, looking through me like I don't exist.

Yannis invites me to his home in Frankston and I invite him to my place. I look at the difference between his cluttered home with all things Greek and my naked flat. I can see large question marks in his eyes as to why I live the way I do. I didn't even know that I live like I don't live there. My walls are bare, except for Mum's portrait, whereas his are covered with posters, paintings (mostly by his nieces and nephews) which he regards as masterpieces, photos and years and years of calendars. 'I like the pictures too much to throw them away,' he shrugs. Every empty space holds model trains, Greek artefacts, Storm (a Melbourne rugby team he tells me) souvenirs and pot plants. His kitchen is a riot of colour and utensils. Each cupboard is painted a different colour; his nieces and nephews each got a cupboard door to paint and decorate how they wanted. I read their names and the dates they painted the doors. 'I'm running out of doors here, so they'll have to start on the bathroom,' he declares with a big grin.

Yannis likes Merv and Melba. He says they are, besides Mum and me, the most interesting and beautiful decorations in my flat. He brings me a poster of what he tells me is the Acropolis in Athens. It's a white ruin with no roof and lots of tall columns perched on top of a big hill overlooking the city. He promises to take me there one day. Me? Overseas? I don't even have a passport! He says I need to get one soon so that I can see the wonders of his country, eat local food, visit his home village and meet his family. 'My father will love you,' he assures me, as he hangs the poster on my bedroom wall, 'as will my brothers and sisters and all of my aunts and uncles and cousins.' *Is he talking about me?* 'I will make love to you in the sea near my home as you look up at the stars.' He stops with a stunned look on his face. 'Sorry, June, I am claiming something I have no right to.'

'No,' I smile, touching his face. 'I think I would love that.'

The distance between our faces narrows until our lips are barely touching. I see his nostrils quiver. Sense his body tremble. Feel his breath. And then his lips close on mine. So gently. He's watching me for a reaction. It's a chaste kiss that assumes nothing but asks permission. I begin to open my lips, wanting to taste him, but he sighs as he pulls away. 'June,' he rasps into my hair as he takes me in a trembling embrace. 'Not here. Not now.'

Monday 8th May

I look up as the doors open at each station but it's too early for the twins, so I settle down with my latest Mills & Boon. I chose this one because the man on the cover has dark curly hair like Yannis's and he looks European.

April's still nagging me to read some of the classics but I just can't get into them or they take me too long to read. It took me forever to read *The Scarlett Letter* but it helped that I saw the film first with Demi Moore in it, which was so romantic and sexy and tragic all at the same time. What a terrible era the story was in; the women were door mats to their overbearing men and if they broke the rules and – god help them – got pregnant, then they had to wear a big letter 'A' on their chest to show they were adulterers, and then they probably got hanged for it anyway in the end.

I'm up to chapter two already in my Mills & Boon and lose myself until the train pulls into Flinders Street. The man has just kissed the girl in chapter seven and they're breathless with lust.

This is my last week before Merv and Trish get back, so I write some reminders in my calendar and think about the things I need to do today. Amy's on leave, so I work on a roster for all of us to take turns at reception. BBB's not happy that Mel will be away from her desk at odd intervals during the coming three weeks. I told him last Friday that he was lucky I hadn't planned on including him in the roster. He's hopeless at answering the phones and his breath would be enough to drive customers away.

Merv and Trish call on Skype from Budapest. 'We've just had some real Hungarian Goulash,' Merv burps, 'and we did a three hour tour of these weird bars and ...' Trish pokes her head into the screen continuing: '...castles, castles all over the place, and a night time dinner cruise where all the beautiful buildings were lit up and, honestly June, you ought to visit this place. Do the river cruise.'

'How's June going to do that!' Merv looks shocked at the idea.

'Why not?' I ask.

'Well, who would you go with? April?'

'Maybe, maybe not. Maybe someone else.'

They both chuckle at the idea. 'You never go anywhere, June. It's just not your style.'

'Just watch me,' I grind out between my teeth. 'I need a couple of days off when you get back.'

I'm at Tony's Pizzeria trying to convince Tony I'm not joking. 'Yes, a pizza with the lot,' I tell him again. He looks at me with misty eyes. 'You've come a long way, June,' he gushes.

Merv and Melba almost shout their joy at my arrival. I tell myself it's not just because I feed them. I wonder if they feel affection or love or pain or happiness. I tell them about my day at work, about Merv's namesake on Skype who thinks I'd have no one to go on a cruise with, and about my secret glee that I think I'm in love with a Greek god who I'm pretty sure would go anywhere with me, including a cruise. My beautiful fish blow bubbles at me, staring through the glass that separates our two worlds, theirs confined and watery, mine bursting with a freedom I had never known existed.

Can you fall in love at my age? Do I dare fall in love at all? What if this thing I have with Yannis is just temporary until the chase is over and we settle into a very new relationship? Will he get a shock when he sees me naked? Will he recoil? Will he tire of me? Will I tire of him? How will I know if he loves me? How *can* he love me? I see my reflection in Merv and Melba's world and try to see what Yannis sees in me. I'm not good looking, that's for sure. Would *homely* be a good description? And what does *homely* mean? A quick search says: ugly, unattractive, plain, unpleasant, uninviting. Is that me? My tears hide in my reflection.

Wednesday 10th May

'What am I going to do without you, *glyka (darling)*?' Yannis looks forlorn when I tell him about my impending visit to Beechworth.

'What did you do before you met me?'

'Wait for you.'

'But you didn't know I even existed ...'

'Yes, I did,' he smiles. 'I've been waiting for you a long time.'

'What?'

'June, my *glyka*, *s'agapo* - I love you - and have always loved you.'

'I don't understand.'

'I never gave up,' he murmurs, touching his heart and then mine, 'knowing that someone special would come to me. I have been very lonely, June, without you.'

'But surely there were other women who ...'

'No, my *glyka*.' He kisses me gently. 'I have been like the priest. No woman. No love.' He smiles. 'Because no woman I met was you.'

If that's not right out of a Mills & Boon book, I'll go he.

I'm sitting between Katerina and Yannis telling her why I'm going to Beechworth. George is holding the back of her chair as he keeps a watchful eye on the restaurant.

'It's very complicated,' Yannis explains, 'about June's father ... well, which father it is, the Charlie or her father.'

'What you mean?' Katerina frowns. 'Her father or the Charlie? It must be the father, no?'

'You've heard of DNA tests?' I ask, looking from one face to the other.

'Yes, yes,' George says. 'It's on Ancestry.com.'

'That's right,' I nod, 'along with many other places where you can look to find your ancestors, including taking samples from your saliva and sending them to a laboratory. What I'm looking for is to find out whether Charlie, or the man who I lived with and thought was my father, is my father.'

'But,' Katerina gestures with open hands, 'why doesn't your *mitera* tell you who he was?' I frown in puzzlement. 'Your mother,' she adds.

'Because she doesn't know.'

Friday 12th May

April comes back to my place after work today. She's going to the footy with Rob tomorrow.

'Do you mind?' she asks, studying my reaction carefully.

'No, not at all,' I say and mean it. 'Actually, I think you two would make a good pair.'

'What about the fact that you and he ... um ...'

'Had sex?'

'Well, yes.'

'If it doesn't bother me, and it doesn't bother him, and if it doesn't bother you ...'

My mobile comes to life. It's Charlie. 'How's my girl?'

'Good thanks, Charlie. April's here with me, as a matter of fact. I'll put you on speaker.'

'You there girlie?'

'Sure am, handsome,' she grins. We hear him chuckle. 'You behaving yourself?'

It's almost like when the three of us were together in Mildura talking like old friends over some drinks and a meal. As we're about to hang up, Charlie hesitates before asking: 'Ah, has that thing arrived yet?'

'They told me it'd take up to two weeks for the DNA test result to arrive,' I say, 'but I'll check with them on Monday to make sure. Fingers crossed it'll get here before we leave on Thursday.'

'What happens if it doesn't arrive on time?'

'Then, I'll just have to call you Dad.'

Saturday 13th May

Yannis asks me for dinner at George & Katerina's with a little more ceremony than I would have expected. He seems nervous on the phone. He hardly talks in the car on the way to the restaurant. He assures me nothing's the matter.

George ushers us to a private booth.

'What...?'

'Sit. Sit,' George commands, very serious. Katerina has a smile wider than the MCG.

Glasses of ouzo appear in front of us. We all drink to what-I'm-not-sure, as it's in Greek.

The entrees appear and so does a flat white and blue decorated box in front of me.

'What's this?' I ask turning it over, surprised at its weight. Something moves inside.

'Wait. Wait.' Katerina backs away, as does George.

'*Glyka*,' Yannis rumbles from his chest, coughs, wipes tears aside.

'You're sad, Yannis!'

'No. No, *glyka*,' he trembles into a smile. 'I am very happy.'

'But ...'

'*Glyka*, I love you,' he says simply.

I look at him, puzzled. Didn't he tell me that the other night? Why is this different?

'I ...'

'No,' he whispers, touching my lips. 'You don't need to reply.'

He takes the box from me and then presents it formally. 'This is a gift to you from me – and my country.'

'Thank you,' I say, equally formally. 'Can I open it now?'

'Of course,' he smiles, opening his hands wide. 'Please.'

A blue and white ribbon falls away as I remove the lid. There is white tissue paper covering something. I look up at him to catch an anxious look on his face. I slowly remove the tissue to find a long necklace of opaque white glass beads decorated with what looks like blue eyes. The beads go from small to large in different shapes. It's like nothing I've ever seen.

'This is ...'

'Old,' he says. 'Centuries old. From Greece.'

I don't know what to say. I realise it means an awful lot to him. Maybe it's quite valuable. 'It's stunning, Yannis.'

'May I?' He takes the necklace from my hands to gently place it around my neck. I feel its weight. 'Now you belong to Greece and Greece belongs to you.'

'He loves you, you know,' Katerina says into my ear. 'He not give you this necklace if he not love you. He never gave it to The Stick.'

I touch the warmth of the beads as they sit comfortably on my chest.

'It been in their family many generations,' she continues. 'Their great-great-great-whatever had it until passed down to the hands of Yannis.'

'I don't understand why he would give it to me, though. I mean, he hardly knows me. I'm not his family.'

'He thinks you are now.'

I start to cry thick fat tears that splash onto the beads and I mop them up with a serviette.

'June! June! What make you cry this way?' Katerina puts her arms around me and hugs me so hard my face is squashed into her ample chest. 'You not happy? You not like the necklace?'

'Of course,' I splutter into her apron which smells of garlic, 'but I feel a fraud. We don't even ... I don't deserve a gift like this.'

'No! No, June,' she pulls me tighter, 'You the *real deal*. You make Yannis happy. That makes me and George happy. We all happy!'

Sunday 14ᵗʰ May

Yannis arrives on the dot at ten o'clock. I've been looking at myself in the mirror trying on different outfits, wondering what I can wear with the beads, if I should even wear them. I mean, they're valuable and perhaps I should save them for special occasions. Maybe he expects to see them on me? Maybe I should mothball them? I don't even know where we're going. What we're doing. He says it's a surprise.

I open the door to this wonderful man who has a smile all over his face that reaches into his eyes sparkling with the light of a thousand stars (did I read that somewhere in a Mills & Boon?). Really. He looks lit up. He smells fresh, clean, yet warm and earthy. I fill my nostrils with his scent as he holds me tight for a moment. He lets me go, pushes me back to arms length, studies me.

'The necklace sits well on your skin. It has found the home it deserves.'

'I don't know how to thank you enough.'

He holds up his hands. 'It comes with no obligation, *glyka*, just a gift from my heart.'

I look at him with tears brimming in my eyes. April would slap me.

He drives me to his place where I find the table set for two. We have a delicious lunch but I can't concentrate. He pours us wine. We laugh as we thread our arms and try to drink from our glasses, nearly spilling the wine. I feel like I'm going to explode with happiness. *June*, I tell myself, *you've come a long way since Beechworth*. I wipe all negative thoughts from my mind, those ones that pick and nag at my self esteem. I'm living in the moment, whatever that might bring.

He takes my hand. Strokes it. Turns it palm up. Kisses it. '*Glyka*, I have something to ask you.'

I stop breathing.

'Will you ... will you ... will you ...'

I wait.

'... come to Greece with me? On a holiday?' He sits back, takes a big gulp of air.

I look at his anxious eyes, feel his trembling hand. Greece? Overseas? Me?

He sees my surprise. I smile in answer.

Somehow he's kissing me.

This is nothing like the slow, measured, educated kisses of Matt. Or the hot, all tongue, brutal kisses of Marty. Or the breathy, wide open, urgent kisses of Rob.

Yannis is controlling a passion that hesitates, waiting for my permission. His lips are gentle as they search my response. Something surges inside me, a longing that comes from past rejections. This is not the awakening Matt gifted me, or the lustful encounters with the twins. Despite the pleasure I enjoyed with them, they never touched my heart, which is where Yannis is right now. I open my mouth and my body dissolves with tingling shivers as this man, this adorable Greek man, kisses me with such passion and – dare I say – love.

We lie back on his bed, exhausted after our lovemaking. Since Katerina told me about Yannis's stick wife, I don't feel quite so self-conscious about my lumps and bumps, though I pull up the sheet to cover myself.

He pulls it back down again. 'No, June. I like to see you. To caress you. To love you.' And then he kisses me again. And again.

The setting sun casts a spotlight on the bed. He looks at me as I lie there sated from this afternoon of lovemaking. 'You are so perfect, *glyka*. You even have aristocratic feet.'

'What?'

'Your second toes are longer than the big toes. In ancient Greece your foot was perfect beauty. I never want you to change.' *Me, of the wobbling body fat? Me, of the ordinary face, multiple chins, big stomach?*

'Stop that,' he commands.

'What?'

He touches my face and kisses me lingeringly. He strokes my eyelids and gently runs his fingers through my hair. He massages my breasts and then down to my stomach which he kisses.

'Here,' he breathes, 'is your heart and your life. You are woman, not skinny girl with nothing to hold onto.' He pauses as he looks at me with concern in his eyes. 'You do not like yourself. You should. You are most beautiful for me. Do not tell the woman I love that you are not worth of that. You are everything for me. Everything.'

I search his eyes for a lie, even a white lie. His eyes fill as he caresses every part of me.

'Yes, June, I do love you.'

That man can read my mind!

'Every part of you, including this silly head,' he smiles, touching my forehead, 'that tells you you are not the most beautiful woman I ever know.'

My eyes leak with emotion. No one has ever told me they love me, other than Charlie and my real mum. No one has ever looked at me with real affection and loved me for who I am. Until now. But, does love, real love, happen that quickly?

Monday 15th May

Yannis has a late shift so he takes me to Frankston Station where I catch an early train to the city. He stands on the platform with me, holding my hand until the train is ready to leave. No hiding or secrets with him. I like that.

I open a Mills & Boon but the words blur as I remember our weekend together. I spend the whole journey to Flinders Street turning over each moment, examining his words, his actions, all the little things he did to make me happy. The way he makes coffee, the way he puts it in front of me like a ceremony, the way he strokes my face as he watches me eat, the way his hand rests on my thigh, the warmth of it reaching into my blood stream sending shivers of longing into every nerve ending. I don't remember anything like this in a Mills & Boon but maybe that's because anything I've read didn't touch me like being with Yannis does. That was fiction. This is fact.

The girl seated beside me scrolls through her emails, sniggering at some, swearing at others. I scroll through my memory bank of feelings. They're good. More than good. They're terrific. I'm scared, though, of falling off this high high pedestal Yannis has lifted me to. I sit up here wondering what the heck happened.

From the first moment I saw him, I was attracted to his dark dark eyes that look like black chocolate, all gooey and warm as they melt into mine. There's something wild and yet tame about him. He's a few inches taller than me so we're a nice fit. He's got a solid, stocky body that's cuddly, warm, and is covered with a good smattering of dark curly hair that I've discovered wraps around my little finger. His skin is olive and smells delicious, especially when we make love. There's not a trace of BO on his clean body so I like to bury my nose into his armpits, into his neck, behind his knees, and close my eyes to capture the memory.

I sense that he's honest. He's SINGLE (!!!!) and doesn't seem to have any baggage that is waiting to tumble out and spoil our new relationship. He loves his family – all of them – and wants me to love them too. He welcomes me openly, as do Katerina & Giorgos, and he wants to be in my life too. He's fascinated about my family mystery and wants that sorted out so that I have a real family of my own as well as his. He hasn't a bad word to say about anyone and, what's more, doesn't swear. (I'll have to warn April when she meets him.)

I exit Flinders Street Station at the same bank of Myki readers where I fell and Yannis helped me up. That's just over four weeks ago and, in that short time, I feel that my life has changed forever having met him. No one notices me in the crowded city streets as we all make our way to work, nor my blushing as I think of the things I've done with the twins and Matt. Sometimes I wonder if I've behaved like a slut, having sex with three men at the same time – well, not at the same time exactly. Over the same period. But, then, I'm single, fancy-free, no strings attached, old enough to know what I'm doing. Well, do I? Did I?

I stop suddenly, two people colliding with me on the footpath traffic, as I think of Yannis. What would he think if he knew?! I clutch my throat in panic as a suited young man shoulders me out of his way. 'Watch where you're going, stupid fuckin' bitch.' I gasp as another nearly spins me around, cursing from her beautifully made-up face.

'Are you okay, love?' a homeless woman stretches her arm out towards me from her pile of belongings and a cardboard sign reading: HARD TIMES | JUST TRYING TO SURVIVE | GRATEFUL FOR ANY KINDNESS.

'Yes, thank you, I ...' and I burst into tears!

She stands up and puts her arms around me. 'Life can be shitty sometimes,' she says patting my back.

'No, actually,' I sob into her shoulder, 'I'm very lucky, very happy.' I splutter a laugh. 'I just thought of what could ruin it.'

She laughs with me. 'I could tell you a few things about ruin.'

I stand back and look at her: probably late 30s, gaunt with a relaxed grace about her, clean despite her situation, lively intelligent eyes. 'I have to go to work, otherwise I'd really like to learn about your circumstances,' I say digging into my bag. I find a $20 note and press it into her hand.

'No,' she says, 'I just wanted to make sure you're okay.'

'Take it. I hope it helps somehow.' There's a glancing moment of connection between us. I have nothing to cry about, unlike her, I realise. 'You've helped me more than you can know.'

Merv sits behind his desk as if he's never been away, glued to his computer screen which displays folders of photos – dozens of folders – that I know I'm going to have to look at. 'Good. Good,' he beams as I settle down beside him. 'You're going to love these.' I turn my head aside as he burps his enthusiasm over a photo of he and Trish poised on bikes in front of a huge castle.

Two coffees later, he sighs and turns away from the screen. 'Trish and I have decided to make up for lost time, go on more holidays, see the world.'

'What about Marj?'

'Well, that's it, isn't it? She's learned she can survive without us, especially since she's got the hots for some old geezer who's probably after her money.'

I'm happy for him. It must be lovely going on holidays with someone you love, sharing so many experiences. 'That reminds me,' I smile, 'I hope you remember April and I are going back to Beechworth on Thursday?'

He nods. 'I couldn't miss it after you put it in red capitals and that huge font in my calendar.'

'Good. I also want to take six weeks off after the footy final for a holiday to Greece.'

His jaw literally hits his chest.

'With my boyfriend.'

April places a casserole on the table that she's warmed up since we arrived at her place after work.

'Here, help yourself, June.' She goes back into the kitchen and brings another dish piled high with mashed potato and broccoli.

'Who else is coming?'

'The king and queen of England.'

'Besides the fact there's no king of England,' I laugh, 'there's enough to feed an army.'

'Well, get stuck into it before they arrive,' she chortles.

Anything April cooks is delicious and she seems to produce it with no effort. I've had a couple of goes, borrowing cook books from the library, but I'm not all that good. Terrible, in fact. But who needs to cook when you're out nearly every night eating at G & K's? And here at April's? And less-often-than-before takeaway? I sit up straighter, sucking in my stomach, bearing in mind how I look with my spare tyre poking out, then I remember I'm at April's so who cares? I help myself to a good-sized serving.

April nods. 'Okay, so what are we going to do if Charlie's DNA test results don't arrive in time?'

I chew a big mouthful, then wash it down with some merlot. 'It'll be disappointing, so we'll just have to go with it – the family reunion ...'

April snorts.

'... without the missing piece.'

'But that's the whole fuckin' ... shittin' ... bloody point of the whole thing,' she says ignoring my frown and plopping another big spoonful of mashed potato onto her plate, 'so aren't we going with an empty gun?'

'Yes and no. At least we'll have some bullets.'

She looks up from her plate. 'Aren't you going to call them tomorrow?

'Of course. They promised they'd send it by tomorrow anyway. I told them we're going to Beechworth on Thursday. Fingers crossed.'

Tuesday 16th May

I'm waiting for BBB to email me the sales figures. Waiting. Waiting. I told him it was today or die. I decide that a visit to the toilet would be a useful enterprise in the meantime. April's just leaving the bathroom as I open the door. Her eyebrow goes up. I shake my head and she slides through the doorway with what I'm sure was an F word. I'm getting a bit touchy myself.

'June, come and have a look at this,' Merv calls from his open door as I try to glide past. 'I found the fancy dress night photos!'

Ages later I feel my eyes glazing and my brain becoming numb as Merv opens yet another folder, this time photos of the Captain's table dinner.

'What about the figures, Merv?' I manage to slur from the side of my mouth.

'Yes, yes, Bob'll have them.'

I settle back into a coma as photo after photo flicks across the screen, Merv's running commentary fading into the background. My eyelids weigh a kilo each. My thumb forces one open as my elbow on his desk takes the weight of my arm. I'm shocked out of my stupor as a vibration in my pocket tells me I've received an email. I look down at my mobile. It's from the DNA laboratory!

'Sorry, Merv,' I say. 'Duty calls.' And I'm out of there, practically running to the kitchen. April runs after me.

'It's the lab?'

I nod as I open the email. It takes me a split second to read what I need to know. I look up at her with happy tears in my eyes. I hand her my mobile.

'Charlie!'

Thursday 18th May

Charlie uncurls from his seat as we arrive in the hotel lounge, a huge smile lighting up his eyes. He opens his arms wide. I rush into them, tears pouring down my face.

'Hello Dad,' I blurt.

April pushes a handful of tissues under my nose. 'I came prepared this time.'

Charlie chuckles as he opens an arm to invite her into a group hug. 'Gidday Girlie. Long time no see.'

We tuck into brunch, all of us as famished as hunger strikers on their first meal.

Charlie – Dad – cocks his head to one side as he looks at me. 'Something's different. You look different.'

April sniggers, 'She's in love!'

I dig her in the ribs with my elbow.

Dad's eyebrows shoot up.

'With Zorba the Greek,' she adds.

Now Dad's mouth drops open.

'And she's drinking ouzo and going to Greece.'

He recovers with a hearty chuckle. 'Well, things have changed,' he says.

Although it's a couple of months since we saw him, and we talk on the phone regularly, it feels like only yesterday we stayed in the same hotel with him. I feast my eyes on my dad, my flesh and blood. I look for similarities between us. Apart from the fact that we both have two eyes, two ears, a nose and mouth, there's not much I can detect.

'It's your noses,' April comments, reading my mind. Both our minds, in fact, as I catch Dad searching my face too.

'Same hair,' Dad says.

'You're white and she's brown,' April laughs.

'Well, it's hair,' he says hopefully.

We plan our strategy for tomorrow when we visit Brenda and the two brats. I ring Wayne to set it up. 'Tomorrow at lunchtime, your mother's place,' I tell him. It's fitting referring to Brenda as if a stranger. I feel nothing for her other than disdain.

Although it's a bit cool today, we decide to go back to the asylum on the hill. I love walking through the Mayday Hills gardens. The tallest tree, a Douglas Fir, is 50 metres high towering over the bunya pines and dogwoods. I wonder what the view must be from the top of the Douglas Fir. I want to hug it. I want to hug everything and everyone because I'm so happy. I have a father in my life, I have a mother, I have half-siblings, I have my friend April and I have my Yannis. What more could I want?

Friday 19th May

We arrive outside Brenda's house at midday, Dad's truck ticking down as the motor comes to rest. I look at the house, a multitude of memories tumbling across my mind, but they don't bother me anymore. That little girl, that unloved and uncared-for little girl doesn't exist anymore. It's the past and it's gone. Pft!

The BMW and Mercedes are on the grass. My so-called siblings are in there with my so-called mother. I'm really looking forward to this and, then, the best thing about it is that I'll never have to see them again. Ever.

We make our way around the back. Barry the Beagle begins to bark and then catches my scent. He's all over me in a flash and then shares his joy with Dad and April. Brenda's on a garden chair with a drink in her hand. Wayne and Sandra are flanking her, likewise with drinks.

'Say what you've got to say,' Brenda spits, 'and then get the hell out of here.'

I look at the fence. 'You might prefer to hear it in private. You don't want it in the papers yet.'

You know the old saying: *If looks could kill...* I'd be blitzed, fried, shredded in an instant.

We three stand back in a line waiting for them to go inside. Sandra flounces past us, Brenda avoids eye contact looking straight ahead, Wayne follows. His look is half-enquiring, half-anxious, as he glances at me. They settle in the lounge room. We remain standing. They refill their glasses without offering us anything, not that we mind.

I pull out photocopies of the DNA results. 'Interesting reading, these,' I begin, passing them out.

'Get on with it.' Sandra glares at me.

'Actually,' I smile at each in turn, 'you're all a mixed bag. But I'm sure you know that already, Brenda.'

She's busy practising the death stare.

'Hmmmm? Cat got your tongue?'

'What's in the results, June?' Wayne looks really puzzled.

'Well, it so happens that you ... Sandra ... and I ... all ... have ... different ... fathers.'

'What the fu...?

'So, dearest Sandra, I'm not related to you at all, thank goodness.'

'Or you, Wayne,' who looks down at the results. 'And we already knew you weren't my mother, Brenda, so that's no loss.'

She's gone from pink to red to purple in the face. I think that there's going to be an awful mess if her head explodes.

'Lies!' she screams. 'It's bloody fucking lies!'

'Really?' I ask, sarcasm dripping most effectively from my mouth. It's a new experience.

Sandra's gone white and is looking from Brenda to Wayne and back again. Wayne looks at his mother with horror on his face.

'Mum?'

Brenda shakes her head.

'Mum?' he asks again, then takes a shaking deep breath. 'Who the hell is my father, then?'

'And mine!' Sandra screeches.

'Well, I know who mine is,' I say with satisfaction.

And with that we make our exit before they ask who. I'd like to leave them wondering. I give Barry the Beagle a parting pat on the head. 'Sorry, Barry, I'll have to leave you with that lot. Good luck.'

'Oh, that felt so good!' I take another sip of my wine as we three go over it.

'The look on their faces was priceless,' April grins.

'It was worth the drive, not even counting how good it is to see you both again,' Dad assures us, 'but Brenda's been a thorn in my side, and Kaye's and your mother's,' he nods at me, 'for many many years. Serves her bloody right.'

'Justice prevails!' April hoots. 'Drink anyone?'

Saturday 20th May

It's hard to say goodbye to my (new) father again. 'Promise you'll come down and stay with me in Melbourne? Soon.'

Charlie – Dad – looks at me with tears in his eyes. 'You think I'll let you go now? Of course I will.'

'Hey, big boy,' April grins, 'don't forget to bring some of your killer tomato sauce down with you.'

His laugh rumbles from his chest as he takes us both in a big bear hug. 'How many bottles do you want?' And then he steps back as we board the bus.

'As many as you've got,' April shouts back at him as the bus motor starts up. 'Get cooking!'

He waves as we pull away from the kerb, looking smaller as we look back. We both sigh as we settle back in our seats.

'That was bloody awesome', April smiles. 'Revenge is sweet, aye Juneeee?'

Yes indeed.

Sunday 21ˢᵗ May

'You're home safe!' Mum practically sings into the phone.

How good is that? A mother who cares. 'Yes, it's a pity we couldn't stay longer with Charlie – Dad – but April and I have to get back to work tomorrow.'

'How was he? Charlie. I mean, how did he take the news about being your father?'

'Really good. Actually, he's quite chuffed.'

She hesitates. 'Do you think ...?'

'That he'll talk to you again?'

'Well, yes.'

I can hear the shame, still, in her voice. 'Hey, you were all drunk.'

'But he and Kaye ...'

'Were an item? Of course. He'll probably never get over that sense of having betrayed her, but I think he'll learn to live with it. Not that we talked about it the other day but I think he's feeling really happy that he has some offspring, despite it just being someone like me ...'

'June! Don't say that. Don't be so negative about yourself,' she scolds. 'He's lucky to have you.'

'Oh, Mum, I feel so humble.' I begin to cry. 'I have you finally and now I have a father. It's so ... so ... incredible. It's almost like a normal family.'

'My poor, poor girl. You've had a rotten trot all your life and now you've been able to get your own back on the Beechworth mob and hopefully can settle down in this lovely relationship you're telling me about with your wonderful Greek man.' She starts to cry too. I really do take after my mother. 'Now tell me all about him.'

Yannis takes me to his place before we go to G & K's for dinner. He shows me another colourful door painted by one of his nephews. This one is in his bathroom, still smelling fresh from a loving paintbrush. It takes me back to Aunty Kaye's studio where her dog stared at me from a canvas, as this turtle stares at me from its vivid green background. No matter where I stand, the eyes follow me.

'Who is this?' I ask Yannis. 'I love it!'

'Ah, Theo,' Yannis smiles hugely, 'he's the artist in the family. Only 11 and he's tops in his class.' He points at another door. 'And this is his little sister. You can see she's good too!'

He turns to me then. 'I missed you at your Beechworth thing.' His eyes wash me with love. 'I work, I sleep, I eat, I see my family, but something very important was missing.' He kisses the tip of my nose, nuzzles my earlobes, my neck, and I feel heat rising, a trembling. My legs feel weak. He holds me so tight I feel the breath squeezed out of me. 'I never want to be apart from you again, my dear June.' He pushes me away to scan my face, every square millimetre of it. 'I love you, *glyka*. I love you so much it hurts me here,' he thumps his chest, 'if I can't see you, can't hear you, can't feel you.'

I don't know what to say. A Mills & Boon heroine would know. They always seem so much more confident than I am. How do I reply to this man who thinks he loves me? How can he?

'Come,' he says suddenly, taking a few deep breaths. 'Not here. Come out of the bathroom.' He leads me back into the lounge room and sits me on the couch. His back to me, he opens a drawer and takes something out of it. He turns and kneels in front of me as he opens a small box in his palm. There's a ring in it that blinds me, its gem caught in sunlight streaming through the window. This is what happens in Mills & Boon. I know what it means. He's going to ask me to marry him! My breathing stops as my heart pounds and my brain screams. This can't be happening!!!

'*Glyka*,' he whispers, 'I love you. You know that.' He clears his throat nervously. 'I am asking you to do me the honour, the great honour, to marry me.'

I look from Yannis to the ring and back. Should I take it? Put it on my finger? What if I say yes and then he changes his mind? He can't be in his right mind to ask someone like me. He hardly knows me. He might think I'm better, much better, than I am. How can I say yes and then he shows disappointment in his eyes? Tells himself off for asking me? Wishes he hadn't? What then?

I look back at the ring displayed in its velvet-lined box, diamonds surrounding a large blue stone that looks like the ocean, deep and clear and yet mysterious. I hesitate, my hand wavering, as I scan my memory for a Mills & Boon response. Take it, my memory yells at me. Take it and rejoice!

I take it. It slips so perfectly over my left ring finger and settles there as if it was made for just that finger, just that hand, just that woman. Me.

I look up at him. 'Yes,' I breathe. 'Yes!' as he breaks into the widest smile, tears pouring down his face, as mine do too. We kiss salty, wet kisses, sealing our promise to each other. How about that, Mills & Boon?

It's hard to wipe the smiles off our mouths as Katerina welcomes us. She searches our faces then breaks into a grin as she picks up my left hand. 'Ah,' she exclaims. 'It is a yes!'

'Yes,' we say in unison. 'Yes!'

'Giorgos!' she calls. 'Come! Come!' She envelopes me in a huge hug. 'It is a yes!'

George rushes from the kitchen to embrace his brother and me. And the children come. And the diners at the restaurant are invited to rejoice with us. It's the biggest, noisiest, happiest, wonderful party I've ever been to. Well, I haven't been to many, but they can't be like this. They don't happen very often in a Mills & Boon, so I'm doing very well.

Monday 22ⁿᵈ May

I can't stop looking at it. MY ENGAGEMENT RING! How it sparkles on my finger! My heart swells so much that my bra feels tight. I'm bursting with excitement and wish I could just stand up and shout: I'm loved! Yes, loved! And by that wonderful man who's taking you to work safely. That man who sits in his tight little cabin, watching ahead, making sure he doesn't hit anyone or have an accident, run the train off the rails. No – he's sitting in his smart uniform, a perfect representative of our public transport system, looking out for you, helping people get to work on time, go to the pictures, do some shopping, meet some friends, go to a concert, the theatre, a restaurant, the footy, go home again safely. There he is where we can't see or hear him, unless he makes an announcement about our journey, that dark and sexy voice dripping from the loudspeakers, telling us what we need to know. And that man, dear fellow passengers, is MINE!

They look at my ring, the females with envy in their eyes. I scan their fingers to see if any of them have a ring that compares. No. Not one of them. Poor things. I almost feel smug. Well, let's face it, I *do* feel smug.

I hug myself as if cold but I'm holding in bubbles of excitement that are running around in my chest, my arteries, my arms, my legs, my eyes, even, that I reckon sparkle like my ring does. I've read I don't know how many Mills & Boon books in my lifetime, but I've never read about *this* feeling. Well, maybe I have but I never *felt* it amongst all those words. Never felt the rush of love and lust mixed with my blood and oxygen, running all over my body, threatening to make me laugh my head off with happiness. I feel quite mad with it.

I rise on the escalators, my left hand resting on the black rubber belt that climbs with me, my ring out there for all to see. Oh, how they stare! I feel giddy with the weight of it on the hand that clutches my bag as I descend the steps under the clocks of Flinders Street Station. I wait for the pedestrian lights and the little green walking man to tell me I can walk with my ring across Flinders Street, up Swanston Street and then into my building where I know there will be oohs and aahs. I marvel at how the sun finds my ring and projects it out to humankind to see what I have. What a handsome, sexy, loving man has given me.

April's relieving at reception so she sees it first, which is only fair. 'What the ...'

I have my left hand sweeping in an arc as Amy, just returning to her desk, spots it. She grabs my hand, almost wrenching it off my wrist, with the loudest screech imaginable.

'June!' she screams. 'June!' She looks from the ring to my face to the ring to my face and again. 'June!'

Mel and BBB aren't far behind.

'What's going on?' BBB demands, thrusting his chest forward prepared for battle. He misses it, of course.

Mel's almost as fast as Amy, spotting it on my hand that Amy hasn't released from her vice-like grip yet. 'June?' Her screech is a few less decibels than Amy's, though equally dramatic.

April's still sitting behind the desk with her mouth dropped open and her eyes wide. Speechless.

A loud burp is followed by Merv's ample belly rounding the partitions. 'Is this a terrorist attack?'

The cork erupts from the neck of a bottle of bubbly, held securely between Mel's legs (making her short skirt even shorter, not missed by BBB – ugh!), hits the ceiling and bounces neatly off Merv's belly to roll under the fridge.

'Never mind; we'll get it later,' Merv says, holding out his glass.

There's a momentary silence as we all sip the sparkling yellow wine, the bubbles tickling our nostrils. Then everyone talks at once again.

'You dark horse.' BBB pretends to be growling.

'Why didn't you ...?' Amy splutters, coughing on the bubbles.

'... tell us you had a boyfriend?' Mel finishes for her.

'Is this who you're going to Greece with?' Merv chuckles.

April stands back clutching her untouched glass. 'I'm happy for you,' she says quietly.

I raise an eyebrow.

'Really,' she nods.

Merv holds his glass high. 'Congratulations, I say,' he declares.

The others join in.

'Congratulations!'

'Happy days!'

'Terrific news!'

'Who'd have thought?'

April insists on cooking dinner for me. We're at her place as she opens a bottle of French champagne. She handles the bottle better than Mel, pushing the cork out with her thumbs. The cork exits with a muted thwack. She wraps a white tea towel around her arm to mimic a waiter. 'Champagne for the celebration, mademoiselle?'

I give what I think a stately nod.

'And the monsieur?'

'He's not able to attend this sumptuous spread,' I nod to the laden table, 'but sends his apologies.'

'Very well, mademoiselle.' She pours for the two of us.

We raise our glasses, touch them gently, take a sip.

'And where the bloody hell is he?' she demands.

'Nightshift.'

'Oh, that's okay then.'

And so we have a wonderful time, my friend and I. We talk about the past, the present and the glorious future. The wedding, the honeymoon. I ask her to be my bridesmaid – or is it maid of honour at my age? I don't care; I just want April to be a big part of it.

'You can choose any colour you want, except black,' I tell her, 'and it has to be something other than jeans.'

'Spoiled sport.' She pulls a face. 'You know I hate wearing skirts or dresses.' She looks at me critically. 'What're you going to wear?'

I go to my handbag and pull out a bride's magazine.

'Jesus, you've got it bad!'

'I'm not going to wear white.'

'Thank Christ for that. What about a veil?'

'I'm thinking of a long train.'

'Six carriages?' she laughs.

'I'm going to surprise Yannis tomorrow morning,' I tell April. 'I'm going to leave early and get on his train. Maybe he'll let me into his driver's cabin and ride to the city with him.'

'That wouldn't be allowed, would it?'

'Probably not, but I just want to tell him I love him and give him a kiss. He'll love that.'

She looks at me doubtfully. 'Be careful. You don't want him to lose his job. Imagine ... you might have to work for the rest of your life keeping him instead of the other way around.'

I look at her thoughtfully. 'You know what? I wouldn't mind at all.'

Epilogue – Tuesday 23rd May

'Where's June?' Merv asked, rounding April's partition.

'I don't know,' she frowned, checking the time on her computer. 'She should be here by now.'

'She's never late, so where the hell is she? Find out, will you, April?'

'She was at my place last night for dinner. She went home around ten.'

'Maybe still celebrating?' Merv grinned.

'Have you seen June?' Amy buzzed April. 'She's not picking up her calls.'

'She's not in yet.'

'What? She's never late!'

'So Merv said,' April frowned again.

'I thought June and I had a meeting this morning,' BBB pointed at his watch. 'She's ten minutes late already.'

April rolled her eyes, holding her breath as she leaned away from him. 'She just might be in the bathroom, Bob. Perhaps you should have a look there.'

'Oh, funny.'

'Has June taken the day off?' Mel asked.

'FIG JAM,' April responds.

'What are you talking about?'

'Fuck I'm good, just ask me,' April scowled. 'I don't fucking know. Why does everyone think I know what June's up to?'

'I was just asking,' Mel pouted.

Merv called April into his office. 'Well?'

April shook her head. 'She's not picking up.'

'Try again.'

'I've tried a hundred times, Merv. She's just not answering her phone. It's going to her voicemail.'

'I'm worried.'

'Me too.'

They stared at each other.

Merv sat back in his chair rubbing his stomach. 'It's not like her. She's like the sun and moon; always turns up when she's supposed to.'

'Yep.'

'Is she a missing person now?'

April hesitated. 'Probably not, at least not yet.'

'What about her fiancée?'

'I've never met or heard about Yannis before yesterday,' April said, not without some hurt in her voice, 'much less have his phone number.'

'Dark horse, eh?'

'You can say that again.'

'Her new family?'

'I've got her dad and mum's numbers. I could try them but, at this stage, I'm not sure I want to worry them. They're too far away. Can't do anything.'

'Why don't you jump in a taxi and go to her place? See if she's sleeping it off.'

April pushed June's doorbell again, hearing it through the door. She banged on it for good measure, making enough noise to wake every one of June's neighbours. When nothing happened, she turned to the next flat and knocked.

'April! It's you making all that ruckus!'

'Oh, Pat,' April sagged against the wall. 'June didn't turn up for work this morning and we're worried about her. There's no answer,' she pointed at June's door.

'What? Hang on ...' she said, turning back into her flat. 'Here's her spare key. I don't think she'll mind.' They entered June's flat, each inspecting different rooms.

'At least she hasn't had a heart attack or stroke and lying on the floor dead,' April commented.

'Well, all looks normal here,' Pat said. 'Nothing out of place. The two Ms are fed,' she nodded at the fishbowl.

'Her shower's still wet,' April called out. 'No handbag. I think she left for work this morning.'

'Hey boss,' April shouted into her mobile as her taxi forced its way into the left lane, trying to dodge a truck that had put itself in the way of a tram that was loudly pronouncing its indignity.

'What'd you say, April? I can't hear you.'

'June's not at home.'

'June's got a comb?'

'No! She's not at home!'

'Oh, she's at home?'

'No! Jesus, boss, SHE'S NOT AT HOME!'

'Christ, you nearly split my eardrums, April,' Merv complained as the traffic noise abated.

April rolled her eyes as she looked out at the traffic. Bumper-to-bumper, and it wasn't even peak hour. *Where is she?* June said last thing that she was going to surprise Yannis. Give him a kiss or something. Maybe they were having it off in his driver's cabin and they forgot about everything and the train crashed into Flinders Street Station? Just like in that film ... what was it ... *Runaway Train?* Or, maybe they arrived at Flinders Street and they went to have coffee? Or, what if they decided to elope right there and then?! No – not without me. I'm her fucking bridesmaid. And she needs me to choose her dress because she has no fucking idea. Her flowers. Her honeymoon underwear, for Christ's sake. And don't forget the shoes.

April's mobile came to life.

'Yes, boss?'

'How far away are you?'

She looked up as they passed the Shrine. 'Minutes.'

'Good. I want you to call the police when you get here. Something's wrong.'

'You reckon?'

The lift doors opened to reveal Amy in tears. 'Oh, April, have you heard anything? Seen June?'

'Look,' April pushed a box of tissues towards her, 'no need to panic at this stage. She's probably at a bride's shop right now choosing her dress.'

'Oh?' Amy looked up hopefully, dabbing carefully at her eye makeup. 'You think so?'

'Sure.'

April pushed past reception to find Mel and BBB hot on her heels. 'Any news?' To which she shook her head and made for Merv's office. He stood up as she entered. 'Tell me why I'm so worried.'

'Because June is never late,' April replied, holding her mobile as she sat in front of him. 'Because June is reliable. June is predictable. June is ... June.' She sucked air between her teeth, jiggling her mobile on her knees. Her heart raced. 'If it was anyone else, I'd not give it another thought. Life gets in the way. But not June's life, though it's taken a big turn I'm the first to admit. But June? June? Yep, I'm worried.'

'Was she unhappy when she was at your place last night?'

'Not at all. She was full of her plans, how she feels about the boyfriend – the fiancée – and, actually, she told me she wanted to surprise him this morning by waiting on the platform for him.'

'Oh?'

'She was hoping he'd get her in his driver's cabin with him and they could make out on the way to the city.'

'*What?*' Merv bounced off the back of his chair and desk and chair and desk, forcing a full-sized burp from his gut.

'Nah,' April grinned. 'Just a love-struck-type of surprise. I dunno ...'

Merv sat in silence absorbing this side of June's character that he had no idea of. 'You think she's in love with him?'

'That's usually what happens when a bloke slaps a big-arsed ring on a girl's finger.'

'I just can't picture it,' he said, shaking his head.

'You said it,' April agreed.

'Big boy?'

'Hello girlie! You hanging out for my tomato sauce?'

'Charlie,' April said quietly, 'June's missing.'

'What do you mean?'

'She didn't turn up for work today. I can't find her.'

'I'm coming.' And he hung up.

'Hello, April, what a lovely surprise!'

'Helen, June's missing.'

'Missing from what?'

'Missing from work. Missing since last night.'

'I'm coming.' She hung up too.

April and Merv slowly descended the steps of the police station. They both felt drained after making their statements.

'What now?' Merv muttered. 'What the bloody hell can we do now?'

April dug her phone out of her bag. 'I'll try again.' It rang until June's voicemail took over. 'June, for Christ's sake, call me! Call me!'

Standing on the footpath, turning left and right, changing feet, watching police enter and leave the building, April came to a decision. 'I'm going back to her flat. See if I missed anything. I might find Yannis's contact details.'

'I'm coming with you.'

Pat let them into June's flat with a worried look. 'I have a bad feeling about this, April. She wouldn't up and leave without telling me ... because of the two Ms. She'd ask me to look after them.' At Merv's quizzical look, she indicated the fishbowl. 'Merv and Melba.'

Merv looked confused. 'What did you say?'

'Oh, she's had Merv for a few years now. Melba's the relative newcomer.'

'But ...'

April's mobile buzzed. She spoke for a short time and then turned to Merv. 'Helen and Charlie have got flights down early tomorrow.'

Pat left them to it to continue with her cooking. Merv looked around the flat. 'You know, I've not once been here since she started working for us. It'd have to be over 42 years. The same address all those years. It's like stepping back in a time warp.'

'Yeah, I know,' April said. 'I've just got used to it.' She looked at the walls and ceiling with fresh eyes. 'I'm surprised this block hasn't been pulled down and developed.'

Merv stood by a window overlooking the street. 'Nothing changes with June, not her clothes ...' he grinned, '... her lunches, her desk – I had to fight her to replace it a few years back when it was threatening to collapse on her. Worried about workers comp, I was. No holidays ... except for the most recent times with you ... and this.' He turned in a circle, taking in the furniture, the neat, clean, drab emptiness. 'She doesn't have any friends ...'

'Hey!'

'Sorry, except for you.' He looked at her searchingly. 'You've been good for her, I reckon. The new clothes, the war paint, the hair style, the jewellery, even taking a few days off to go up to Beechworth and then the family thing. It'd have been a bugger, her doing all that without you helping her.'

Merv sat balancing a beer on his belly. A tear rolled down his face. 'I can't get over the coppers' attitude.' "She's not been missing for 24 hours yet," he mimicked. 'You'd think they'd have listened to us. We *know* June; let's face it, she's worked for me the past umpteen hundred years. She was a kid when she started. Not much younger than me, really. Bloody good worker. Honest, too. You could trust her with your life, as well as your business.' He took a long swig of his beer, wiped his mouth with a sleeve. 'This is just not bloody June,' he muttered. 'Not June at all. She wouldn't just piss off like that. She'd have called. Emailed. Something.' He blinked away more tears. 'I can feel it in my gut. Something's not right.'

'It's the fiancée thing I don't get,' April sniffed. 'Just out of the blue. She always tells me everything, and I mean *everything*.'

'Apparently not.'

'Huh! But how do you disguise a budding romance and then *that* thing ... the huge rock on her finger. That doesn't come from nowhere. I can sort-of understand a train driver; I mean she sees them for a nanosecond every weekday. But where do you hide a Greek train driver in your life, much less his Greek family and their Greek restaurant? Why wasn't I invited? I *love* Greek food!'

'A pity there was no mention of him in her flat. A phone number would've been good.'

'Well, there's that poster of Athens,' April offered.

A waiter hovered. 'More drinks?'

'I'm going for another beer,' April murmured.

'Well, bugger it, I may as well too,' Merv said, smothering a burp. 'You hungry?'

April shook her head. 'You?'

'Nope.'

April's mobile suddenly jumped into life. 'Mel?' Merv watched as she listened. 'What? What?' She quickly looked around the walls of the lounge, her eyes finding a TV. 'I'll call you back.' She dropped her mobile and darted over closer to the TV. 'Quick! Quick!' she called Merv.

They were in time to hear a TV journalist summarising an item on the day's news. '*...and, as you can see behind me, the Frankston line is still closed, since early this morning, in fact, after a woman was tragically sucked under a city-bound train as she fell from the platform at Mentone Station. It appears she was attempting to talk with the driver who has been taken by ambulance to the Alfred Hospital, uninjured, but in shock. The woman, believed to be in her 60s, died at the scene.*'

Wednesday 24th May

Charlie looked at the policewoman blankly, his skull tight, tense. He felt he might topple over, right in front of Helen and April, the officer and the morgue person. 'What?'

'Can you, Charles Dixon ...'

'Yes. Yes,' he recovered. 'Yes, this is my daughter, June Cooper.' He looked down at her face, remarkably spared by the train's wheels, surprisingly youthful, her hair and forehead cocooned inside a large blood-stained bandage. 'This is my daughter, my own daughter, and I only just got to know her.' He choked as tears made their way down his weathered face. A glass of water appeared within reach. He took it gratefully.

Helen's sobs intruded into his befuddled mind. How could June be placed on this cold slab, a sheet draped over her body that didn't quite look right? How could she not be breathing? Not moving? He felt someone lean into him and turned to support Helen whose legs buckled. Someone pushed a chair under her and he found himself patting the top of her head. His leg felt wet where she cried into his trousers.

'I can also identify her,' he heard April. 'June Cooper has been ... has been ... has been my close friend for approximately three years.' She took a shuddering breath. 'I'm April Snowden, her best friend.'

She put her arm around Charlie, silent tears mingling with her runny nose. She let go of him reluctantly to blow her nose, then leaned over to kiss June softly on the cheek. 'No,' she whispered to June's still face, 'I'm not going soft on you or else Merv would never let me hear the end of it.' She closed her eyes as tears seeped from between her lids. 'I miss you already. Oh, Juneee, why? Why? How am I going to live without you?' Her head dropped onto June's chest which wasn't there anymore. She recoiled in horror. 'Jesus, June! What have you done?!'

'You can come and stay at my place, if you like, Helen, or here,' April indicated June's bedroom. The three of them looked at each other. No one wanted to leave.

'Okay,' April decided. 'You and I sleep in June's bed,' she indicated to Helen, 'and you can sleep on the couch.'

Charlie nodded. 'Fine by me.'

'What do we do now?' Helen took another handful of tissues from April. 'Shouldn't we do *something*? Try and find her fiancée maybe?'

'I reckon so,' Charlie agreed. 'What if he doesn't know?'

'What if he was the driver?'

They looked at April in shock.

'You mean ...?' Helen's face said it all.

'If he was the one who ran her over.' Charlie added slowly.

They picked over the segments of pizza without enthusiasm.

'Do goldfish like pizza?' Charlie asked.

'I don't think so, big boy.'

Helen cleaned up the remains of their dinner to return to June's couch facing her TV.

'Here it is,' April said, turning up the volume.

Today's tragic incident at Mentone Station, where June Cooper lost her life, has local residents wondering whether this was, indeed, another act of suicide or just an unfortunate accident. Metro officials are investigating whether ...

A photo of a middle-aged Greek man covered the screen and then panned to a video clip of the same man leaving the Alfred Hospital.

'That's him,' April confirmed, 'going by June's description.'

'We have to talk with him,' Helen sniffed behind a tissue. 'Find out what happened.'

'... but can you ask him to call us? We need to speak with him to understand the circumstances ...Yes. Yes. I understand that ... privacy ... Yes, I know ... Look, our hearts are breaking here. She was a daughter, a friend.' April's voice cracked. 'Well, can we have her handbag? Her phone? ... My name's April Snowden. I was at the morgue earlier with her parents to help identify her ... her body. Yes, my mobile number is ...'

April turned to the others. 'We wait.'

They sat there, desperately flicking through any channels showing the news, waiting for another glimpse of the driver. April held out a stubby in each hand. Charlie took one.

'Wine?' she asked Helen who looked up at her, eyes brimming with tears. 'That's something June had in common with you,' she said wryly, 'crying all the time.'

'I know! I know! I just can't help it.'

Charlie put his arm around her shoulders as April sat down beside her. 'Hey, it's not a crime.' April looked up at Charlie. 'You remember how much June cried before she met Helen? And then after? She cost me a fortune in tissues.' She suddenly pointed at the TV. 'There he is!'

'Ah, it's the same news ...' Charlie stopped.

'*... and she leaned over from the edge of the platform, holding her hand up at me. There was a flash from a ring, I think, on her finger. It was blinding.*' The driver shrugged with an anguished face. '*Not that it would have made any difference. It was too late too quickly.*'

Thursday 25th May

They spent more time staring at the ceiling than sleeping. Helen got up to make a cup of tea and the others joined her.

'What time is it?' Charlie asked squinting at the kitchen clock.

'Two thirty,' April yawned.

An hour later they got up again.

'And the time now is?'

'Three forty.'

'And now?'

'Four fifty-five.'

'And this time?'

'Don't ask.'

'Do you think we're disturbing the fish?'

'Helen, I think they'd rather join the vigil than sticking their heads under their gills and pretend nothing's happened.'

'April, you're priceless.'

'Is that a compliment?'

April looked at her mobile. 'Unknown number.'

Charlie placed his cup carefully in its saucer. Helen turned from gazing out of the window.

'Hello?'

She made the thumbs up signal.

'Yes, thanks for calling me. Yes, I'm June's friend. Yes, her parents are here with me. Yes, I know. It's awkward on the phone. Can we meet for a coffee?'

They sat at a table overlooking Mordialloc Creek's exit into the bay. Norfolk Island pines and boat masts rose over white and coloured boats bobbing and glugging in orderly lines, like so many students at rollcall. Reflections of the bright blue sky on the calm water glittered and dazzled, confusing the eyes. The peaceful scene was lost, however, on the sombre trio as they gazed into their cappuccinos.

'Excuse me?'

They looked up to see Yannis, who they recognised from the TV news.

Charlie stood. 'Please, sit, sit. Can I get you a coffee, tea or something else?'

Three pairs of eyes studied the man who'd asked for June's hand in marriage. They liked him instantly. His honesty, warmth, vulnerability, shone through. No wonder, they thought, that she'd loved him.

'I'm so sorry ...' he began. 'I ... don't know what to say.' His eyes were bright with unshed tears.

Helen, likewise tearful, leaned across to take his hands in hers. 'We don't either, Mr ...'

'Call me Nik, please.'

'Nik,' she said, her voice breaking, 'we don't want to make this difficult for you. We understand – we think – what you must be going through too. You're grieving as we are.'

'Yes,' he replied haltingly. 'I have never had someone die from my train.'

She stopped to search his eyes. 'Yes, but ...'

'For the family it must be terrible. Sad.'

Charlie cleared his throat. 'For you, too, mate. Jesus, you'd only been engaged five minutes.'

Yannis sat back in his chair in surprise. 'Engaged?' He looked from face to face. 'To who?'

'June, our June, of course,' Helen sighed.

'Sorry? You are saying I am engaged to your June?'

There was an uncomfortable silence. Almost as one, they all picked up their cups and sipped, each placing the cup back in its saucer carefully.

'I don't understand,' he said.

'June told us that you were engaged. You were going to get married soon, in fact, and go to Greece for your honeymoon. June asked me to be her bridesmaid. We were to buy her dress on Friday night after work.'

'You are playing a joke on me?'

'Hey, steady on, mate. Why would we joke about that? It's not a time for joking.' Charlie's voice grated to a halt.

'I still don't understand,' Yannis frowned. 'How could I be engaged to your June?'

'The ring!' April almost shouted. 'What the fuck was that about?'

'April!' Helen frowned, just like June.

'Sorry, the bloody ring,' April acquiesced, 'the one she turned up with last Monday at work. Her engagement ring that you gave her.'

Yannis shook his head as if to clear it. 'April, I have not given your June this ring. April, I have never met June before in my entire life.'

The need to piece together June's life, and the mystery of the engagement with Yannis, spurred the trio to search June's flat. Charlie was allotted the kitchen/family room area. April and Helen took one half of June's bedroom each.

'There's a thick notebook here,' Helen said, holding up a book from the bedside table drawer. 'It looks like ...' she mused, scanning through it, '...a diary.'

'Now, that could be handy.' April rounded the bed to look over Helen's shoulder. 'She never told me she kept one.'

As Helen leafed through it, a piece of paper fell out. She opened it to reveal a receipt from a jewellers in Collins Street, the details of which were:

1 x Sapphire Engagement Ring 4.20tw
Diamond/Sapphire Halo
18k gold Dinner Ring
$2290.00

'That's the ring!' April exclaimed.

'So why's she's got the receipt and not him?' Helen frowned as she read it. 'Surely June wouldn't have paid for it herself?'

'That's totally, f ... weird.'

Charlie walked into the bedroom with a large pile of papers clamped with a bulldog clip. 'There are some receipts here too.' He held them out. 'From a dance studio. Train and bus tickets to Beechworth and back. Pizza shop receipts. Books. Myers. A bar in the city. Phone bills. Op shop receipts for books and DVDs. Invoices and receipts from Little Malcolm. A receipt for Melba, assuming she's the goldfish. Tickets to the footy.'

'Look what I found,' April said from inside June's wardrobe. 'A humungous pile of Mills & Boon books! Probably every one that was ever printed!'

'Hang on,' Helen said. 'Did you say Little Malcolm?'

Charlie looked down at the bundle he held. 'Yep, a couple of them.'

'Shouldn't we tell him about June? That she ... died?' And then she dissolved into tears again. 'Sorry. I just ...'

April thrust a tissue box under her nose. 'Go nuts.' She grabbed a couple for herself to blow her own nose.

'Did Little Malcolm represent June?'

'Well, he was sorting out the problems with Kaye's estate and so on,' Charlie explained. 'April and I went with June.'

'Did June make a will?' Helen asked.

April and Charlie looked at her.

'I don't know,' April shook her head. 'Did she have one?'

Charlie shrugged. 'It didn't come up.' Memories of those wonderful days getting to know his daughter and April flooded his mind. His breath shuddered out of his chest as he fought for composure.

'Let it out,' Helen said, patting his arm. 'It helps.'

'She should know,' April nodded.

Helen looked up from June's diary. Her eyes were tired and dry from the day's tears and scanning June's spidery handwriting. April had almost finished sorting the papers from the bulldog clip into piles on the kitchen table. Charlie was snoring softly on the couch. 'Have you heard of a man called Matt?' Helen asked quietly.

'Matt? No ... in what context?'

'According to June, she was having a pretty torrid love affair with him.'

'What?!'

'Here, read for yourself.' Helen handed her the diary.

Friday 26ᵗʰ May

April and Helen spent most of the night and early hours of the morning reading June's diary. It raised many questions, the answers to which they could only guess at.

'I don't think we should show this to Charlie,' Helen said softly, pointing to the February entries. 'There are these dancing lessons with Rob that end up in some scorching sex. It's pretty graphic.'

'I think I'm too young for this,' April grimaced.

'I think I might be too.'

'I don't get it,' April frowned. 'I know that these twins existed. I saw them get on the train one morning. They're identical. She didn't speak with either of them.' She gazed absentmindedly at Merv and Melba who were throwing kisses at her image on the other side of their watery world. 'We'd talk about them sometimes. Imagine why they never sat together. Never spoke. They were a bit of a mystery, really. June made up stories about them.'

'But,' Helen said, thumbing through the pages, 'they seemed to play a pretty large part in her life.'

'News to me,' April shrugged.

'And this Matt.'

'How the hell did he come into it? I never saw him. She never talked about him. He didn't exist, as far as I know. But,' she looked down at an entry of dinner in a Japanese restaurant, 'it seems so real. To her, at least.'

'Are you saying she made these men up?'

'I don't know what I'm saying.'

Helen looked up at April. 'You were so close and yet how could she hide love affairs like these from you?'

April shook her head which was beginning to ache. 'I could have sworn I knew her in and out ... and yet ...' She thumbed through the diary pages to 14ᵗʰ May when Yannis and June had made love for the first time. 'You know, she must have dreamed her version of the perfect man. Listen to this bit:

'Here,' he breathes, 'is your heart and your life. You are woman, not skinny girl with nothing to hold onto.' He pauses as he looks at me with concern in his eyes. 'You do not like yourself. You should. You are most beautiful for me. Do not tell the woman I love that you are not worth of that. You are everything for me. Everything.'

April sighed. 'Maybe she read something like that in her books. Wouldn't we all like a man like him?'

Helen grimaced, then yawned expansively. 'I can hardly see anymore.'

'Why don't you go and lie down and stare at yourself on the wall for a bit.

A weak smile quivered across Helen's lips. It didn't reach her eyes. 'I wonder what would have happened if I'd stayed at Kaye's, brought June up there, met a nice Mildura man and settled down. June and I would never have been separated all these years. She'd be alive today.'

'Go on,' April urged Helen into the bedroom, 'No matter how many what ifs you come up with, they'll never change today.'

Helen touched April on a shoulder as she left the table. 'I'd never have met you though, dear April.'

April watched her go, the older version of June, older than the young woman who smiled at the woman who painted her, older than she was three days ago. Much older. *Poor June*, April thought, *she'd only just discovered her mum. I wish I'd still had one — one like Helen would have done me fine.*

She refilled the kettle and leaned against the kitchen bench, looking around her as she waited for the kettle to boil. Charlie snored on. Her eyes took in the old-fashioned clock standing on top of the fridge. Like the nights she'd spent sleeping on the couch, she could hear it relentlessly ticking, a sound that she'd cursed in the past as she'd covered her head with a cushion to escape it. A scorched oven mitt hanging from a hook; it looked a hundred years old. She'd already bought one for June's birthday next month, along with matching tea towels and hand towels. And a lovely edition of *Great Expectations* in the hope that Dickens would further educate and mature June's choice of books. *Those bloody Mills & Boon books filled her head with romance that only the characters in the pages live. It doesn't exist!* April smiled at June's love of those books and romance movies.

She idly opened the cupboard doors, feeling a sense of guilt and invasion. The usual stuff: canned food, salt and pepper, crockery, a few vases, saucepans, etc. Not much. However, the door closest to the oven revealed a surprise: an assortment of neatly arranged recipe books. April frowned. *June doesn't ... didn't ... cook!* She removed one labelled: *Japan — a people, food and cultural journey.* Curious, she took the book over to the kitchen bench — kettle forgotten — where the pages opened to a bookmark. Lavish full-page photos of Japanese people in traditional dress, country and city landscapes, restaurant scenes, food displayed on traditional dinnerware. Interviews with restaurateurs, chefs, patrons, produce growers.

April flicked through the pages to discover some underlining, highlighting and sticky notes marring them. There was something familiar about those notations. *Hang on!* She darted over to June's diary. Flipped through it. Found 15th March when June wrote about her dinner date with Matt at a hi-rise Japanese city restaurant.

'Japanese chefs work with the best ingredients and do as little to the food as possible to bring out the colour and flavour,' Matt tells me as we sip on sake, an interesting flavour that I like. The waiter pours the sake until it spills over into a saucer as a token of appreciation for our visit. How lovely! Imagine an Aussie restaurant doing that with beer; the customer would probably complain and ask who was going to pay for it!

Matt goes on to tell me that to add contrast to the food, simple condiments are provided to enhance the flavours. This is my first experience with miso and wasabi. There is a small green ball on the side of my plate and, thinking it is a mere pea, I pop it into my mouth. A kimono-clad waitress throws her hands up in front of her face in horror and asks me if I am all right. I don't at first know what she's talking about until it hits me. The wave of agony that explodes into my sinuses reminds me of Gran's horseradish that she would get me to grate to go with the roast beef.

This is almost word-for-word what's on the pages of the recipe book, April realised as she matched commentary about food preparation, serving, ingredients, an interview with a waitress who watched a patron eat a ball of wasabi. She leaned back against the bench, stunned. Was June making this up? Was it an elaborate plan to create a fictional relationship with Matt? If Matt existed?

She remembered a previous dinner when June tried oysters for the first time. Found the entry on 8th March. Went back to the recipe books. Found one on seafood. Examined the index. Found oysters on page 27. Opened the page. *There!* Oysters in all their glory along with commentary that matched June's diary entry. *That accounts for her sudden liking of oysters,* April mused.

... sniff it, then tip it into his mouth ... 'Bring it to your nose and inhale.' 'The aroma should be super-fresh, instantly transporting you to the sea. Slurp the meat with its juices and give it two or three good chews,' he encourages. 'Then tell me what you taste.'

April caught herself poking her tongue between her front teeth and stopped immediately. She'd read enough instances of June writing about her weird tongue/teeth habits that now made her acutely aware of them.

Oysters ... pearls ... She went back to the 15th March entry to read again about the pearls Matt gave June. They were in a long red velvet box. She tiptoed past

Charlie to stand in the doorway of June's bedroom, her eyes scanning every possible place where June might have kept valuables. Tears sprang to her eyes as the thought hit her – again – that June wouldn't be coming back. There'd be no more nights sharing dinner and wine, no more soppy movies, no more trying to educate her friend with classic books, no more poring over the internet trying to find Helen (who was sleeping fitfully), eating snags with Charlie sitting outside on his broken-down chairs, discovering family secrets hidden in that magnificent tree outside Kaye's art-filled house, no more fun times shocking Brenda and the brats, no more missions to Myers (June's version of the singular Myer), no more making plans, sniggering at BBB, no more ... no more ...

She sank down to the floor, leaning against the doorframe, head and arms on her knees, sobbing. Only later was she aware that two pairs of arms were around her, Helen and Charlie sharing in her grief. They cried until there was nothing left, and then more. 'I don't know what to do,' she wailed. 'June's my only friend. I don't know how to go on. I don't know,' she shook her head. 'I don't know.'

Charlie pulled out a hanky, dried his face, blew his nose. He cleared his throat. 'I know we're a poor substitute ... and can't possibly be ... but you've got us,' he said looking over April's head at Helen. 'We'll be here for you.'

'Until you go home, both of you,' April began crying again, 'and then I've lost you too.'

Helen handed her a wad of tissues. 'My turn this time,' she shuddered a smile that became a hiccup, as fresh tears coursed down her face.

'I think we should call Little Malcolm,' Helen said later. 'There's the issue of next-of-kin, executor ...'

Charlie nodded. 'June might have arranged something with him, especially after Kaye's will getting lost.'

April shrugged. 'You want to call him? You know more about these things than I do.'

They found the number on one of the invoices. Charlie spoke with Little Malcolm briefly, then hung up.

'He's going to call me back when his ditsy secretary finds June's file,' he told them. 'He knew about June. He'd been ringing her mobile after he saw it on the news, but of course it was just going to her message bank. He was glad I rang as he didn't have contact details for any of us. Sends his condolences.' He turned to sit down at the table again but jerked in pain as his neck caught, slapping his hand around it. 'I know. I know,' he held up his other hand in surrender to April. 'I'll see the quack sometime.'

'Even if I have to go up to Mildura myself and drag you to a doctor, I'll do it.'

'Now wouldn't that be something,' Charlie managed to smile.

April was making June's bed, tucking in the sheets, when she stopped suddenly. She'd never noticed drawers that were almost concealed, part of the fabric of the base. Curious, she slid one out to find bed linen, doona covers. Another with pillows and cushions. She walked around the other side of the bed to open another, sat back on her haunches to exclaim, 'Here!'

Helen and Charlie joined her in the bedroom as she took out a long red velvet box and opened it to disclose the pearls and earrings. 'Yes, these are the ones I saw her wear a couple of times,' she said holding them up. 'Said she bought them in an op shop.'

'I think I saw a receipt for some pearls somewhere,' Charlie said, bringing the bundle into the bedroom. 'Yep, here they are.' He whistled as he read the receipt. '$1299.00 for the necklace and earrings!'

April caught her tongue before it poked its way out between her teeth. 'So … that means, like with the ring, June paid for these. They weren't gifts.' She pulled the drawer out to its full extent to find a flat blue and white box, some blue and white ribbon. 'Geeez, it's heavy!' She took the lid off to reveal a beaded necklace.

'Here's the receipt for this one too,' Charlie offered. 'Imitation Phoenician necklace – blue/white glass eye beads. She got it on eBay for $230.00.'

'These are the ones June wrote about, saying that Yannis gave them to her and he said that they were *'Centuries old. From Greece.'* Helen said, finding the entry for 13th May.

'I don't get it,' Charlie frowned. 'As far as you knew, April, June never had a boyfriend, except for suddenly becoming engaged to Yannis who says he never met her.'

She pushed her hair back behind her ears as she cast her mind back to June's last days. There hadn't been a hint of a change in her romantic life, if she even had one, much less April knowing about any of it. If Yannis had existed, she'd have been happy for her friend. He sounded … nice. Awesome, in fact. It was just so sudden. So secretive. So weird. They'd said goodnight after dinner, planning for the wedding with the help of the magazine. She'd even found something to her liking that didn't include jeans. As she'd drifted off to sleep, there was still a nagging sense of hurt and loss, some doubt about their friendship.

'I'm beginning to wonder about the whole Rob/Marty thing too,' April added.

'Who?'

April and Helen exchanged a look, eyebrows raised. 'A set of twins,' Helen said, clutching the diary close to her, 'who June wrote about. An awful lot.'

'Should I read it?'

'Oh, no!' Helen shook her head. 'April and I are too young for it and you certainly are.'

'X-rated?'

'You could say that,' April grimaced. 'It's interesting, though, how she has one of the twins going to the footy with her and yet, on those dates – I looked them up in my calendar – I went with her. On 18th February she went on her own, I think, because I've got no record of having gone.'

'And there's the dancing twin,' Helen added.

'Yep, those receipts you found, Charlie, for a studio, show her having private lessons with a tutor there called Tim. She went the first time on 24th February, then 27th February, 17th March, and 7th April. The dates in her diary correspond to the receipts. But she paid for those lessons; no person called Marty gave her free ones like she wrote. I helped her get clothing in Myer for the dancing, as well as the footy, the gym, as well as to go to Beechworth and stun those lowlifes who, thank Christ, aren't related to her at all.'

April put the jewellery back in the drawer and they went back out to the kitchen, emotionally exhausted, their bodies heavy, eyes dry and sore. They sat with their elbows on the table, their hands supporting their heads, saying nothing as they collectively stared at the diary in the middle of the table.

'What about the flowers?' Helen mumbled.

'You mean did Matt send her any?' April pulled the diary to her and flipped over the pages. 'There are at least six or seven times when flower arrangements arrived at the office. I saw them. Looking through these pages during the night, I noticed they were usually after she wrote that she'd been with Matt the night before. Then I checked against the receipts for flower deliveries to herself at our work address, and they correspond. Not only that, she says here, when we were in Beechworth together the first time, that Matt was going to courier the

DNA test kits to her in Beechworth. That didn't happen as we ordered them online while we were in the hotel.'

'You've done an enormous amount of work while we slept,' Charlie looked at her. 'Did you get any sleep?'

April shrugged. 'I wanted to understand what the f ... was going on with June. It's been like getting to know her all over again. She had a secret life but, you know, I think it was all pretend. It just doesn't add up with the twins and her, having a relationship with both of them without any of the triangle knowing about each other. Her fantasies seem like bullshit to me, almost like dreams that don't make sense. There's the story but it's got huge holes in it. I'm convinced there was no Matt, no Rob or Marty, no Yannis.'

'But that Giorgos & Katerina's Restaurant actually exists,' Charlie said, holding out some dinner receipts.

'I'm going to call them,' April said, taking the receipts from him. After a lengthy conversation, she turned to Charlie and Helen. 'June ate there quite a few times. She got to know the owners, George and Katerina, and their kids. They felt sorry for her, as she was always alone, but they liked her and had a sort of friendship with her. Katerina would sit with her in quiet times and talk about their families. She told June about her brother-in-law whose name is Yannis. Apparently June talked a lot about me ...' At this April's voice faltered and she took a deep breath, fanning her face. 'She talked about me, about work, even about the DNA tests and her shitty family in Beechworth. Katerina was so surprised when I rang. It was f ... bloody weird them knowing so much about me. She said that they saw the news about ... about ... about June,' she cried, 'and that they were afraid it was her. And it *was* her. It *is* her.'

Helen pushed a tissue box under April's nose as Charlie cracked open some beers and poured a glass of wine. 'For what ails you,' he said quietly.

As one, they raised their glasses. 'To June,' they said.

'And Mills & Boon,' Helen added.

'That rhymed,' Charlie commented.

'You know,' April continued, 'I told Katerina about the train driver and how we realised after he'd left us that he said his name was Nik. She said, yes, that would be short for Nikolaos. They saw him on TV and thought how distraught the poor man looked but he wasn't her brother-in-law.'

Charlie's mobile vibrated and danced across the kitchen table. 'Hello?' He listened intently. 'Yes. Yes, of course. She's right here beside me.' He passed the phone to April who looked at him in question.

'Hi Malcolm. Yes.' She jerked back in surprise. 'She what?' A pause. 'You're shittin' me.'

One Year Later

'Well, what do you think?' she asked, standing back to survey the latest brushstrokes. 'A bit more warmth around the cheekbones, I reckon.'

They gazed at the canvas from their big adoring eyes.

'And the highlights in the eyes'll make a big difference.'

They turned around and came back again, taking another look.

'I can tell you're impressed.'

She noticed the light had gradually withdrawn from the window where the easel stood.

'Time to shut up shop, though. We'll have another go tomorrow.'

She turned as she heard footsteps coming through the kitchen.

'Are you talking to those bloody fish again?' Charlie grinned at her.

'Of course,' April smiled back, 'where else would you get such sage advice? M&M are the best.'

'You up for a snag or two, girlie?'

'Tomato sauce? Onions?'

'Is the Pope a Catholic?'

April cleaned up and followed Charlie past the gum tree with the table surrounding it and over to his place. They carried the food outside and sat on the wicker chairs in companionable silence, tomato sauce dripping down their chins as they devoured April's favourite food.

'Ahh, Charlie, they're up to your usual standard. Thanks.'

They clinked stubbies. Watched the sun sashay behind the orange groves, the local birds squabbling over who claimed what branch to fall asleep on.

'Remember we're going to the doctor's tomorrow about your bloody neck?'

'After your driving lesson.'

She pulled a face. 'Do I have to?'

He smiled at her. 'You'll get it eventually, that's if my poor bloody ute survives it. Helen'll think you're the ant's pants when she sees you driving finally.'

'She already does.'

'Two more days, eh?'

'Yep. Can't wait to see her again.' April took another sip of beer.

'You've almost finished the portrait now.'

'Such as it is.'

'Don't run yourself down, girlie. You'll knock her socks off with June's portrait. She'll love it.'

'I can't believe I'm actually painting.'

'I reckon Kaye's talent rubbed off on you seeing as how it's your home now.'

An hour or so later, April said goodnight to Charlie and made her way back to Kaye's – well, her place now. She sat underneath the gum tree, listening to the landscape rustling under its night-time blanket, each noise more familiar than when she first arrived.

After the shock of learning June had left everything to her, she'd gracefully accepted Charlie's offer to move into Kaye's house. She could afford to pay for it but he said who the bloody hell else could he leave it to; he'd rather see her enjoy it while he was still upright and vertical.

Helen had her life up in Port Macquarie but had visited four times already, staying with April, when they'd sit up in bed, like Helen had done with Kaye and April with June, talking into the night until M&M complained.

'That's ridiculous, April,' Helen would say, 'fish don't talk.'

April would look at her in the moonlight and say, 'Are you sure about that?'